Cash turned toward the mystery woman.

Her legs were long and sleek and shot up to heaven. Short denim cutoffs rode high on her thighs, and with each step she took, a hint of her well-rounded buttocks peeked out.

Cash swallowed. There were no tan lines.

Several men formed a fan club behind her. Cash looked away, immediately thinking of Rainy and feeling guilty. Acknowledging the feeling, he swallowed again. Where had that come from? Hell, he wasn't married and he wasn't dead. He forced himself to take one last look.

Her shorts rode up another fraction. Cash tried to keep his eyes at chest level. A big mistake, he found, when she turned toward him.

Cash raised his gaze to her face.

Rainy?

He blinked several times. Irrational relief galloped through him. It was Rainy. He didn't have to feel guilty.

Rainy? Relief then turned to shock.

Dear Reader,

Ever wonder what it would be like to meet not one but *four* fabulous handsome hunks? Well, you're about to find out! Four of the most fearless, strong and sexy men are brought to their knees by the undeniable power of love—in this month's special VALENTINE'S MEN.

Meet Cash McCloud in *The Cowboy and the Centerfold* by Debbi Rawlins. He's by far the sexiest cowboy in all of Texas (a mighty big claim), and he's just itching to have himself an adventure. As far as how he gets himself mixed up with a centerfold... I'm afraid some secrets are just too good to tell. The faster you read, the sooner you'll know!

We don't want you to miss out on any of these sexy guys, so be sure to check out *all* the titles in our special VALENTINE'S MEN.

Regards,

Debra Matteucci
Senior Editor & Editorial Coordinator
Harlequin Books
300 East 42nd Street
New York, New York 10017

THE COWBOY AND THE CENTERFOLD

DEBBIE RAWLINS

Harlequin Books

TORONTO • NEW YORK • LONDON
AMSTERDAM • PARIS • SYDNEY • HAMBURG
STOCKHOLM • ATHENS • TOKYO • MILAN
MADRID • WARSAW • BUDAPEST • AUCKLAND

To Bonnie, Jan, Jolie, Kathleen and Kim—my critique buddies. Thanks for keeping me straight.

And special thanks to Bonnie Crisalli, editor extraordinaire, for hanging in there with me.

ISBN 0-373-16618-4

THE COWBOY AND THE CENTERFOLD

Copyright © 1996 by Debbi Quattrone.

Chapter One

It was the last one.

Rainy Daye's gaze riveted on the glossy magazine cover barely visible behind the store counter. The cola she was about to sip stalled inches from her lips. A bag of M&M's she'd picked up slipped from her other hand, and she made a quick grab for it before it beaned the sweet-looking, gray-haired lady standing in line in front of her.

They weren't supposed to sell things like *that* in here. This was a small, west Texas general store. The sign outside read Bait, Beer And Ice, for goodness' sake.

Rainy shoved the sunglasses more securely up the bridge of her nose, then swept a casual glance around the near-empty store. Catching another glimpse of *Midnight Fantasy*'s taunting cover, she reached around the elderly lady and her young companion to grab three more packages of soothing chocolate.

She'd made a mistake. Rainy knew that now. Here she'd driven more than fifteen hundred miles and her problems had managed to stick to her like road tar. She snatched another bag of M&M's. And sighed.

"Can I help you?"

I doubt it. Rainy shifted her focus from the brazen strip of magazine covers to the curious store clerk peering at her over his glasses. The elderly woman, her companion and their purchases had vanished.

Rainy pasted on a passable smile and dumped her assortment of goodies and aspirin on the counter. Maybe this was only a nightmare. Or possibly she had read the map wrong. Perhaps she was still hundreds of miles from her destination, where, hopefully, such trashy magazines were unheard of.

"How far is Maybe?" she asked.

"Two towns over."

Rainy nodded slowly. The man didn't look up. He punched the price of each item into the ancient register, while Rainy, taking total leave of her normal, rational senses, decided what she had to do.

"Is that it?" The man licked the tip of his finger and peeled off a small paper sack.

"And that." Rainy aimed a relatively steady finger at the bane of her existence. "I'll take that last copy, please."

The man jerked his attention to the small selection of magazines tucked discreetly behind a strip of plywood. "You mean this?"

She could've sworn his glasses fogged.

"Yes," she murmured and darted a sideways glance toward the back of the store. Two teenage boys approached the counter.

"You want *Midnight Fantasy?*" the man asked in a voice designed to carry halfway across Texas.

No, she didn't want the damn thing. But she certainly didn't want it available to the good citizens of nearby Maybe, either.

"Yes," she repeated through clenched teeth, bending her head to count out her money and to avoid any stunned looks. Her humility could only be tested so far.

But one less copy was, after all, one less copy.

CASH MCCLOUD, barefoot and bare chested, crouched down and peered at his green cotton prey through the glass window. Timing was everything, he reminded himself as he froze, his hand firmly wrapped around the clothes dryer handle. As soon as he saw the shirt start another pass, he opened the door and yanked it out. He had a bunch of things he needed to do today, but ironing wasn't one of them.

"Son of a..." He tossed the shirt from one hand to the other until it cooled, then slipped it over his head. He adjusted the collar and pulled the hem down over the jeans that were still too tight from their earlier bout with the dryer. With a satisfied smirk, he headed for the kitchen.

"Dang, that's hot." Smiley Ferguson threw the wooden spoon down near the simmering pot and fanned his exposed tongue with fervor. "Too many jalapeños. Pass me another can of tomato sauce, will ya, Cash?"

Cash shook his head, ignoring his ranch foreman's request. "Damn it, Smiley. I told you this place has got to be cleaned up before Miss Daye arrives." He eyed the red splatters dotting the white kitchen walls and the smears beginning to dry and cake atop the stove.

"Who?" His eyebrows drawn together, Smiley lifted a shoulder to rub at his whiskered chin. "Oh, you mean Aunt Bea?" He nodded and stuck the wooden spoon back into his brew. "Hope she knows somethin' about chili. I ain't lettin' Violet Pickford win again this year."

"Don't call her Aunt Bea." Cash retrieved a sponge from the sink and swept it across the spice-dotted counter. A medley of unfamiliar aromas erupted and he sneezed. "Jeez, what have you got in there?"

Smiley chuckled. "Pretty near everythin'. Wanna taste?"

"Pass. Now start cleaning up this mess."

"Aunt Bea ain't gonna mind. Might be darned impressed that us bachelors can cook." The foreman scrunched up his face. "Course, bein' a Yankee, she might not cotton to my chili. Gimme the ketchup, will ya?"

"Don't call her Aunt Bea. I mean it, Smiley. Just because a woman's over sixty doesn't mean she can't be vain. And this is Maybe, not Mayberry." Cash took another swipe at the counter, but this time leaned back and angled his nose away. "We need her. Josh needs her. I don't want you ticking her off."

"I ain't gonna tick her off. When she's not teachin' Josh, she can help me with this here recipe. I only got two weeks before the competition."

Cash exhaled a large breath. It had taken him more than a month to find a full-time tutor for his fourteen-year-old son. He couldn't afford to screw up the deal now. Josh had only two months to get his academic act together. Cash leaned against the counter and watched the older man dump another can into the pot.

"You know, it wouldn't hurt if you invited her out to dinner sometime soon. Try to make her feel welcome," Cash added.

Smiley nearly spat out the sample he'd just deposited in his mouth. "Aunt Bea?" He puffed out his sixty-something chest and shoved back his ever-present Stetson. "You gone plum loco? Don't go gettin' no ideas, boy. I ain't takin' her, or Violet Pickford, nowhere."

A grin tugged at the corners of Cash's mouth, but he refrained from pointing out that he hadn't mentioned Violet at all. Smiley had gotten busy cleaning up and Cash knew better than to look a gift horse in the mouth.

He tore a paper towel from the roll and followed behind Smiley, swiping and blotting the misses for the next twenty minutes. But as soon as Cash plunged his hands into a sink full of soapy water, the doorbell rang. He swatted the suds from his elbows and cursed under his breath.

It couldn't be her, he thought, eyeing his bare toes. It was too early. Hell, he hadn't even gotten his boots on yet. Probably one of Josh's friends, he assured himself. But when the bell pealed again and his son hadn't come bounding down the stairs as he usually did, Cash sighed and headed for the door.

Rainy tugged the baseball cap lower over her eyes. A defensive move she recognized as ludicrous, since she'd be living here for the next two months. But the newly acquired habit reassured her, nonetheless, and she pushed the doorbell one more time.

Before she could withdraw her hand, the door swung open. Rainy took an automatic step backward and tipped her head to look up into a pair of dark, emerald green eyes. At five foot nine, herself, she seldom had to look up to anyone, but her head angled considerably in order to meet the man's surprised gaze.

"Yes?" He swept a long black lock of hair off his forehead. His dark eyebrows puckered, a small scar bisecting the left one.

Rainy glanced down to the slip of paper in her hand and gripped it for all she was worth. One single word and she'd recognized the voice. Low and gravelly, it reminded her of a crackling fire, warm brandy, satin sheets... Chocolate— she needed another chocolate fix... bad.

The man's displeased expression snagged her wayward attention. "I'm looking for Cash McCloud," she said as she shot a glance to the black script numbers, high to the left of the door. "Do I have the right house?" she asked, suddenly wishing she didn't. Phone voices never matched the actual person. Wasn't there some kind of rule about that? She had counted on that rule, damn it.

The man frowned. Rainy repositioned her feet. She didn't like the way he was looking at her. He couldn't possibly recognize her. Could he? She shoved her sunglasses up the minuscule fraction they had slipped.

"I'm Cash McCloud." He stood with his arm stretched across the screen door, holding it open, but making no attempt to welcome her inside.

Rainy's confidence took a brief nosedive. She adjusted her cap and lifted her chin a notch. "I'm Rainy." She gritted her teeth at his deepening frown. "Rainette Daye. You *are* expecting me?" Her tone was a little too clipped, so she forced a weak smile for her prospective employer.

"Well, yes." Cash McCloud blinked. She watched a convulsive movement make its way down his throat. When he dropped his arm, the screen door nearly slammed in his face, but he caught it in the nick of time. Instead he stepped outside and let the door slam behind him.

That was when Rainy noticed that his feet were bare. And that the jeans he wore were tight. Not just tight. Sprayed on. The soft, worn denim clung to every muscled curve of his thighs, his hips, his...

Rainy drew in her lower lip and briefly shut her eyes. She cocked one open, then the other, grateful for the very dark glasses she wore. "Mr. McCloud? I distinctly told you I'd be arriving today. I don't understand..."

He was regarding her with such open surprise that Rainy lost track of her thoughts. Once again, her confidence faltered. Oh, God. How could he possibly recognize her?

"What the dickens is goin' on out here?" An older man came to a halt at the door. His oversize hat shadowed his thin, weathered face. When he transferred his puzzled gaze from Rainy to Cash McCloud, she saw the long black braid, liberally threaded with silver, hanging down the older man's narrow back.

No one answered, and the man looked back to Rainy. "She ain't the tutor."

Cash merely nodded without taking his solemn gaze from her, and Rainy felt the M&M's she'd just inhaled do a tap dance in her stomach. She held her breath. They had recognized her. Way down here, in the middle of nowhere... even with the hat, the sunglasses. But how...

Rainy swallowed back the small bit of hope she'd brought with her from Boon, Michigan, and wondered if she had enough money left to make it to Siberia.

"Holy smokes... And she ain't no Aunt Bea." Gaping, the older man pulled off his hat with one bony hand. Then a huge grin cracked his sun-beaten face. "I'd be Guy Ferguson. But everyone calls me Smiley. Pleased to make your acquaintance, ma'am."

Rainy smiled. She was glad *somebody* was. Her attention immediately drew back to Cash McCloud. One black brow lifted in an arrogant arch, while an impatient hand tumbled into his thick, collar-length hair. Her smile faded.

"Look, Ms. Daye. I think there's been a mistake." Her almost-new employer rolled his shoulder a half turn while adjusting the collar of his shirt.

Déjà vu. The action felt like a lightning strike to Rainy's frazzled nerves. One after another, the members of the Boon High PTA had taken a similar posture...right before Rainy had found herself out on her well-publicized butt.

But not this time, she told herself, she was *not* going to let it happen again. "Mr. McCloud, I don't believe there has actually been a mistake *yet*." Rainy gathered her renewed confidence around her like armor. She was qualified for this job. He had extended the offer, and she had accepted. She was not going to be pushed around anymore. "So let's not be too hasty, shall we?"

Cash McCloud lost the baffled look. His strong, square chin came up and his lids lowered to half-mast. In a low tone, he said, "Lady, I'm not the one who made it."

"Well, neither did I, Mister."

"Yeah? And if you have forty years' experience under your belt..." He ran a slow and deliberate gaze down her body making her feel like her long, baggy T-shirt was invisible. "Then I'll eat my hat."

"Glad you didn't say shoes." Rainy forced her gaze off his bare feet. She kept her eyes level with his.

Cash McCloud pursed his lips. He didn't look down, either. He simply crossed his arms over his chest, leaned against the open door and trained his disturbing green eyes directly on her.

Smiley chuckled, and Rainy and Cash reluctantly gave up their silent combat. "Seems like someone's got some explainin' to do," he said, chuckling again. He plopped his hat back on his head and let the screen door close behind him.

Rainy felt foolish all of a sudden. It wasn't at all like her to go on the attack like this, and being obnoxious certainly wasn't going to save her job. A job she desperately needed, she reminded herself. But if he had recognized her, she wished he'd just come out with it. "Mr. McCloud?" Rainy squelched a sigh. "I'm not trying to be difficult—"

"And I'm not the one who lied about having forty years' experience," he cut in. He looked totally relaxed—except his toes, which curled tightly into the cement floor of the wraparound porch.

"I don't know what you're talking about." She pulled off her glasses. Not much use for them now. Not that she'd ever believed they'd serve any purpose other than giving her a temporary reprieve. She looked up into his expressionless face and threw up a hand. "I really don't."

Slowly, he uncrossed his arms and tucked his hands into his back pockets. Although how he'd managed to find room for them Rainy couldn't figure, the soft denim stretched so...

She abruptly switched her attention to his face. "What forty years?"

"In your newspaper ad."

"My ad?"

"I've got it right inside."

"My ad said four years."

Cash shrugged. "You want to see it?"

Rainy stared at him in disbelief. Then she realized this was the mistake to which he'd been referring. Giddy relief, like bubbles from a newly opened bottle of champagne, frothed up inside her. She pulled off her baseball cap and caught herself just short of throwing it up into the clear blue Texas sky.

"Sure, Mr. McCloud." Rainy flashed him a brilliant smile. "I'd love to see the ad."

He pushed away from the door. "Well, you'd better come in, then." Rubbing the back of his neck, he gave her one last wary, yet slightly resigned, look before stepping aside. "And I guess you'd better start calling me Cash."

Cash watched Rainy precede him through the door, her long, dark blond ponytail bouncing behind her. Damn, but she didn't look like any tutor he'd expected.

"Have a seat. I'll go get the ad." Cash paused at the door to his study, while Rainy sashayed toward the pine green leather couch in the living room. Well, that wasn't exactly a fair description of the way she walked, it only looked that way because of the ridiculously big T-shirt she wore. But as she moved, the shirt snagged briefly on an interesting curve or two. And although her legs were covered to the ankle, the clingy leggings hugged the head-turning curves of her calves.

Maybe she thought she was hiding things, but as far as Cash was concerned, she was dead wrong.

It only took him a few minutes to locate the ad and another couple to pull on his socks and boots. When he got back to the living room, her head was bent over a notebook full of scribbled pages.

As soon as she heard him, Rainy put the notebook aside and looked up. An arrow of tension zapped Cash right about navel level. She had extraordinary eyes. They were large and brown and shaped like two perfect almonds. Her skin wasn't too fair—more warm and golden, as if she might have a speck of Indian in her.

"Here it is. Forty years." He handed her the clipping and was surprised to see the slight tremble in her fingers as she accepted the piece of paper.

Cash sat in his usual tan recliner and tried to find a comfortable position as he watched her scan the ad. After a moment, her shoulders slumped a little and she nibbled at her lower lip.

She sighed. "You're right. There has been a mistake." She gave him back the ad with an apologetic smile. "It should have read four years. I had no idea..." She shrugged. "There was no way of checking all the papers I'd sent it to."

"I understand," he lied. He didn't understand any of this. Just how many newspapers had she advertised in and why? And what in the hell was he going to do about Josh? "As I'm sure you can understand my position."

"Your position?" She lounged back in her seat, the passive posture putting him on edge rather than reassuring him. "What I understand is that you offered me a job. I accepted. Then, in good faith, I drove all the way here from Michigan. Mr. McCloud, you owe me this chance."

"Actually, Ms. Daye, I don't owe you a thing."

"Really? I think the courts might disagree. Ever hear of breach of contract?" Rainy asked sweetly.

Great. Just what he needed. First his ex-wife manipulating the legal system to muscle him out of custody of Josh. Now this new tutor—who had the nerve to not even look like one—threatening him with a lawsuit.

Cash studied her another moment, waffling between throwing her shapely little butt out of his house and giving in to reason. Time was running out. "That offer was based on misinformation."

"Look. I need a job, and you need me."

Wrong. She was trouble, and Cash didn't need trouble. He watched her in silence for a lot longer than he cared to, except he couldn't quite come up with anything to say. Because the hell of it was, he and his son really did need her.

Finally, he shook his head in slow and deliberate repetition and said, "It's not going to work."

Rainy let out an exasperated sound. "What exactly are you afraid of?"

Was she kidding? She was too young, too pretty, and he had a hormone-raging son who was too fourteen. Cash closed his fist around the chair's worn leather arm. Hell, his son's father's hormones weren't exactly out to pasture, either. Hiring Rainy was becoming less and less a hot idea.

"Not a thing," Cash finally forced himself to answer.

"Then give me a chance. Let's agree on two weeks. If it doesn't work out, no hard feelings. What could go wrong?"

What could go wrong? A lot. He'd be up a creek without a tutor for one, yet he didn't have a barn full of choices, either.

Jeez, he didn't want to think about this. He wanted to think even less about the blatant challenge in her eyes. Subtle, but no less potent than the dares he'd received as a twelve year old. He'd had enough trouble ignoring them then and found he liked them no better at thirty-five.

When he didn't respond, she leaned forward, bracing her elbows on her knees, her hands clasped together in front of her, her short, well-groomed nails making small ridges in her skin.

"I'm a darn good teacher. My references are impeccable." She nailed him with those almond-shaped eyes. "I can help your son, Cash."

He'd never heard his name said quite that way before. Soft and slow, like it got caught on the tail end of a sigh. Again, he wondered why she'd sent out so many ads, and he wondered if his recent celibacy was about to make a fool of him. "Okay."

"Okay?" She straightened.

"It's a deal. For two weeks, at least."

Rainy let out a long breath, her chest rising and falling in rapid succession. "You won't be sorry."

Yeah? Too late. Cash rubbed his jaw. "About the living arrangements. I told you it was live-in."

Rainy smiled. His gut tightened and he knew for certain he'd just made a grave mistake.

"I think you'd be more comfortable near town." He pushed out of his chair and headed for the hall phone. "We don't have a motel, but Violet Pickford usually rents out rooms. I'll foot the bill."

"But I was counting..." She paused, a small frown settling above her troubled eyes. Then she got this skittish look all of a sudden, like a brand-new colt who'd just come into the world. "Can't I stay here?"

Cash rocked back on his heels, weighing his answer. She couldn't be that naive, and if she was, he wasn't crazy about explaining the situation to her. "Violet's place is closer to town. You'll be happier there."

Her eyes widened a fraction, then she got up and paced a few steps to the window. "I don't consider this a vacation." She sent a pleading look his way. "I'd rather stay here."

"Look, Rainy, it's just Josh and me here. Smiley's my foreman and lives out in the bunkhouse with the other hands."

Her teeth caught at her lower lip. She twisted her hands together.

"And our housekeeper only comes out three days a week." He gave a slow shake of his head and wondered why he felt like the bad guy all of a sudden.

She seemed to clearly sense his hesitancy, because what looked like hope tugged cautiously at the corners of her mouth and she gave him an expectant look.

"Well..." He cupped the back of his neck and blew out a puff of air.

"Great." A wide, radiant smile spread across her face, as if everything was settled, and she strode toward him.

"Darn it, Rainy. I don't know..." She stopped a couple of feet away from him and squinted at his mouth. He reared his head back and brought a hand to his chin. "What?"

She peered closer. "Right there. Something red. Just a speck. Catsup maybe."

Cash swiped at the area where she was pointing.

"No. You missed it."

He tried again.

"Almost."

Cash was about to take another run at it, but Rainy dabbed a finger at the corner of his mouth.

Heat rushed through him. With a lightning reflex, his hand jerked up to capture hers.

Their eyes met and hers widened in horror. "I am so sorry." Her free hand worried her shirt neckline. "My nephews—my brother's kids—I do it to them all the time." Her shoulders sagged. "I wasn't thinking."

Cash cleared his throat. "No problem." The problem was, he was still holding her hand. A soft, warm, fragile hand. He dropped it like a hot-handled iron skillet and beat a quick retreat toward the hall.

"Cash?"

She was doing it again. He stopped at the door and faced her.

"I really do want to stay here." She tilted her head to the side. "Please."

With any other woman, Cash would've been irritated by the manipulative, coquettish tactic. But Rainy looked so earnest, almost pleading. He didn't know why, didn't want to know. He had his son to think about. And Rainy didn't even appear a whole lot older than Josh. Four years' experience, she'd said. That would put her at about twenty-six, maybe twenty-seven, he figured.

He looked into her clear, hopeful brown eyes, glanced at the ponytail draped carelessly over her narrow shoulder. She barely looked twenty.

"I'll call Violet Pickford and get you a room." He turned away to avoid the disappointment clouding her gaze.

Chapter Two

"No, Violet, I am not sending a spy over for Smiley," Cash said.

Rainy made one last entry into her notebook and closed it. She scooted forward on the couch and strained an unabashed ear toward the hall. From this new vantage point, she could see Cash's profile and the frustrated hand plowing into his dark curling hair.

"I promise you, Violet. She's a tutor I hired for Josh. Smiley only met her today." Cash paused and grimaced. "She's from Michigan, Violet. Maybe she doesn't even like chili."

Rainy bit at her lower lip to keep a grin in check. If Cash managed to sweet-talk Violet Pickford into giving her a room, Rainy knew just how to get uninvited.

"Now, Violet, when have I ever lied to you?" Cash's shoulders rose, then fell on a sigh. "That's okay. I understand." He pursed his lips in silence for several moments, angling the telephone slightly away from his ear while he listened. Irritation showed in the hard set of his jaw. And then he grinned.

Rainy's breath caught. As if his looks weren't lethal enough, white teeth gleamed against his tanned, beard-roughened face. Rainy decided Violet Pickford's place was sounding better.

"Thanks, Violet. Thanks very much. And, yes, I'll tell Smiley." He replaced the receiver.

Rainy scooted back in her seat and reopened her notebook.

"She'll take you." Cash stopped in the doorway and leaned against the frame. "But, for God's sake, don't mention the word chili."

Rainy brought her innocent gaze up to his warning one. "Why?"

"Tell Smiley what?" The foreman appeared out of nowhere, his hands planted on his aproned hips.

Cash slapped his thigh. "Hell, Smiley, you're not messing up the kitchen again, are you?"

"What did that ol' battle-ax say? Tell me what?"

Cash sighed. "I called to get Rainy a room, and she thought I was sending out a spy for you. To check up on her chili entry."

Smiley let out a gleeful howl. "Got her worried, do I?" Then he sobered. "The nerve of that ol' bat thinkin' I need to stoop to spyin'." He set his scheming black eyes on Rainy. "You cook?"

"Sure." Rainy grinned. "And I love chili." She cast a playful glance at her new boss.

Cash passed a hand over his face. "Great. Now you both need to promise me you won't discuss Miss Pickford's chili."

"Why would I, when I got the winnin' entry right here?" Smiley hooked his bony finger toward the floor for emphasis, then slid a glance to Rainy. "What do ya put in your chili?"

"Don't start," Cash interrupted. "First and foremost, Rainy is here to tutor Josh, not help you win your chili contest. Second..." Cash stared at Rainy staring at him. "Uh, second..." What the heck was second, anyway? Smiley waited, frowning.

"Second," Smiley continued for him, "this poor gal just drove a far piece. She don't wanna stay at the ol' bat's. I'll bring in her things." Smiley moved toward the door.

"Hold it." Cash caught him by the tip of his braid. "She's going to Violet's, and I don't want to hear another word about it. Now call Josh so he can meet her before I take her on over."

Smiley muttered under his breath as he headed for the stairs.

When they were alone again, Cash stuck his hands in his pockets and slowly swiveled toward Rainy. The denim of his jeans appeared to have relaxed some and, for that, Rainy was grateful. She watched him toe the carpet with his scuffed boot for a few moments before he looked up.

"Don't listen to Smiley. You'll like Violet. I'm doing the right thing by you."

"Thanks."

He arched a brow at her sarcastic tone.

Rainy sighed. "Don't worry about me, Cash. I'm here to do the job you hired me for. And I'll be the judge of what's right for me." She picked up her purse and stood.

"Fine." Cash reached for the bulky canvas tote she'd brought in with her.

"Fine," Rainy repeated and snatched it up ahead of him. She'd had enough of people deciding what was good for her. First the school honchos, then her parents and, worst of all, Richard. Of course, Richard had been more concerned with what would be good for him. And, for Rainy, that had been the final blow.

"There's no need to get all bent out of shape over this." Cash stood in her way.

She glared up at him and had the sudden desire to know just how tall he was. With his dark hair and wide shoulders, he was nothing at all like Richard. Her old boyfriend was fair and slight, more a pretty boy. Far too pretty, in fact, to be a stodgy associate professor. But that hadn't stopped him from aspiring to a full fellowship. Even when it had meant throwing her away to get it.

"I'm not. It was a long drive." Rainy transferred the bag to her other hand. Stuffed full, its weight dragged within an inch of the floor.

Cash said nothing. He leaned forward and pulled the bag from her. A whiff of pine and soap emanated from him. His biceps bunched as he swung the bag to his side. They weren't big designer muscles, but nice chiseled ones that resulted from everyday, hard-earned sweat. Sweat that came from working a ranch, Rainy reminded herself. This wasn't Boon. She'd left the whispers and the pettiness behind. She had no cause to be jumpy here. Not yet, anyway.

She started to smile and caught Cash's darkening green gaze, the fullness of his lower lip. Then again, maybe she had plenty of cause.

Rainy straightened her oversize T-shirt before it threatened to swallow her whole. She noted with wry amusement that if all else failed, she could pitch it and camp outside. She *was* tired, she realized at once.

"Cash? I'm really not trying to start an argument."

He pursed his lips, his expression serious. "Neither am I. It's just that this is so important." He turned up his palm in a show of helplessness. "Josh is my only child—"

She laid a soothing hand on his arm, impressed with how seriously he took his responsibility. "Don't worry, cowboy, I work with kids all the time, remember?"

His gaze lingered on her hand. Rainy felt the heat of it, felt the moment that reassurance turned to a spark. She gave him a tight smile and dropped her arm to her side.

Cash shifted. "Look, Rainy—"

"Dad."

They heard the cracking voice long before nearly six feet of lanky teenager flew off the last stair. He skidded across the hardwood foyer floor past the living room door. Within seconds, he backed up and popped his dark head into the room.

"Dad?" Josh's gaze darted between his father and Rainy.

"Josh, come meet your new tutor." Cash crooked his finger. His attention zoomed in on his son's every move.

Rainy warmed at the concern Cash showed, and some of the unwarranted jumpiness she'd been feeling fell away. Anonymity and a normal loving family in the middle of west Texas was just the balm she needed.

"Son, this is Ms. Daye."

The young man shuffled in obediently. He played with the headphones of his Walkman as it dangled from around his neck, his gaze bouncing around the room before falling on Rainy.

Typical shy teenager, Rainy thought. No problem here. She smiled and extended her hand to him. Josh studied first her sneakered toes, then his own, before he finally looked up.

His fingers stilled at the headphones. Then he wiped the back of his hand across his eyes as if he'd just awoken.

Rainy cocked her head to the side and caught Cash's dumbfounded expression out of the corner of her eye. He gave his son a none-too-subtle nudge from behind.

She felt his cold fingers connect with hers, felt the dampness creeping into his palm. And when his eyes widened in shocked and telltale disbelief, she knew the jig was up—he'd recognized her.

Cash watched his son dumbly greet Rainy and felt the first sting of regret. It wasn't that he hadn't expected some sort of reaction on Josh's part, but he hadn't expected the boy to go catatonic on him. "Josh?"

"Uh, yeah, D-Dad." Josh blinked as though coming out of a trance, then looked down at Rainy's hand, which he had enveloped in a death grip. He dropped it and rubbed his denim-clad thigh.

"Why don't you take this bag out to Ms. Daye's car?" Cash suggested quietly as he handed Josh the tote. He wasn't pleased with the boy's behavior, but he felt obliged to bail him out.

"Sh-sure." Josh gave Rainy one last glazed look, then made a befuddled retreat.

Cash let out a large sigh and turned to Rainy. He could tell she was trying her damnedest to keep a smile on her face, but there was a slight quiver to her chin and her eyes were dark and wary.

"I don't know what's gotten into that boy." Cash drove a lock of hair off his forehead. "He'll be fine, though."

She didn't say anything. She merely gave him a small nod that looked as if she didn't believe a word he'd just said.

"Some of it's our fault," Cash tried to explain. "He was expecting . . . You see, Smiley's been calling you Aunt Bea and I'd figured with forty years . . ."

Rainy's eyes widened. The corners of her mouth twitched. She was either going to burst out laughing or crying—he couldn't tell which. Ah, hell, what had he gotten himself into?

He stared at her for several moments longer, then grabbed his hat and headed for the door.

RAINY PULLED HER little white MG to a halt in back of Cash's monstrous dark green pickup. Violet Pickford's house was set back twenty yards behind three tall rows of gigantic scarlet roses. Each row formed a perfect line, and the entire area was sealed off with barbed wire.

As near as Rainy could tell, there wasn't another house around for at least a mile, and that suited her just fine. She needed the peace and quiet, along with time to regroup. What she didn't need were any more stares and whispers.

And this place looked perfect...if Josh's reaction truly had nothing to do with the centerfold, as Cash had implied.

Cash came around the back of the truck and reached into the convertible for one of Rainy's suitcases. He followed her idle gaze toward the roses and grinned.

"There are two things you don't mess with when it comes to Violet Pickford. You already know about the chili." He nudged his chin in the direction of the roses. "And those. American Beauties, she calls them."

Rainy climbed out of her car and scanned the menacing barbed wire. It was at least three feet tall with no sign of a gate. She was about to comment, when the front door creaked open a crack. The barrel of a shotgun appeared in the gap. Then she caught a glimpse of unruly red hair, followed by a pair of bright blue eyes.

"It's just us, Violet." Cash swung the suitcase to the ground, then winked at Rainy. "And we're not armed."

The woman's high-pitched laugh was cut off by another loud creak as she swung the door wide and anchored it open with the butt of the shotgun.

"Neither am I. I haven't had any shells for this old relic since the sixties," she said in a surprisingly cultured tone, then pulled out a large straw hat adorned with a single sunflower and plopped it atop her head. Stuffing her hands into the pockets of her white overalls, she strolled toward them, giving a wide berth to her fortified garden. "You two came quick. Did the smell of Smiley's chili send you running?" Chuckling, she presented a perfectly manicured hand to Rainy.

Cash gave Rainy a warning look, which she decided to accept gracefully—for now. She smiled at Violet Pickford, shook her hand and asked, "What chili?"

"Don't tell me that old buzzard isn't experimenting night and day, because I simply won't believe it." With a show of total unconcern, she picked a sage twig off the bandanna around her neck. "Not that it will help him any."

"Now, Violet, Rainy doesn't know anything about the chili contest. She's here to help Josh."

"As long as she understands that." The woman gave Rainy a sharp look and pushed back the unruly hair that sprang from under her hat. "I'm working in the shed out back. I've left the green room open for her. You know the way, Cash." She inclined her head toward Rainy. "Breakfast is at six each morning, tea at four, rain or shine. You're on your own for the rest of your meals." Then she carefully detoured around her roses and disappeared behind the house.

Rainy looked back to Cash and found that he'd been watching her. She sent another quick glance in Miss Pickford's direction before picking up the tote Cash had placed on the ground.

"She's a little high-strung but harmless," Cash said as he claimed two bags and started toward the house. "You can have lunch and dinner with us. Our housekeeper makes most of our meals, but otherwise Smiley and I are pretty fair cooks."

Rainy followed him, enjoying her own private showing of his attractive rear end. His tight jeans hugged each well-developed curve, while his long, lean legs cut a lazy path around Violet Pickford's prized roses.

She sighed, wondering how much longer she'd be around to enjoy the view.

Cash stopped and looked at her over his shoulder. "Something wrong?"

Rainy straightened, trapping a mournful sound in her throat. She cleared it. "The roses," she said quickly, spreading an expansive hand. "They smell heavenly."

Cash frowned, as if he didn't understand what the fuss was about, but nodded and continued toward the house. "Enjoy them. This is as far as they go."

"You're kidding." She hurried to catch up with him.

"Nope. Except for the competitions. And the occasional joker who raids the garden—kids usually."

"Is that the reason for the barbed wire?"

"That, and the fact that she doesn't want the soil contaminated."

Rainy laughed. One side of Cash's mouth lifted. He stopped at the front door, set one suitcase to the side and carefully stomped the dust off his boots. "She takes this competition stuff seriously." He stepped aside, bracing the door open with his arm. "We all humor her."

"Hey." She put up a hand. "Keeps her off the streets, doesn't it?"

He chuckled, gesturing her to precede him.

Rainy stepped forward and was immediately accosted by Cash's musky pine scent. She bowed her head and made a hasty job of wiping her feet. She put a palm to the door in the hope of relieving him of the job of propping it open. But he maintained his stance, his exposed biceps tensed and bunched, restraining the heavy wooden door. Her gaze moved to his well-toned forearm, to the sprinkling of fine dark hair across his knuckles—the knuckles of his long, slender, capable-looking fingers. She shot a glance at his face and was immediately drawn to his intense green gaze. His breath warmed her cheek.

Oh, boy. Talk about jumping out of the frying pan into the fire. She took too quick a step over the threshold and nearly tripped on a colorful woven rug. But Cash's fingers proved their capability by anchoring around her forearm and steadying her.

Rainy gave him a faint smile of thanks, then shied away from his touch. He accommodated her with insulting speed.

She held the door, her eyes scanning the living room, while he reclaimed the bag he'd set aside. It was neat and clean, the hardwood floors polished to a shine. The pink settee and pair of Queen Anne chairs were merely old rather than antique.

"Veer to the right," Cash said.

She did as she was told, resisting the urge to dawdle over the numerous framed pictures covering the hall walls.

"The open door on the left," he further supplied. As Rainy entered the room, a tart whiff of green apples tickled her nose, and she noted the baskets of potpourri scattered about the room.

She exhaled deeply. "Whew. No wonder she calls it the green room."

"I guess, but I'm not asking." A slow grin made the corners of his eyes crinkle. "Where do you want this?"

She gestured to the double bed, and he swung one bag up and set the other on the floor.

"I've got to talk with Violet a minute, then I'll bring in the rest of your things."

He retreated before Rainy could offer to get her own stuff, so she wandered over to the window for a look at the backyard.

Beyond a small fenced-in area, acres of lifeless pasture land stretched as far as she could see. A none-too-friendly-looking dog prowled the confines of the yard, but as soon as Cash entered through the gate, the dog wagged his tail and darted over. Cash obliged him with a few scratches behind his ears, then threw a stick for him to fetch before striding toward the far end of the yard.

Rainy didn't see the shed at first, tucked away behind a tangle of overgrown mesquite. A large sign warned visitors to trespass under penalty of buckshot.

Cash stopped several feet away and brought his cupped hands to his mouth. Violet Pickford appeared seconds later.

Rainy smiled and left the window. This place was looking better and better all the time. Her landlord obviously liked to be left alone—Rainy's sentiment exactly.

And spending any more time than was necessary in Cash's house sure wasn't a good idea. He did extraordinary things to her nervous system. This reaction had to be due to the stress of the past few weeks, she decided, and started opening the dresser drawers. They were all empty and lined with lime green shelf paper.

She flipped open her suitcase and emptied it of her supply of extra-large T-shirts, when she heard a knock at the open door.

"Is this all you have?" Cash frowned, balancing a laptop computer in one hand and a briefcase in the other.

"That's it." She relieved him of the computer.

He gazed in narrow-eyed suspicion at her stack of T-shirts. "For two months?"

"I didn't expect I'd have to dress up for home tutoring. Do you have a problem with that?"

"Not as long as you understand that after two weeks, *if* we agree that you stay, there's no pulling out before Josh takes his exam."

Rainy hadn't missed the emphasis he'd put on "if" and she lifted her chin. "Mr. McCloud, I have no intention of reneging on my part of the bargain."

"There's not a whole lot of excitement around here. You may find Maybe a little stifling."

"I've already told you, I don't consider this a vacation. I'm not here to be entertained."

"Good, because you won't be."

"Good." Rainy yanked out the last batch of clothes.

"Look, I'm not trying to be contrary—"

"Thank goodness. Imagine if you actually tried." She closed a dresser drawer with her hip and opened the closet door.

Cash shoved the empty suitcase aside and swung the other one up beside it. "I don't want you to have a mistaken impression, is all. Hell, the town has just one movie theater and it only opens on weekends."

She took a deep breath and faced him. "Then I guess I'll feel right at home. Okay?"

"What?" His eyes traveled over her face, then came to rest on her lips.

She moistened them. "Boon, where I'm from, isn't much different." His gaze intensified. She swallowed and turned back to her unpacking. "Okay, you caught me. Our theater opens four days a week."

His chuckle was deep, seductive, and she peeked back over her shoulder at him.

"Is Boon really that small?" he asked.

She nodded. "You look surprised."

"I am." He pulled off his Stetson and a thick lock of dark hair fell across his forehead. He swept it up in a lazy motion. "I figured you for a big-city gal."

She drew her head back. "Me? Thanks, but no thanks."

A shadow of relief crossed his face and she relaxed against the bedpost. She wasn't sure why this information pleased him, but she was glad it did. She didn't need any more strikes against her.

"And you don't mind the quiet?"

"Believe me, that's just what I'm looking for."

Silence and a skeptical look were his initial response. Then he slapped his hat against his hand. "Well, it looks like we've got a deal. At least for the next two weeks."

Rainy didn't much care for his qualification, but she smiled. "You can count on me, Cash, I'll take good care of your son." He gave her a slow, heart-stopping smile and she almost stumbled, reaching for her tote bag.

"Right." He backed up a step. "One more thing...about, uh, well..."

Oh, no, here it comes. He knows about the centerfold. Rainy grabbed one of the bedposts and leaned on it for support. "Yes?"

"About Josh." His almost sheepish gaze strayed out the window. "He's a good kid. He won't give you any trouble." Cash returned his attention to her, his gaze traveling up her body, stopping to rest briefly on her mouth. He grinned faintly. "Once he gets over the infatuation part."

If anyone else had looked at her in the past few weeks like Cash just had, Rainy would have been tempted to sock him, but she knew he hadn't meant the raw intensity the way she'd felt it.

Every one of her nerve endings went on red alert, even as the relieved realization that she'd jumped to conclusions dawned on her. She clutched the sides of her baggy T-shirt and twisted them around her closed fists.

Cash's gaze flicked down to her chest, then he shifted his attention back to the window.

Rainy straightened. She felt the shirt hugging her breasts and she disengaged her hands from the fabric.

"Let's see, what else do you need to know... I made an office out of an upstairs bedroom for you." Cash looked back at her, his eyes trained at a precise area above her eyebrows. "Like I said, you can have your meals with us. We eat at around six-thirty every night."

"Sounds great."

"I'm out on the ranch most of the day. Most evenings I spend in my study."

"Okay."

"Saturdays I go into town for groceries and supplies. It takes most of the day."

"I see."

Cash stepped closer to the door. "When a rodeo is nearby, I could be gone an entire weekend."

"Oh."

"Any questions?"

"Yeah." Rainy bit back a grin. "And Josh?"

Cash cast a quick glance to the ceiling. She could almost see him mentally shaking his head. "Of course, Josh will be at your disposal."

If he wasn't too busy avoiding her, like his father obviously planned to, Rainy thought with wry amusement. So much for worrying about unwanted attention.

Rainy nodded, making up her mind. She was going to take her own advice and not worry about a problem that may not exist. Maybe Cash's interpretation of his son's behavior was accurate. Maybe Rainy was seeing things that weren't there. Just maybe, no one in Maybe had seen that damning centerfold.

"How does Josh feel about giving up his summer?" Rainy asked. Having made the decision to tough it out, she needed to get a feel for what she was walking into.

Cash laughed. "Ticked. Big time. You may have trouble getting him to buckle down at first." His lips thinned. "But he knows it's serious. If he doesn't pass that test at the end of August, the court could reconsider his custody arrangement. And Josh doesn't want to leave the ranch." He rubbed a palm against his faded denim-encased thighs.

Rainy studied her hands, the same hands in which Cash was placing his son. She pushed back a cuticle. She had more questions—questions about Josh's mother, questions about Cash, questions that didn't concern her.

She brought her head up and smiled. "Don't worry, as they say back in my hometown, I'll learn him good."

"You all say that in Boon?" Cash laughed. It was a slow and easy sound. Rainy liked it. "Maybe I'd better think twice about having you as a tutor."

"Oh, no, I'm perfect for you." As soon as the words were out of her mouth, she wanted to call them back...especially when he gave her that bone-melting look. She fumbled for her tote.

Cash was quick. He hauled it off the floor and onto her bed.

"Thanks," she mumbled. Her reluctant gaze made her way to his. He hadn't stepped back and she could smell the pine and soap again. It settled around her like a warm cocoon. She noticed again the small scar that bisected the arch of one brow and the shadow on his strong jaw.

"More catsup?" Cash put a finger to his chin.

"What?" She'd been staring. "No, no." She swung her eyes forward and flipped open the top of her suitcase.

"After you've settled in, come on back to the ranch." He backed toward the door. "But before you do, I've got one more word of advice. Don't let Smiley talk you into any cooking experiments. The man can be lethal in the kitchen."

"So can I."

"Yeah?" A slow smile spread across Cash's face.

"Yeah," Rainy confirmed, enjoying their easy rapport. She smiled back at him and pulled out a red see-through negligee.

A negligee? Rainy jerked her attention to the filmy creation. She didn't own a negligee. Or a teddy. She untangled the black contraption clinging to the red number. Especially one with a cone-shaped bra. And a gold fishnet crotch. A groan bubbled in the pit of her stomach.

She caught Cash's stunned expression in her peripheral vision, before slowly turning in his direction.

She felt the smile quiver, then die, at the corners of her mouth. And for one of the few times in her miserable life, she was utterly speechless.

Cash erased all reaction from his face. As calm as you please, he leaned against the doorjamb and asked, "Boon's latest fashion?"

Chapter Three

If Rainy Daye wasn't the most confounding woman he'd ever run across, Cash really would eat his hat.

He poured his third cup of coffee and sat down at the kitchen table. It had been an hour since he'd left her to unpack, yet he still couldn't shake the image of that red nightwear from his mind. Hell, you couldn't even call the black thing nightwear. He cursed under his breath and punished his tongue with a steaming sip of coffee.

God knows what you'd do with something like that. A totally inappropriate image flitted through his mind and he cursed again.

"Got a burr up your rump, boy?" Smiley asked, ambling into the kitchen in his typical bowlegged fashion. He poured himself a cup of coffee and leaned against the counter.

"Shut up, Ferguson." Cash dragged a hand through his hair, ignoring the odd look Smiley gave him. "Has the vet called about Darth yet?"

"Nope. But I ain't worried. That bull's too ornery to be bad off." Smiley blew at the steam coming from his mug.

"Someone clear a space for the new teacher's things in the library?"

"You mean Aunt Bea?" The foreman howled with laughter until Cash glared at him. He coughed into his hand.

"Yeah, Josh did," he said, scratching his head. "He straightened up the guest room for her, too, just in case."

Cash slammed down his hand and spilled his coffee. "Damn it. She is not staying here."

"What the dickens is wrong with you? The boy was trying to be nice, is all."

Yeah, right. Cash blew out a puff of air. "Sorry." He got up and yanked off a stream of paper towels, then set to soaking up the mess he'd made on the table.

"It's that filly, ain't it?" Smiley asked after eyeing him for a long moment.

Cash tossed the soggy towels into the trash and made a casual show of settling back into his chair. "What do you think of her?"

"Real looker, as far as I can tell. But why she'd wear them big ugly clothes is beyond me."

Cash clung to his patience. This information was no news flash. "I mean from a character standpoint. You've always been a good judge of that."

Smiley shrugged. "Only talked to her a minute, but she seemed okay. Didn't you git all that reference stuff before you sent for her?"

"Well, yeah." Cash had talked to a number of people. They'd all spoken well of her, said they'd miss her. But they never said why she was leaving.

"If you still got questions, seems to me ya'd better ask her. She comin' back soon?" Smiley waited until Cash nodded, then emptied his cup into the sink and placed it in the dishwasher.

When he reached into the spice cabinet, Cash said, "So help me, Smiley, if you so much as think about messing with that chili again, I'm going to string you up."

"Fine. 'Cuz if I don't win the contest this year, I ain't gonna be fit to live with."

"You aren't already."

"Gosh dang it. I ain't seen you in this foul a mood since you caught Josh smokin' last year."

Cash returned Smiley's glare, then noticed a movement near the door.

Rainy stood at the threshold, her hands twisted together. "I knocked. Twice. The door was open." She switched her gaze from Cash to Smiley, then back again. "Am I early? Shall I come back?"

"Not if ya got a lick of sense." Smiley pulled his hat off a peg and grumbled all the way out the back door.

Cash sighed. He couldn't blame the older man. At the moment, Cash couldn't even stand himself. He pushed out of his chair and pulled out the one across the table for her as he went to get more coffee. He raised the pot to her. She nodded.

"Cream or sugar?" he asked.

"Black."

Cash took his time retrieving a mug and watched her take several uncertain steps toward the table. She'd hiked her ponytail up tighter and higher on her head, but the severity of the style was softened by honey-colored tendrils dancing about her cheeks. Her face was flushed and Cash's unruly memory grasped a fleeting image of something red and filmy.

"Nice kitchen." Rainy's gaze scanned the designer cream-and-burgundy wallpaper, the butcher block island.

"Serves its purpose." Cash slid the mug over to her. He grabbed the ceramic cactus cookie jar and offered her the home-baked goodies his housekeeper kept in constant supply.

She unclasped her hands and took the last chocolate chip cookie. Cash settled for a handful of oatmeal raisin ones.

"It's nice and homey. A lot like my folks' kitchen in Boon." Her eyes slowly met his and she smiled. Her long curly lashes caught on a stray tendril. She brushed it away with the back of her hand. "I like it."

Cash rested his elbow on the table and took a bite of his cookie. He liked chocolate chip better.

"I hope you won't mind if I putter around in here sometimes." She broke off a walnut and nibbled it. "Cooking's one of my hobbies."

If they'd had this conversation earlier, he might have bought it. She looked nervous, which should have softened him up a bit. But he knew, sure as it would rain come October, this woman was not who she seemed.

"About Josh," he began, sidestepping the small talk.

"Wait." Rainy snatched a napkin from the dispenser on the table and set her cookie on it. She raised serious brown eyes to his. "I need to clear something up." Even as her voice lowered, the color in her face rose. "About that…that…" Her eyes widened. "I don't even know what to call it."

Cash kept silent and looked straight ahead. He knew what she was talking about, but he refused to give her the slightest break. He had his son to worry about.

"It's not mine," she said simply.

"That's entirely your business."

"Yes, it is." Her tone was so sharp, Cash couldn't help but look at her again. "But in view of the nature of my position here, I thought you should know." Her chin lifted and she added, "It's a long story, nothing I want to get into. But I suspect my sister put that thing in my suitcase. She has a warped sense of humor." Rainy made a wry face.

Each time she had referred to *that thing,* a pretty pink stained her cheeks and Cash wanted to believe her. "Like I said, it's your business. I don't expect you'll be wearing that to tutor Josh."

"I don't expect I'd be wearing that at all."

She looked so indignant, Cash felt the corners of his mouth itch to curve up. He finished his cookie instead.

"Look, Rainy. There's a damn good reason Josh needs to be in top form by the end of the summer. His mother doesn't just want him out of Maybe. She wants custody. If Josh doesn't pass the court's test, she could win. She has a lot of influence. If anything is out of line, she *will* win."

He paused and gave her a long, hard look. "Now, please tell me I have nothing to worry about."

Rainy dove for the last chunk of her cookie. She gulped it down under Cash's curious stare, fantasizing about an array of painful ways she could do away with her sister. What a fine mess she'd stirred up, the lingerie being the least of Rainy's problems.

"No," she lied. "You don't have a thing to worry about." And prayed it was true even as the first hive surfaced on her shoulder. The second blossomed behind her left knee.

Cash drained his coffee, the movement in his throat lasting long after the brew had been swallowed. "I hope you're right."

"Me, too," Rainy muttered to herself, before licking the remnants of chocolate from her lips.

"You say something?"

She shook her head, eyes widening. A third hive had popped out on her lower back. Unconsciously, she scraped her chin over the one on her shoulder and tucked a hand behind her knee.

"Are you all right?"

"Fine." She smiled and swiped at her shoulder again. What the heck was happening? This nuisance had started about a month ago, just about when everything else had hit the fan. But this was the worst attack she'd had yet. As if she didn't have enough reason to wring her sister's neck.

"Are you sure?" Cash scraped back his chair, lines creasing his forehead.

"Absolutely." She jumped when the one on her back made contact with the chair. It was huge and itched like crazy.

"Rainy?" He rose, peering down at her through narrowed eyes.

"Uh-huh?" She casually hooked her arm up the back of her shirt, trying to apply the soothing pressure of her fingers, while doing her best to erase the panic from her face.

Cash was beside her in a flash. "What the devil is wrong?" He circled her upper arm with one hand and hauled her up out of the chair.

"Oh." Rainy recoiled and dove for the back of her knee. She held one trembling hand to her lower back, the other pressed to her leg. She looked up into his shocked face. "I'm okay."

"The hell you are. You look like a pretzel."

"Thanks." She managed a small laugh and tried to straighten.

"Are you in pain?"

"Not exactly." Rainy grimaced as she came to an upright position. She should have ignored the itching. She should have excused herself. She should keep her mouth shut. "It's my back . . ." she began, searching for an easy explanation. And my knee, my shoulder and who knows what next? But he didn't need to know all that.

"Your back?" He paled. "God almighty, I should never have grabbed you like that. I wasn't thinking."

"No, Cash, really it's not that." Actually, the commotion had gotten her mind off it, and at the look on his face, Rainy wanted to laugh. She twisted around and administered pressure to the lusty welt instead.

"I didn't hurt you?"

"Of course not. It's not even what you think."

Cash narrowed his gaze. "Let me see."

"Pardon me?" She laughed.

"Show me."

Rainy turned away, still laughing, and rolled her shoulder slightly forward while looking over it at him.

But Cash wasn't happy with that. He circled his arm around her waist, spun her around and pulled her toward him. Gently, he drew her T-shirt up just above the top of her leggings.

Rainy gasped and squirmed when she felt cool air hit her bare skin. "What the heck do you think you're doing?"

"Hold still. You're as bad as Josh." He tightened his hold around her middle and probed the inflamed area with gentle fingers. Indignant as she felt, she noticed the calluses on his hands against her naked waist. And as big and baggy as her shirt was, it had managed to ride up in front and she swore she could feel every coarse hair on his tightening forearm.

Rainy finally gathered enough wits about her and let out a hiss. "I'm not Josh. So would you quit handling me?"

"It's a hive." Cash circled it with two fingers—two warm fingers, which combined with the heat from the hive, threatened to burst her into flames. The rest of his splayed fingers whispered against the surrounding skin and brought instant bumps to the surface.

Rainy sucked in her breath. "No kidding. Now would you let me go?"

"Have you had this long?"

"It comes and goes." She clutched his arm and levered it away. With the effort, her T-shirt slipped off her shoulder.

She felt his breath dance across her afflicted and very bare shoulder. Then his gentle fingers trailed the exposed area.

"You have another one here."

"Really?" Rainy yanked at her top and covered the hideous welt. She took two giant steps back and leveled him a warning look.

He ignored it. "Have you got some lotion?"

"I don't need any. I'll be fine."

"We probably have something."

Rainy stopped rearranging her shirt. "Thanks, Dad, but I said I'm okay." She glanced up to see if her sarcasm had hit its mark.

The look Cash was giving her was anything but fatherly. His lids drooped as his darkened gaze traveled the front of her shirt. He'd stuffed his hands into his pockets and rocked back on his heels while letting out a harsh breath. His eyes abruptly met hers. "Did you say you needed some lotion?"

"No. You did," Rainy snapped. "But I don't." She tugged her shirt down over her thighs. She resented his accusing tone and expression.

And then a deliciously nasty thought occurred to her. With a nonchalant hand, she smoothed back the many wayward tendrils that had escaped her ponytail, and said, "Gee, I hope I'm no longer contagious."

"You're what?" Cash inclined his head forward as if he hadn't heard right. When his fingers reflexively scraped a few times across his neck, Rainy pressed her lips together.

"Just kidding." She grinned and rubbed one of her very real hives. It had already shrunk a degree or two but it still itched like the dickens.

He glared at her with an obvious lack of sympathy. "Are you going to be able to start with Josh tomorrow?" he asked.

"Of course. I thought we'd keep regular school hours, unless you have a problem with that."

"I wouldn't care if you kept him at it all day, but you couldn't hold his attention for that long." Cash straightened the chairs they'd managed to knock around in their tussle.

"Oh, you might be surprised." She crossed her arms over her chest. "I have a way with kids."

Cash allowed his gaze a fleeting romp over her body. The look wasn't insolent—more unthinking—but it was enough to make her feel uncomfortable. She reached behind her and grazed the subsiding hive.

"Well, maybe so," Cash conceded. "Josh isn't exactly a model student. Don't let him stall you. Believe me, he'll try."

"Two-second warning." A disembodied voice caused both Cash and Rainy to turn to the doorway. Josh leapt across the hall, his eyes directed at a baseball spinning in midair. He caught it with one hand behind his back, then stuffed it into his jacket pocket.

"Josh."

"I know. No ball playing in the house." He grinned at his father and headed straight for the cookie jar. "So, Ms. Daye," he said, rubbing his palms together and sending Rainy an enthusiastic look. "When do we start?"

Cash nearly dropped his jaw. Who was this strange kid wearing his son's jeans and Nirvana T-shirt? He caught the triumphant look Rainy slid him and shrugged.

He watched Josh gobble down two cookies, then go to the fridge for milk. He waited to make sure Josh used a glass before returning his attention to Rainy.

She had reclaimed her seat and, although a smile was in place, he could tell she was trying not to attack the hives. God only knew how many she had. They'd looked red and painful against her creamy satin skin.

Cash gave himself a firm mental shake. Skin. Plain, ordinary skin. Not creamy, not satiny. Just plain skin... that smelled like lavender.

Oh, jeez. Why did she have to smell like lavender? His ex-wife hadn't smelled like lavender. Mrs. Parker, their housekeeper didn't smell like lavender.

Rainy had no damn business smelling like lavender.

No wonder Josh was so eager for his lessons. Cash pulled out his chair so hard it hit the wall.

Two pairs of eyes flew to his. "What?" he all but barked as he positioned the chair on the tiled floor, sat down and crossed his arms.

Rainy transferred her inquiring gaze from Cash to Josh. "How about we start tomorrow morning at…" She glanced back at him for a brief moment. "Eight?"

"Sounds cool." Josh joined them at the table and turned to Cash. "Does this mean no chores for a couple months?"

A slow grin threatened the corners of Cash's mouth. With Josh, there was always an angle. Maybe Cash had been jumping to conclusions about Rainy being the reason for his son's sudden zeal. Maybe Josh saw this as a way out of his daily chores.

After all, though Rainy was attractive enough, his son hadn't seen what Cash had seen under that massive excuse for a T-shirt. He hadn't felt how small her waist was, how her hips flared to just the right proportion. Josh hadn't been close enough to smell the lavender…

Cash passed a hand over his face. "Worry about studying and I'll let you know about the chores."

Josh let out a huffing sigh at Cash's abrupt tone.

Cash glanced at Rainy, who watched the exchange with faint amusement in her warm brown eyes. "You know how important this is, Josh."

"I know, Dad. I'm not going to let you down."

"No, we aren't," Rainy said and both men looked at her. "In view of our limited time, I think we'd better plan a six-day schedule." When Josh groaned, she gave him a stern look. "Look, Josh, I've seen your transcripts. I'm not going to lie to you and claim this will be easy, but as your father said, you have a lot riding on this."

Her schoolteacher expression softened with a smile. "And

it doesn't have to be boring. I've never put a student to sleep yet." Her lashes swept down and briefly brushed her cheek as she sent Cash a sidelong glance, her catlike eyes meeting his wary ones. The gesture was so innocent, so provocative, Cash felt his mouth go dry.

And not for a minute did he doubt her words.

"Yes, m-ma'am." Josh swilled down the rest of his milk.

"Tell me, Josh." Rainy leaned forward, her elbows resting on the table, stretching the thin fabric of her shirt across her breasts. Generous breasts, Cash noted and forced his attention to her face. "What do you consider your weakest subject?" she asked.

Josh pursed his lips for several thoughtful moments, then grinned.

Cash got a sinking feeling all of a sudden. He knew that look. He knew that grin. It wreaked of adolescent impishness. He sent his son a warning frown.

"Sex," Josh answered. "Sex education." Enormously pleased with himself, he flashed a challenging look at Rainy.

She stared back. Shock, then fear, registered in her eyes before she schooled her expression back to bland. Cash noted the movement of her throat as she quietly cleared it.

Josh didn't seem to notice the undercurrent he'd caused, but in the ensuing silence, his cocksure grin faltered. He slouched in his chair.

Cash let out a disgusted sound and opened his mouth to speak. Rainy laid a hand on his arm.

"Since that subject won't be covered by the court exam, I don't think we'll need to review it," she said, and Josh half nodded. Her lips took a slight upward curve that belied the earlier unease Cash had witnessed. "But since I never discourage natural curiosity, I think we should discuss it right now."

"Now?" Josh's voice cracked.

"Sure. I'm certain your father would like to partici-pate."

The hell he would. Cash shifted in his chair. The in-creased pressure of Rainy's fingers against his forearm made him glance over at her. Mischief sparkled in her eyes. Re-alizing what she was up to, he tamped down the grin that threatened his authoritarian pose. He let his son hem and haw a few more seconds, then asked, "Where shall we be-gin?"

"Do you know where babies come from, Josh?" Rainy asked with perfect innocence.

"Jeez, you guys." Josh jerked out of the chair. "Can't you take a joke?"

"Josh?"

The boy had already zipped to the door, but turned re-luctantly in his father's direction.

"Aren't you forgetting something?" Cash inclined his head toward the nearly finished beverage on the table.

Grumbling under his breath, Josh shuffled back in, grabbed the glass and deposited it in the sink before disap-pearing down the hall.

Rainy kept her gaze on the table, her lips pressed to-gether. At some point she'd removed her hand from Cash's arm and clasped it with her other. Her lashes fluttered, then she eyed the empty doorway.

"Guess who won't be getting an apple tomorrow?" she whispered.

Cash laughed. "He deserved it."

Rainy sighed. "Not exactly how I hoped we'd get started, but I had to call his bluff."

"Believe me, I understand." And he did. She'd done a good job of setting a boundary. He admired that. Still, he wondered what had spooked her earlier.

"I guess you would." She unclasped her hands and toyed with her napkin. "How long have you been divorced?"

"Ten years."

"And you've had Josh the entire time?"

Cash didn't really want to talk about this, but the circumstances being what they were, she might need to know. "Except for six weeks each summer and one week during Christmas. Then he travels with his mother. The rest of the time he's here on the ranch."

"It's unusual for a mother not to have custody." Her gaze flitted away from his and he could tell she was sorry for having pried.

"She didn't want to be tied down. Besides, I wanted to keep Josh." Cash shrugged. "Maureen's not a bad person. She just wasn't meant to live in a small town. She can't understand why anyone else would want to, either. Too bad we hadn't figured that out before we graduated from college."

"Small towns do have their drawbacks." Rainy gave an instinctive shake of her head and drew a hand up and down one arm.

"They do," he agreed, watching the strange play of emotions cross her face.

"But you chose to come back after college," she said, regarding him with open curiosity. "You must really love it here."

"Sure," he said in a slow, dismissive tone, because some reasons were best left buried in the past.

"I'M TELLING YOU, it's her. Why would I lie to you guys?" This was the biggest day of Josh McCloud's life and his idiot friends were having a dumb attack. Leaning back on his seat, he picked up the front of his bike and watched the dust fly from the tire.

"I didn't say you're lying. You're just wrong." Seth Johnson skidded his bike to a stop next to him.

"You've been drooling over that dang magazine so much, now you're seeing things." Jimmy Ray Hassett laughed.

Tom Martin did, too.

"Shut up, you guys." Josh had a good mind not to let his so-called friends get a look at his new tutor. Except then he couldn't prove it to them.

"Besides," Seth insisted, "you said her name is Rainy. The centerfold babe's name is Sunny."

"You guys are really stupid." Being the second oldest of the group, Josh shook his head with mature disgust. "Those women never use their real names. They make 'em up, you idiot, everyone knows that. How many Bambi's and Tammy's and Sunny's do you think there are in the world?" He shook his head again.

"Don't act like you know so much about it." Tom Martin laid down his bike. "I happen to know that's only the second magazine you've ever seen."

"Says who?"

"Says me." Tom jabbed a thumb at his chest. "And only because I ripped it off from my brother."

Josh kept his mouth shut on that point, not keen on getting into arguments he couldn't win. He toed the kickstand of his bike into place and set it up near the barn.

"Okay," he said, facing the group. "I say it's her. You say it isn't. How about we place a small bet before we go inside?"

Seth tossed his long blond hair out of his eyes and glanced at Jimmy Ray and Tom. "How small?"

"Oh, let's see." Josh studied the top of the large oak tree shading part of the corral. "Fifty bucks?"

"Fifty bucks?" Seth and Jimmy Ray bellowed in unison.

"Keep it down." Josh scanned his front porch over their shoulders. A cat rolled out from one of the sagebushes in search of the midafternoon sun. "If you're so sure of yourselves, what's fifty bucks?"

"Well, you must be pretty damned sure to bet that kind of money." Seth wiped the palm of his hand down his denim shorts and frowned at the other two. "I believe you, Josh."

"Either one of you wanna bet?" Josh spread his hands.

"I ain't bettin'." Tom kicked his bicycle tire.

"Me neither." Jimmy Ray shook his head.

"Okay." Josh grinned, satisfied that he once again had their rapt attention, and herded them toward the house. "Just remember that in the picture, she's all done up." He thought about that ugly, oversize T-shirt she was wearing and about how tight her ponytail was. He hoped she'd changed her clothes since he last saw her a couple hours ago. "But you'll know it's her. You'll see it in the eyes and the smile."

"Yeah, right." Chuckling, Seth flung out his arm and landed it across Josh's belly. "As if you ever looked up that far."

Josh hugged his middle, pitching his torso forward. He laughed, then straightened before actually doubling over. "Keep it up and I'll charge admission." He punched Seth's arm.

And then the idea came to him.

"Eyes and smile. Right." Jimmy Ray snorted, then fell into step with his three friends. "Maybe we should rethink that bet."

"Gentlemen," Josh said as he circled one arm around Seth's shoulders, the other around Jimmy Ray's. He acknowledged Tom with an inclination of his head and a confident grin. "What I'm about to suggest will make fifty bucks sound like chump change."

Chapter Four

"Sorry I had to dash out like that. Got a sick bull." Cash appeared at the doorway and removed his hat. A light sprinkling of dust filtered through the sunlit air and settled about him. "This room going to be okay?"

Rainy set down the portable computer she'd brought with her. "Fine. It's certainly big enough."

She eyed the antique oak desk, the computer station in the corner, the bookcases crammed with everything from science fiction to travel magazines. Many travel magazines, she noted, and asked, "This isn't your study, is it?"

"I don't do the ranch books here, if that's what you mean. I have an office on the first floor. No one will bother you here."

"The thought never entered my mind." Rainy smiled to herself at his quizzical look. Him bothering her was about the last thing she had to worry about. After showing her the room, Cash had disappeared so fast it would have put a dent in her feminine ego, if she had been so inclined.

"As long as Josh has that exam to study for, this place is yours," Cash said.

Rainy accepted the information while walking across the room to a closed double door. "Is this a closet or a bathroom?" She opened it.

It was neither.

A king-size, four-poster bed was centered between large twin windows and covered with an attractive handmade quilt. A pair of jeans lay in a careless heap in one corner.

"This is my bedroom." Cash's voice came from near her left ear. His shoulders blocked the light from the study behind her and cast a shadow on the hardwood floor. It pointed to his bed.

"Oh, I'm sorry." Embarrassed, Rainy closed her hand around the knob and was about to pull it shut, but Cash leaned around her and held the door open.

"No problem. This area where you'll be working used to be a sort of sitting room or parlor."

He stood close as he spoke, too close. Rainy could feel the heat from his body, his breath fanning her cheeks. If she moved forward, she'd end up in his bedroom. If she backed up, she'd be in his arms.

"I converted it into a study a few years ago so anyone could use it." Cash edged past her and sailed his hat toward a low armoire. It landed next to two other Stetsons, one black, the other tan. He grinned at his success, then looked at her. "I promise I won't disturb you."

Right. Rainy took a step back. "I was thinking it might be the other way around."

"See that." He gestured out one of the massive windows. Rainy took a few reluctant steps toward him to see what he was referring to.

Acres and acres of green pasture stretched before them. Cattle grazed in the distance. Several men on horseback galloped across the range. To her Yankee eyes, it looked like a scene from a movie, or from some romantic time long ago. A thrill of excitement bubbled within her.

"You won't be bothering me," Cash continued. "This is no dude ranch. Plenty of work to be done." He sank down on the bed and tugged at his boots. His voice sounded weary, not full of pride like Rainy would have expected, and once again she wondered about him.

It suddenly occurred to her that she should probably leave now. He was, after all, taking off his boots. But she was fascinated with the view of the ranch.

"Do you usually ride a horse?" Rainy asked, craning her neck for a final glimpse of a lone rider disappearing along the horizon.

Cash kicked one boot near the foot of the bed and looked up at her with amusement in his green eyes. A slow grin lifted his mouth and, once again, Rainy was subjected to that see-all gaze that combed her body.

"Not always." He tugged the other boot free. "Sometimes I even ride a car." His eyes glittered with devilment—highly attractive devilment.

Oh, heaven help her. His lips twitched and Rainy's gaze fastened on his mouth—his very attractive mouth—and that chin so square and strong it dared her to look away. A flash of heat sent a shiver from her boneless neck down to her weakened knees.

She focused her attention on the intricate quilt framing his lean hips. "Who made this?"

Cash blinked at the abrupt change of subject, then surveyed the bed on either side of him. "This?"

He pinched one of the squares between his fingers. His nails were wide, blunt and clean. But when he glanced back up at her, it was the color creeping into his face that caught Rainy's interest.

He stood mumbling something about no one she knew.

His strange reaction made Rainy all the more curious, so when she inspected the piece a bit closer, she saw the abrupt changes of pattern, almost as if the work had been done by several different people.

"This is interesting." She peered even closer. "At first I thought the squares repeated themselves."

"Yeah." He fished in his pockets and threw some keys on the dresser.

"In fact, they aren't even all squares." She squinted at the odd pieces holding the quilt together. Some were triangles, a few looked like distorted hearts. She wasn't quite sure what to make of it. "Did more than one person do this?" Toward the center of the bed, she found a circle attached to the other pieces by a series of crocheted webs.

"Uh, yeah, I think so."

"This is really extraordinary." She leaned in closer to trace the stitching with her fingers.

"Well, if you don't need anything right now..."

The peculiar tone in Cash's voice made Rainy look up. It took a few seconds to remember where she was—in his room, practically sprawled out across his bed.

She'd been so interested in the strange quilt, which was beginning to look more like some Andy Warhol creation, that she had ignored propriety and the fact that she barely knew this man. And, more importantly, that she had no business with her nose to his bed.

Slowly, she straightened and rearranged her T-shirt. A door slammed somewhere downstairs, distracting them both. She heard the echo of voices and lowered her gaze for a few composing moments. Then she lifted her chin and gave the quilt a swift and purposeful glance.

"Fascinating work," she said with the air of an art critic, her dignity firmly back in place. Then she took a step toward the door and promptly tripped over the boot he'd discarded near the foot of the bed.

She grabbed the air and, for a split second, eyed the hardwood floor, then tumbled in the direction of the welcoming mattress.

If she hadn't had a close enough look at the quilt before, she had an excellent view now with her chin flattened against a particularly scratchy piece of fabric.

"Sorry about the boot." Cash stood above her, silent laughter shaking his shoulders as he offered her a hand.

She ignored it and flipped on her side in order to lever herself up. At that precise moment, she heard the murmurs—and the dead silence that followed.

Her attention flew to the open doorway and the four pairs of silver-dollar-size, adolescent eyes staring back at her.

Rainy briefly closed her eyes and prayed for a miracle. None came. Josh's three friends practically bounced off one another as they tried to scramble for a better look at her, while Josh merely leaned against the doorjamb, his arms crossed, a satisfied smirk on his face.

And here she lay sprawled across Cash's bed like a...like a...

She gulped and bounded to her feet.

"All right. Everybody outta here." Cash's booming voice made everyone start. Josh opened his mouth to speak, but Cash asked, "Done with your chores?" Josh promptly reconsidered and did an about-face.

"You'd think they'd never seen anyone trip before," Cash added loudly, winking at her, while the boys shuffled away.

She stopped trying to straighten her shirt and hair. The boys hadn't seen her graceless encounter with the boot and he knew it. She gave him a small, grateful smile.

"Talk about not putting my best foot forward." She shook her head. "I'm sorry if they got the wrong—"

"Don't worry about it. You know how kids are." He rubbed the back of his neck and gave her a long, hard look. "How old are you?"

Rainy lifted her chin. She'd been accused of being too young looking for a teacher before. "Twenty-seven. How old are you?"

A lazy grin lifted his mouth. "Thirty-five." He headed for the door then pivoted slowly toward her. "You still want the job?"

"I still want it." Want it? Heck, she needed this job. And more than the job, she desperately needed the distance and independence it would provide.

CASH USHERED RAINY through the barn, keeping one eye on the reaction of two ranch hands pounding nails into a beam on the rear wall. He didn't have to watch them for long. The hammers stopped swinging in seconds and the silence grew. First one man wiped a forearm across his forehead and stared at Rainy, then the other pushed his hat back for an unencumbered view.

But only when Cash heaved a sigh did Rainy react. She transferred her inquiring gaze from the row of horses to him.

He saluted the two men and called across the barn, "Joe, Nathanial, this is Rainy, Josh's new tutor."

Each raised a hand in greeting. She waved back. Even from clear across the barn, Cash couldn't miss their dumb-struck looks. You'd think they'd never seen a woman before. He glanced back at her. Well, actually, they probably hadn't. Not one like Rainy anyway. And certainly not here.

Jeez, this was a big mistake.

"Don't mind them," Cash said and swung a saddle out of the way.

"Huh?" Rainy poked her head forward to peek at the stallion in the next stall, oblivious to their ogling.

Cash rubbed the five-o'clock shadow forming at his jaw as he watched her fascination with the horse. Either she was so used to male attention that it didn't faze her, or she just wasn't the flirty type. He hoped it was the latter.

"Feel free to ride anytime. Either Smiley or I will find you a horse and saddle."

She turned wide eyes on him, an intoxicating blend of awe and excitement mirrored in their depths. "I don't know how."

He watched her longing gaze return to the beautiful animal, and he ordered himself not to make the offer. He had far too much work to do. And she was here for Josh. Period.

"But I'd love to learn."

He shook his head, knowing he was making a mistake. "Seven tomorrow morning."

"You'll teach me?" Her smile made the surrounding hay look like spun gold.

He kicked at a bale of the stuff. "I said so, didn't I?"

"I don't know." Her smile faltered and her eyes narrowed. "Did you?"

Cash swallowed. Here was his chance to renege. He could ask Smiley to do it. "Meet me here at seven sharp."

"Fantastic." She smiled again before bracing herself against the stall gate and leaning in on tiptoe.

Cautiously, she stuck two fingers between the wooden slats. The stallion pushed his enormous nostrils at her, searching for sugar. When he found none, the animal continued to nuzzle her hand.

"Looks like you've made a friend." He reached into his pocket for sugar cubes. "With Montoya, that's no easy trick, and almost impossible without these."

"I like the name. It suits him," she said, peering into Cash's open hand. Delight lit up her face when she saw the sugar. "Can I feed him?"

Cash looked down at her outstretched palm. Moisture glistened from her fingers, yet she seemed untroubled by Montoya's sloppiness. Instead, her rapt look disarmed him and Cash felt a pull in his gut. Reflexively, his fingers curled around the cubes until the corners began to crumble.

"Cash? You're teasing Montoya." Rainy grinned and he wondered how he'd managed to miss that tiny dimple. "Not to mention me."

He quickly opened his hand and dropped the cubes into hers. He barely brushed her palm with the tips of his fingers, but he might as well have touched a lit match.

He immediately drew back. Something had to be wrong. This woman was drop-dead gorgeous, liked kids and animals, seemed as guileless as a kid herself and actually didn't seem to mind living in a small town.

He took two comforting steps backward.

Something was wrong all right. Now even his damn barn smelled like lavender.

"WAS I RIGHT, or was I right?" Josh leaned back into the tall grass, his hands clasped behind his head, a stalk of hay between his smug lips.

"This is totally awesome." Seth shook his head in utter reverence, his eyes fastened to the glossy magazine pages. Tom Martin and Jimmy Ray hung over his shoulders, their bug-eyed expressions echoing their obvious agreement.

"She'd look better in something besides that crappy T-shirt she's wearing today." Josh smirked at his pals' slack-jawed expressions.

"Hell, she looks damn good without it." Seth seared an imprint of his gaze on the revealing pages before raising disbelieving eyes to his loco friend.

"Yeah." Josh sat up and discarded the hay stalk. "No kidding. That's why we gotta hurry and buy up the rest of the copies. Jimmy Ray, can you hit Colesville, Dune and Baker counties by the end of the week?"

"How am I supposed to get there? On my bike?" Jimmy Ray shook his head. "Besides, I don't see how you're gonna get her to autograph all those magazines."

"Me neither." Seth went back to turning pages.

"Don't sweat the small stuff, boys. You worry about buying up every copy from here to Houston, and I'll figure that out."

"Houston. Yeah, right," Tom added. "Besides, there ain't no way we're gonna get her to do that."

Josh leapt to his feet. He knew that, but he was determined to figure out an angle. "Look. This is last month's issue. There won't be many copies left as it is. Are you guys in or out?"

"Tell me again how much you're figuring we'll get on the resale?" Seth asked.

"At least five times." Josh watched their frowns turn to grins and relaxed. "Well, gentlemen, time's a wasting."

"REALLY, MISS PICKFORD, I can get my own breakfast." Rainy smiled at the woman while sneaking a look at the wall clock above her head. It was her third morning of riding lessons and Cash's mood had been so unpredictable, she didn't want to jeopardize their deal by being even one minute late.

"Like I told you yesterday, breakfast comes with your rent." Violet Pickford put a kettle on to boil and turned to the refrigerator. "I also told you to call me Violet."

Rainy shuffled from one foot to the other. "Okay if I just have a piece of toast…Violet?" Rainy broadened her smile.

The older woman's pursed lips softened until they began to curve up. Looking Rainy up and down, she pulled out a package of English muffins from the freezer and set it on the counter. "Such a pretty young thing you are. I don't know why you insist on dressing like such a ragamuffin."

Rainy followed Violet's gaze from her striped, oversize T-shirt to her baggy drawstring jeans. She glanced back up at the older woman and shrugged. "They're comfortable."

Violet shook her head. She set out butter and orange marmalade. "Not an ounce of vanity, either. Polite, too," she went on as if Rainy weren't there. "Not always common for youngsters these days."

Rainy hid a smile. She was hardly a youngster, but she wasn't about to disagree with Violet. They'd gotten along fabulously so far. The woman had even allowed her in the kitchen while she'd made a batch of chili. Rainy had the feeling that was a gigantic step in their relationship. Especially since she'd figured out that the moonshine Violet made in her shed was a major ingredient. And Rainy was fairly certain Violet knew she had guessed her secret.

"You know, Cash has been single quite a while." Violet fidgeted with the ancient toaster, but slid Rainy a glance. "He'd make a fine husband."

Heat climbed Rainy's face and she gratefully turned to the kettle the second it started to whistle. She had no doubt that was true, only she wasn't in the market. And if he knew about *Midnight Fantasy*...well, she wouldn't even be in the running. Not that she wanted to be, she assured herself.

"Yup. He needs himself a wife. Maybe then, all those silly women would quit making him those god-awful quilts."

Rainy stopped the tea bag in mid-dunk. "What?"

"Every year before the Swing Festival, they all try to outdo one another with their entry into the quilt auction." Violet chuckled. "Cash always places the winning bid, and they all get so fired up to impress him, most years they end up not finishing in time. Last year he made them attach it all together. What a sight it made. Two of them still aren't speaking."

Rainy digested the information with mixed emotions. It shouldn't surprise her that Cash was considered the town catch. In fact, if her sister were here, Sunny would snap him up in a heartbeat. The sudden thought would have unsettled Rainy, if she hadn't known her twin was a couple of thousand miles away. Besides, Sunny was way too flamboyant for Cash.

"You're looking mighty pleased all of a sudden. Thinking about entering a quilt yourself?" Violet pushed the plate of buttered English muffins she'd just toasted toward Rainy and chuckled. "Course, the festival is in one week. You'll have to get mighty busy if you want to make Cash's heart sing."

Rainy made a face. "I was thinking no such thing." She looked at the older woman's cagey smile and gave her a saccharin sweet one back. "Actually, I was thinking how nice a bouquet of your roses would look on this counter."

The smile faded from Violet's face and her eyes narrowed to crystal blue slits. "Don't even think about it, Missy. Those flowers will be Swing Festival winners, just like my chili. And if you know what's good for you, you won't even eyeball them."

Rainy swallowed her laughter and surprised Violet with a swift kiss on her unlined cheek. "Yes, ma'am," she said and snatched a muffin half. "See you tonight." She caught a glimpse of Violet's smile as she went out the kitchen door.

She laughed halfway to Cash's ranch, thinking about the look on Violet's face. She spent the rest of the time thanking her lucky stars she hadn't overly antagonized the woman. Her response to Violet had been pure Sunny. Her twin normally had the last word or witty comment. Sunny was the one to whom everyone immediately warmed up. Rainy's unflappable and lovable sister was the one who took the risks and got the attention.

Strange, Rainy had never identified with Sunny's characteristics before—even on this small a scale. Of course, this was the longest they'd ever been apart, and with Sunny around, Rainy had never had much time to think, much less act on her own. And now that she did, the feeling was both weird and exhilarating.

Rainy leaned back into her seat and flexed her hands on the wheel. She felt only a smidgen of guilt for not missing her twin too terribly since leaving Boon. And most of that guilt had to do with their birthday next week, which, for the first time in their lives, they'd share only in spirit.

It was a small price, Rainy decided, for the freedom of finally being able to spread her own wings.

"WHAT DO YOU MEAN you don't have a bellman?" Sunny Daye tossed back her luxurious mane of honey blond hair and drummed her long red fingernails on the motel counter. She started to look over her shoulder to complain to Rainy, but remembered that her twin wasn't there. Her breath caught in her chest. Smart, dependable Rainy had always been there before. The empty blackness that encased Sunny's heart grew a little bleaker.

She took a calming breath, gave her hair an extra toss and asked, "Well, *who's* going to carry my bags?"

The young man snapped his widened gaze up from her tight leather minidress to her incredulous and dramatically made-up eyes. "Sorry, ma'am. But this isn't even a motel no more." He looked out the window down the row of faded turquoise bungalows. "It's been closed for nearly two years. We use it to store equipment for our annual Swing Festival."

"Oh." Sunny pursed her full, red lips and was pleased to see that her effort received the desired result. "Where can I find another motel?"

The young man gave her a toothy grin. "Colesville."

"No, I mean here, in Maybe."

He shook his head. "We don't have one. Violet Pickford usually has a room or two to rent, but I heard she already has boarders."

Sunny blinked. Could one of them be Rainy? The urge to rush over there nearly had her on her knees begging for directions. "How do I get to Colesville?"

She started to write down the directions the helpful young man eagerly supplied, but realized quickly that even she could remember twenty miles straight down the road.

Smiling, she thanked him and hopped back into her rented red convertible. It was going to be a blast surprising Rainy for their birthday.

Chapter Five

Cash yanked the saddle off the sawhorse with a little too much force and it landed with a thud, disturbing two stacked bales of hay. A difficult week had just gone farther down the tubes.

"I'm not late, am I?" Rainy's soft voice came from the direction of the barn door.

He pulled off his work gloves and slowly turned toward her, shaking his head. "Sorry, Rainy. No riding lesson today."

Her eyebrows drew together, and she pushed the last of her hair into her usual ponytail before glancing at her watch. "It's just now seven."

He hated the look of apprehension that colored her peachy complexion. It reminded him that he hadn't been the best of companions the past four days, snapping at Josh and Smiley for no good reason...well, Smiley's worsening chili disasters might qualify. But, all in all, Cash had been a jerk, yet she'd continued to show up on time, smiling and excelling at everything he taught her.

She was even keeping Josh at his desk for hours on end, something Cash had never been able to accomplish. Hell, even his own stubborn horse was taken with her.

"That's not it." He wiped an arm across his forehead. "My housekeeper had to leave town unexpectedly this morning. Her daughter up near Dallas is about to have a baby."

"Mrs. Parker? I didn't know she had a pregnant daughter." The apprehension fell from Rainy's face. A radiant smile took its place, and Cash knew instantly what had him so bent out of shape.

He picked up the lopsided bale of hay and slammed it atop the other one. "I just didn't know she was that pregnant. I haven't made arrangements to have someone cover for Mrs. Parker yet."

Rainy moved into the barn and bent down to try and straighten the bales. They wouldn't budge. "No problem. I'll help out. Dinner shouldn't be hard to whip up." She lifted her face to him and blew a blond tendril out of her eyes.

Cash was sorely tempted to kick the hay to shreds. "That's not what I'm paying you for."

"I would never shortchange Josh's studies, if that's what you're implying." Her expression became stern as she stood facing him not four feet away.

He stared back, contemplating the way her youthful ponytail draped carelessly across her shoulder. "Don't you ever wear your hair down?"

"What?" She stepped back.

He stepped forward.

Rainy put a nervous hand to her hair and smoothed it. When she edged to her right, she bumped into Montoya's stall. The horse whinnied and Rainy jumped.

Cash put a hand out to steady her, even though it was hardly necessary. Only when his fingers let up on her upper arm, and he felt the warm flesh, the firmly toned muscle, the energy that undermined his good sense, did he know that touching her was what he needed to do.

"I'm all right," she said with a weak smile.

"Yeah." Hell, she was more than all right. She was damn near perfect. And he still wondered what the devil she was doing here in Maybe. He let his hand slide down her arm and wondered if she realized that she'd come a little closer.

His attention snagged on her pouty lower lip, and he told himself that kissing her would be a stupid move. He was a responsible adult with a son to worry about, but her eyes were round and luminous, her parted lips enticing. And Cash decided that refusing the invitation would be the stupidest thing of all.

He slipped his fingers under her ponytail, cupping her nape, pulling her face forward. Her warm and minty breath seduced him, drawing him closer. She stretched up the last few inches to meet him and their lips joined in a gentle union.

He brought his other hand up to her waist and fitted her against him.

She stiffened at first, but as she leaned into him, her soft breasts pressed into his chest and the kiss gained urgency. He teased her lips open with the tip of his tongue and, just as a heat wave threatened to dissolve the rest of his common sense, a car door slammed outside the barn.

Guiltily, they jumped apart.

Rainy's hand made a beeline for her hair. The semblance of a ponytail barely remained. Long strands of silky blond hair clung about her face and neck. The pulse at her throat ticked wildly.

Cash loosened the bandanna at his neck. He rotated a shoulder a couple of times before forcing his eyes to meet hers. "Guess I'd better go see about replacing Mrs. Parker."

She averted her eyes and said, "Good idea."

He picked up the work gloves he'd discarded and slapped them against his open palm. "Rainy?"

She strode off. "I think I'll go see if Josh wants to get an early start today."

He hung back for a few seconds, then took off after her. "Wait a minute."

They reached the door at the same time and he grabbed her arm. She turned in agonizing slowness to face him.

The confusion on her face almost had him apologizing...until he saw the Cadillac. Mint green, painfully familiar and parked only yards away. He let out a succinct curse, glanced back at Rainy and apologized for that instead.

She followed his gaze toward the car. "Who is it?"

Coming toward them from the front porch was a petite, slightly plump, impeccably dressed redhead. A casserole dish lay across her outstretched hands and appeared to be helping her balance as she picked her way across the gravel driveway on absurdly high heels.

"Now would be a good time to go find Josh." He lifted a warning brow in Rainy's direction, then mentally braced himself for the advancing redhead.

Rainy arched a brow back. "Oh, I don't know." She grinned at the exasperated sound he made right before he returned his attention to his unexpected guest.

"Josh told me you'd be out here." The woman took a careful step over a particularly rocky strip of ground and stood before Cash with a well-practiced smile. "I've brought your favorite dinner—my chicken and dumplings." She widened her smile, then gave Rainy a brief, sidelong glance. "Why didn't you tell me Ida had to leave? You know I would have been here in an instant."

"Thanks, Della." Cash rubbed the back of his neck. "I didn't know her daughter was having the baby so soon. Anyway, I got it covered."

Della blinked, then studied Rainy again, this time slowly and thoroughly. She frowned. "Oh."

Cash gave Rainy one last helpless look before he faced the inevitable. "Della, this is Rainy Daye, Josh's new tutor. Rainy, Della Weatherspoon, owner of Della's Boutique."

"Hi." Rainy offered the woman her hand and a warm smile.

"Did you say Rainy? As in rainy day, sunny day?" As Rainy cringed, Della chuckled. "Your parents must have a wonderful sense of humor."

"Yeah." Rainy yanked the hem of her T-shirt farther down her thighs. "Guess I'll go find Josh. Nice meeting you."

"Same here. And, hon?" Della's eyes traveled Rainy's body. "Stop by my boutique anytime."

Rainy forced a parting smile. She hurried to the house, leaving Cash to squirm alone. She wondered if Della had had a hand in Cash's quilt and had her own chuckle.

But by the time she had located Josh, confiscated the gooey brownies he was about to have for breakfast and made him some hot cereal, she felt exhausted. Being a morning person, she knew her condition had little to do with the activities and everything to do with Cash's kiss.

No doubt about it, the man was a black-belt kisser. Not that she was any expert, but holy moly... She put her hand to her mouth. And she was a black-belt idiot.

The kiss had no business happening. Getting involved was nowhere on her list of goals. Remembering her ex-boyfriend's betrayal, her feet labored as she ascended the stairs to prepare for Josh's lessons.

Not to mention that this job, this town, was her only safe haven. If she did well, it might be her whole future. She couldn't blow it now, not even for Cash McCloud.

As sweet as kissing Rainy had been, Cash decided it wasn't worth the cold shoulder she'd given him for the past day and a half. She'd even canceled her riding lesson yesterday.

He tried not to think about it. He had too much work to do to be worrying about kissing her or her reaction to him...or lack thereof, he thought as he chuckled humorlessly. She was doing a great job with Josh and that was all that mattered. Throwing a kiss into the mix had been a damn fool thing to do.

He leaned into the open refrigerator and surveyed their choices for lunch. Apart from Della's leftover chicken and dumplings, there was Sue Ellen Kramer's lasagna, Bonnie Brown's stew and Mae West Mayfield's ham-and-cheese something or other.

Cash sighed. He hoped he hadn't sounded ungrateful when he'd finally had to put a stop to the parade of widows and divorcées bearing enough food for the entire county. It had started to get downright frightening. And Rainy's obvious amusement over the whole matter didn't sit well with him, either.

He'd made his decision and was putting the stew into the microwave when the doorbell rang. He arrived to answer it about the same time Josh and Rainy came downstairs for their noon break.

"Got your latest issue of *Traveling Man* here," Kathleen Mason said, waving the magazine at him. "It's the issue on Alaska I know you've been waitin' on, and who knows when Clarence would have gotten around to deliverin' it. And since I was in the neighborhood..." Her interested gaze wandered past him to Rainy, who had just left the last step and was headed for the kitchen.

"Thanks, Kathleen." Cash took the magazine from her. "I appreciate it."

"No trouble." She smiled, then sent a slight frown in Rainy's direction. She looked back at Cash and flicked out a tuft of strawberry blond hair from behind her ear.

"Uh, we were about to have lunch." Cash gritted his teeth. He knew he had to make the offer, and at least she didn't have a casserole with her. "Care to join us?"

"Actually..." She gave him a sly smile accompanied by a wink. "I brought that, too. I'll be right back." She dashed out in time to miss his low groan and returned a minute later with two covered dishes.

Rainy and Josh had already set the table, Smiley was washing his hands and the microwave had just dinged. Cash walked over to hang his hat on the peg near the back door.

As Rainy withdrew the steaming bowl of stew, she noticed Kathleen's two dishes and her disappointed pout.

"What have you got there?" Rainy asked. She discreetly placed the stew on the counter and approached the woman.

"Cash's favorite." Kathleen's smile was beatific. "Turkey and dressing, and an apple pie for dessert."

"Wow! That's got my vote." Josh ripped back the foil. Smiley agreed.

Kathleen purred with pleasure.

Cash managed a weak smile and pulled out his chair.

Rainy covered the stew. "Sounds like you've made a hit."

"Hope so." Grinning, Kathleen set the food in front of Cash and took the seat beside him. "Figured it just might get me an invite to the dance Saturday night."

Cash took a large gulp of water and slid Kathleen a wary glance.

Smiley chuckled, scooping up a huge mound of cornbread dressing.

Rainy nudged the salad she'd brought to the table toward Josh. "What dance?"

"Rainy..." Cash scolded in a playful tone. The brief and pointed look he gave her, however, was pleading. "You already said you'd go with me. Now don't go teasing."

She held his stare for a second or two, then dropped hers and arranged the napkin on her lap. When she looked up,

Josh had stopped in mid-chew and was darting puzzled glances from her to his father. Kathleen had pushed her plate away, thinly veiled disgust marring her pleasant features. And Smiley kept shoveling in dressing, his black eyes sparkling with amusement.

Cash's mossy green gaze hadn't left her. She fidgeted with her fork, reminding herself she didn't owe him a thing. In fact, after the kiss the other day, committing to anything social could be professional suicide. And Rainy was a sensible, intelligent person. Everyone said so. She looked back up into his beautiful green eyes. "Oh, *that* dance. I thought it was *next* Saturday."

She forced a smile and raised her water glass so quickly it clanged against her teeth.

There wasn't much conversation at the table after that. Cash did send her several grateful looks. Oddly, Josh sent her several salty ones, which she was hopeless to interpret.

Kathleen declined to stay for the apple pie and, after she left, they all voted to save it for dinner. Smiley closed the back door behind him on his way out and Josh disappeared down the hall.

"Thanks for bailing me out," Cash said as soon as he and Rainy were alone. They both reached for the plate of turkey at the same time. When their fingers brushed, Rainy pulled back. Just casually touching him was dangerous. It made her think of the kiss.

She picked up the bowl of salad instead. "No problem." She let him finish clearing the table and began stacking the plates in the dishwasher. "But I guess you'd better explain what this dance business is all about."

"It's part of the Swing Festival. Hey, I don't expect you to do that." He came up behind her and reached around to take a plate from her hand. She felt his breath on her neck. When she started to resist, she felt her fanny rub against something delightfully solid.

"I said I'd help." She snatched the plate and sidestepped him. "Now tell me about this Swing Festival." Her fingers trembled as she jammed the plate into the rack.

"It's an annual fair. Three counties participate and it opens with a welcome party on Friday night. Then the chili cook-off starts the next day, and there are rides for the kids, games, bake sales, that sort of thing. The dance is Saturday night. Then they wrap up with an auction on Sunday."

"Oh?" Rainy lifted a brow and kept a smile in check. "What kind of auction?"

Cash put the last of the dishes to rinse in the sink and turned the water on full blast.

She really should let him off the hook, she thought, pursing her lips. Nah. She leaned slightly toward him and said a little louder, "I asked, what kind of auction?"

"It varies." His color deepened and she was glad to know he was a lousy liar. "The money all goes to the town council for civic programs."

"Sounds like a good idea."

"Usually. But not this year."

"Why not?" She stopped what she was doing, curious about his disapproving tone.

"They've all got some crazy idea about using this year's proceeds to get involved with a cattle drive some Dallas hotshots are trying to get started."

"Who is 'they' and is that bad?"

Cash shook his head in disgust. "'They' is most of the town, and they have no idea how much time or money hooking up with this damn cattle drive would require."

"Sounds intriguing."

"We don't have the resources. So it's a moot point, Rainy. No sense talking about it."

"Well, so is the dance." She noticed his skeptical expression. "I mean, you don't really expect me to go?"

"Well, yeah." He tossed the dish towel past her toward the counter. When it missed, he lunged to catch it.

She tried to back out of the way, but the open dishwasher door hit the back of her calves and kept her a waiting captive for his open arms.

Cash braced himself with one hand on the counter. The other he anchored at Rainy's waist. The towel lay in a heap beside her foot. "Actually, I do," he said in a voice just above a whisper.

"Do what?" Her voice caught and came out weak.

His devilish grin was pure suggestion as he paused before answering, "Expect you to go to the dance with me."

"Oh. Why?"

"Because it'll be fun."

"I don't dance."

"You can try."

Rainy put her hand on the counter to steady her sagging knees, except it was his hand she found under hers.

His grin widened. "Does that mean yes?"

She pulled her hand back. "No."

"Come with me, Rainy."

"It wouldn't be like a date, right? I mean, I *know* it wouldn't be a *date*. People would just think you were being polite because I'm new in town . . . right?"

"Sure." Amusement glittered in his eyes. His thumb stroked her waist, reminding her that he was far too close, that her pulse raced out of control.

As gently as her frazzled nerves would allow, she placed her hands on his shoulders. Out of the corner of her eye, she thought she saw a shadow at the doorway. She glanced over, but no one was there. Turning her attention back to Cash, she lightly pushed him away.

She allowed her uncertain gaze to linger on his seductive mouth for another instant and wondered at exactly what point sensible Rainy Ann Daye had lost her ever-loving mind.

JOSH JERKED BACK from the kitchen door and flattened himself against the wall. What the hell did his father think he was doing? He was way too old for this stuff. The woman was likely to give him a frigging heart attack. If his father saw Rainy's centerfold, Josh knew for sure he'd have a heart attack.

He let out a huff of air. Although he truly liked Rainy, his loyalty was to his dad. And Maybe High's PTA president couldn't afford to get mixed up with someone who'd... who'd... Josh's heart pounded just thinking about those glossy pages.

He squared his shoulders and pushed off the wall. He couldn't allow himself to get distracted now. It looked as if saving his dad was up to him, and he knew just how to do it.

Chapter Six

Cash opened the door of his truck and loaded in the first three bags of groceries. He was about to return to the store for the last two when the owner, Jeb Haller, came through the door, balancing one bag in each arm.

"Hey, Jeb, you didn't have to come out in this heat." Cash quickly relieved the elderly man of the heavy sacks.

"It sure was worth the trip." Jeb shaded his eyes against the bright July sun and looked past Cash toward the far end of Main Street.

Cash turned to see a woman with long honey-colored hair and an obscenely short denim skirt briefly survey the sign outside of Maribell's Beauty Shop, then disappear through the doors.

"Never seen her before." Jeb wiped the sweat from his brow. "You?"

Cash stared at the empty doorway. A shiny blue pickup zoomed past and he blinked. The woman bore an incredible resemblance to... Ah, hell, now she had him seeing things.

"Nope, never seen her before."

"Not the likes of her, neither." Jeb shook his head. "Wonder what she's doing here? Wouldn't be that tutor I heard you got staying at your place?" He chuckled.

"Yeah, sure. And anyway, she's staying with Violet Pickford." Cash offered up a grin he didn't much feel like. "Not with me." The idea of Rainy staying with him and Josh had been bothersome enough when she'd first arrived. Now it just about scared him to death. "Jeb, you know anything more about what Thelma's plans are?"

"Going to live with her daughter." The man clasped his hands together and rested them on his round belly, narrowing his eyes on Cash. "You thinking maybe that tutor of yours could take her place?"

Cash casually rearranged the grocery bags until he was sure they wouldn't tip. "Maybe."

"Qualified, is she?"

"To teach ninth graders? We'd be lucky to have her." Cash climbed in the pickup. "Anyway, it's just a thought."

As he waved to Jeb and maneuvered the truck down Main Street, he admitted to himself that it was more than just a thought. Rainy had an incredible knack with kids. Josh had never been so attentive to his schoolwork before. He'd watched them several times unobserved and had witnessed her patient, yet stern manner, how she got Josh to think on his own. She was a good teacher. He had no doubt about that.

What he did doubt was his own objectivity. He was a PTA member, one who had long been known for his sound judgment. Before he could recommend Rainy for the open position, he had to make sure she wanted the job and would be willing to stick around for it. Although she seemed more than at home in their sleepy little town, it was too soon to tell whether she could adjust to living here permanently.

Cash didn't want to make that mistake again—personally or otherwise. During the short time his ex-wife had lived in Maybe, her disdain for the town had grown to the point of causing them both a lot of pain. And the hell of it was, when it came right down to it, Cash couldn't really blame her. If not for his obligations, would he have stuck around?

He pulled the truck along the driveway to the kitchen door. Then he quickly unloaded the supplies and refrigerated whatever was necessary, hoping he'd picked up everything Mrs. Parker would have. After assuring himself that Rainy and Josh were in the middle of their session, he considered doing something he hadn't done in years.

He stared at the piece of paper outlining his endless list of chores, then allowed his gaze to stray out to the barn that was in desperate need of painting, the corral that needed a new gate. He was out of his mind. He had far too much to do, especially with Mrs. Parker gone. The timing was all wrong.

"Ah, hell." He folded up the list, stuck it in his jeans pocket and grabbed the issue of *Traveling Man* Kathleen had brought over yesterday. He cast a guilty look over his shoulder, then slipped into his study and locked the door. For just a little while, Cash would allow himself to dream.

"YOU AIN'T TAKIN' Rainy to the dance in that ol' pickup, are you?" Smiley asked before bringing the wooden spoon up to his nose and taking a whiff of his latest and spiciest batch of chili. He pulled back and twisted around just in time to let out a horrific sneeze.

Cash laughed and slid the can of black pepper across the counter toward him. After spending several hours hiding out in his study with his travel magazines, he was feeling pretty good.

"Doggone smart aleck," Smiley grumbled, pushing it away and reaching for a large can of tomato sauce.

"Oh, no," Cash groaned. "You keep that up and you'll have enough to feed all of Maybe."

"Nope. Just us. This is tonight's dinner if it don't turn out right." Cash groaned again, but Smiley ignored him.

"Now what are you goin' to do about gettin' that gal to the dance?"

"What's wrong with the pickup?" Cash turned back to pouring himself a cola. He hadn't been on a date in so damn long that he hadn't even considered the truck a problem. Now he wondered. Hell, this wasn't a date. "I took Bonnie that one year. I used it then."

Smiley gave him a wry look before turning back to his doctoring. "She's not like Bonnie." He paused for a moment, then slid Cash a brief sideways glance. "She ain't like the rest of 'em, either."

"Yeah." Cash set the cola aside and opened a beer instead. He took a large gulp and forced back a sigh. "But it's just a favor she's doing me. The dance is no big deal."

Smiley raised his black brows, but said nothing.

"Are you really going to the dance?" Josh strode into the kitchen and snatched up the cola his father had discarded. Cash nodded.

"With *her?*" Josh faced his father, frowning.

"You mean, *Rainy?*" Cash frowned back. "Yeah."

"I suppose you'll stay longer than half an hour, like you usually do."

Cash didn't like his son's tone one bit. "So?"

"Do you really think you should be, like, dating my teacher?" Josh took a casual sip of his drink, but Cash knew him too well. The boy was nervous.

"It's not exactly a date, Josh." Cash could feel the heat at his collar. Why the hell was everyone so interested? "Why don't you tell me what the problem really is?" He blinked, thinking he may know the answer to that question. Although Josh had been circumspect in his interaction with Rainy, maybe he did have a crush on her. Cash thought back to when he was fourteen. Ah, great. "Josh?"

His son shrugged. "You're out of practice, Dad." He pursed his lips and the serious look on his face was just about Cash's undoing. "I don't want you to get hurt."

"Thanks, kid." He took another pull of beer, not sure whether he should be happy with his son's answer or not. "Maybe my ancient memory won't embarrass me too badly."

Josh opened his mouth, ready to deliver another argument, when the doorbell rang. He made a dash for it and Cash let him, glad for the interruption. The only thing worse that could happen was if it were Rainy, and Josh gave her an earful about dating his father....

"Oh, hell," Cash said out loud, netting himself a puzzled look from Smiley. He put down his beer and hurried to see who it was.

"Come in, come in, ladies," Josh was saying, his face wreathed in a smile. He opened the door wide and in pranced Melissa Sue and Kimberly Faye, each holding a covered dish.

Cash held back a huge groan. He thought he'd made it clear to all and sundry that supplying his meals was unnecessary. Word spread far too fast in this town for everyone not to have heard. He forced a smile for the short blonde and tall brunette as they headed directly for him.

"I think it's awful that Ida Parker left you without any notice," Melissa Sue said, then breezed past Cash and zeroed in on the kitchen. Nodding her agreement, Kimberly Faye followed her. Cash threw up his hands and followed, too.

"Melissa, Kimberly, this is real nice of you, but—" Cash barely got the words out.

"Oh, hush, Cash McCloud. Don't think another thing about it. I know how you love my fried chicken." Melissa winked at Josh, who grinned back until he caught his father's eye. A nasty-looking shade of red began to blotch his son's jaw.

"And I came through with my famous bean and wienie casserole," Kimberly said. Cash cringed, then plastered a grateful smile on his face just as she, too, winked at Josh.

Cash gave his son a long, suspicious look, but Josh was too busy inspecting the dishes the ladies had brought and trying to avoid his father's eyes. When the doorbell rang once again, Josh tried to bolt for it.

Cash put a hand on his shoulder. "Hold on. I'll get it." He gave Josh a we-need-to-talk look before hightailing it out of the kitchen.

Rainy stood waiting at the door, attempting to pull her hair into her normal ponytail.

Cash let out a giant sigh of relief. He glanced back over his shoulder at the giggling coming from the kitchen, took her by the shoulders and walked her backward until he could close the door behind him.

He grabbed her free hand. "Come on."

She let out a sound of surprise and her fingers slipped, causing her hair to tumble forward. "Where are we going?"

"A riding lesson."

"Wait a minute. I have something important to discuss with you."

"Later." He pulled her along with him, realizing that this was the first time he'd seen her hair down. It was magnificent. Shimmering like a field of sun-kissed wheat. The faster they walked, the more the silky strands fluttered about her shoulders and pink-tinged cheeks. Her beautiful eyes sparkled with confusion and excitement. The possibility that he might be getting himself in even deeper water crossed Cash's mind.

Quickly, he saddled their horses. He helped her mount Ginger, her favorite mare, and led them out toward the open range. After they'd been riding for about five minutes, he slowed down his horse to a leisurely canter abreast of her.

"Want to tell me what this is about?" Rainy tossed her hair away from her face. She hadn't had time to tie it back yet, and if Cash had his way, she wouldn't ever again.

"I felt like a ride."

"Right." She gave him a bland smile and glanced at her watch. "Shouldn't we be seeing to dinner about now?"

He wasn't sure why yet, but he had a feeling he was going to kill Josh. "I don't think we have to worry about that."

"Why?" She finger combed her hair back and tilted her head toward him. The sun shone in her brown eyes, reminding him of warm caramel. When he was too busy looking at her to answer, she added, "You know Josh and Smiley expect to eat by six-thirty."

"Yeah. And the horses have to be fed twice a day, the cows need to be milked each and every morning and the hands have to be paid every Friday." His tone was so sharp he got an odd look from Rainy.

Cash sighed, feeling the weariness close in. "Did you know the sun never sets in some parts of the world?" He gazed up into the cloudless July sky. "And that it's winter in Australia right now?"

"Well, yes, as a matter of fact, I did." She stared at him long and hard. "Cash, is something wrong?"

He didn't answer her. Instead, he led them over to a nearby brook, climbed off Montoya and tethered both their horses to a low-slung mesquite branch.

Slowly, Rainy dismounted. When she got her footing, she slipped her fingers into the pocket of her jeans and produced the pink elastic band she used to secure her hair.

It had barely left her pocket when Cash put his hand over hers. "Leave it down."

Her almond-shaped eyes grew round. "I—I don't like it down."

His gaze traveled to where she'd hiked up her customary, large T-shirt in order to reach her pocket, and where the fabric had remained snagged. Her waist was small, her hips seductively flared. But he'd already known that—by touch. "Why?"

She lifted a shoulder. "It's impractical."

A slow smile curved his lips. She couldn't be for real. He let go of her hand, and as her breasts rose and fell in seeming relief, he grabbed a handful of the gleaming hair cascading about her shoulders.

A surprised gasp escaped her.

"Leave it...for a while...for me." Cash slid his other arm around her and pulled her closer. She put both her hands on his chest and nodded slowly, her gaze fastened to his, a slight quiver in her lower lip.

He let some of the silken strands slip through his fingers and brushed his thumb across her mouth, wishing she didn't have to feel the calluses years of ranch work had put there.

"Cash?" she whispered. "Do you think this is a good idea?"

"Definitely not." He lowered his mouth to hers and tasted her sweet hesitancy grow to an even sweeter urgency.

Her hands inched up his chest until she had circled his neck with her arms. He hugged her to him, stroking her back, angling his mouth over hers, finding his own urgency spiraling out of control. He slipped one hand under her shirt and rested it on the curve of her buttocks.

Her nails dug into his back through the thin cotton of his shirt. Her stomach muscles tightened against his hardness. She leaned into him, her breasts pressed against his pounding heart, and as quickly as the promise had been made, it was broken.

"Cash," she said, shaking her head as she stepped out of his embrace. She seared his mouth with one last longing gaze before she pressed her own lips together. She took another step back until she'd run up against the tree. "I need to talk to you, but not if... well, we can't do this." She shook her head again. "Not with what I'm about to tell you."

It took Cash several seconds to gather his wits. He stood there, his arms suddenly empty, his desire evident. But except for a few trees, they were standing in the middle of several acres of open land and there wasn't a hell of a lot he could do about his obvious arousal.

When her words and demeanor finally registered, Cash's heart mushroomed into his throat. She looked nervous, lines forming between her brows. Whatever she had to say, he had a feeling it wasn't going to be good. "Go on."

"I suppose you've heard about the opening for a ninth-grade teacher." She fidgeted with her hands, but the worry lines had softened and the beginnings of a smile played at the corners of her mouth. "Violet told me about it, and... well, I'd be a terrific replacement."

The tightness in Cash's chest dispersed and he let out a relieved breath of air. "I agree."

"You do?" She splayed her connected fingers and smiled. Then her mouth drooped a bit and her eyebrows furrowed once more. "But not because..."

"No, Rainy." He took her hands, pried them apart, then gave one a brotherly pat. "I think you're a good teacher."

She let her hands fall to her sides and he had no choice but to let her go. Her expression turned oddly wary and she said, "So my qualifications are what matter."

"Among other things."

"Such as?"

"Character, primarily."

"Have I passed the test?"

Funny, it seemed as if he were the one being tested. "If I didn't think you were a good, responsible person we wouldn't be having this conversation."

She seemed to relax a bit, then her hand fluttered in a nervous gesture. "I just want to get this straight. Your decision—Maybe's decision—will be based on my credentials and character alone? Period."

He frowned. "Yes. And like I said, I already know that you're a good teacher."

"You don't actually know that," she argued.

"Oh, yes, I do. When it comes to the welfare of my son, I'm not above eavesdropping." He shrugged. "And when it comes to Maybe, I'm not about to let my hormones ride roughshod over my common sense."

A faint rosiness seeped into her complexion and her gaze swept the front of his jeans.

She looked like the old Rainy again, and Cash laughed. When she tried to turn away in embarrassment, he touched her arm. "Look, I'm going to be honest. I think you'd do a great job, but I have to admit to having some reservations about endorsing you."

She returned anxious brown eyes to his, her shoulders wilting slightly. "Why?"

"This is a small town."

She looked relieved. "I already know that."

"You haven't even been here two weeks. Believe me, in two months it'll seem even smaller."

"I've already told you, I come from a small town."

"But you didn't stay, did you?"

Rainy's shoulders recoiled against the trunk of the mesquite as if she'd been struck, and Cash cursed himself for his accusing tone.

"Look, that was... I didn't mean..." He lifted his hat, then tugged it back down again.

She held up a hand and ducked between him and the tree. "I don't blame you for being curious about that." She sighed and sank down at the edge of the brook. "It's a long story. Nothing I want to discuss now." She let out a soft, humorless laugh, while unsuccessfully trying to skip a stone across the water. "Maybe someday when my sense of humor returns I'll tell you about it."

"Are you kidding?" Cash sat beside her. "You have a great sense of humor. That's one of the things I love..." Love? His boot heel nearly lost its hold on the sloping ground and he kicked up a spray of dirt trying to keep his balance. It was a figure of speech, for God's sake. Wasn't it?

With enormous reluctance, he glanced over at her. Her knees drawn up, arms folded atop them, Rainy rested her chin on her wrist and paid him not one drop of attention. Her gaze was snared on some faraway thought, and his anxiety settled into relief... and curiosity.

"Okay, Rainy, we'll set your reasons for leaving Boon aside." For now. She'd angled her face toward him, and her look told him it couldn't be any other way. "But I still say you could get tired of this place real fast."

She smiled then, a slow tolerant smile, as her head lolled to the side and her warm look touched first his mouth, then his eyes. "I don't think so."

Cash's heart slammed against his chest. Did she have any idea how she was looking at him? What her eyes, her smile, her tone, implied? He gulped in a staggering amount of air. "What about your family, friends?" he asked slowly. "Wouldn't they be upset?"

"It's not like I'd be moving to Russia." She laughed and closed her eyes, lifting her face toward the sun. Even in the direct light her skin was smooth and flawless. "Besides, they'd understand."

He wished he did. Despite her repose, tension puckered her eyebrows and her lips had tightened. Something troubled her, something she had no intention of telling him. And he suddenly realized he wanted to share her burden.

She continued to face the sun, her hair a silken waterfall down her back. He looked at the strong, slim column of her throat, his lips burning to follow the path.

"Wouldn't you miss them? Miss being close to a city?" he asked, wanting the right answer far too much.

"Oh, right." She wrinkled her nose and faced him. "I guess I'll just have to hire a jet for weekends at the opera." She grinned, shaking her head. "There's not a whole lot I'd do in a city. And if I ever have that burning desire, Dallas or Houston are only hours away. Violet said I could go on some of her monthly jaunts."

Cash let out a snort of disbelief. "Violet invited you to go with her?"

"What's so surprising about that?"

"Let's just say, Violet doesn't take to most folks that quickly." That was an understatement. He narrowed his eyes. "You say Violet told you about this teaching position?"

She nodded. "And she told me I could stay with her as long as I want." Her tongue stole out to moisten her lips and she darted him a quick glance. "She also told me that you had a lot of influence."

Rainy, obviously, had Violet's stamp of approval. Cash drew a hand over his face, covering his mouth for a minute. There was no question Rainy could do the job. The fact that he wanted her to stay was beyond question. And she hadn't once complained about the town's meager offerings...

"Now I won't say any more about it," she added when he didn't respond. "I just wanted you to know I'd like to be considered for the job." She rose to her feet and dusted off her bottom. "And that I'd really like to stay."

Cash stood, too, doing everything in his power to tap down the hope flaring within him. He poked his Stetson back with one finger and looked down at her earnest face. "Okay," he said slowly, ramming his hands into his pockets in an effort to keep them off her. "You've got my vote."

"Violet said you'd say that." Rainy's brilliant smile lit up her face. She aimed it at him and he felt his gut somersault to his groin.

"Yeah?" Grinning, he withdrew his hands from his pockets. "She say anything else?"

"Uh-huh." She took a small tentative step forward. "Said I might as well go for it. The commitment is only for a year."

Cash's grin faded. He ignored her quizzical look and dejectedly eased his hands back deep into the safety of his pockets.

SUNNY HAD YET TO FIND a gift for Rainy, and their birthday was only three days away. She'd looked in every store in Colesville and half the ones in Maybe—which hadn't been difficult considering there were only three...four if you counted the beauty shop.

And now she peered into the window of the last untried store. None of the displayed merchandise was appealing, but a sign in the window advertising the Swing Festival caught her eye. It started tomorrow and boasted handmade crafts.

Rainy would like something homemade, she decided, contemplating the festival. Besides, Sunny wanted to keep her presence scarce in Maybe. Knowing her twin like she did, she figured her sister would hardly spend any time in town, but Sunny didn't want to risk bumping into her.

She brought a finger to her lips. The festival could be another story. If she didn't find a gift during this brief trip to Maybe, she'd have to think long and hard about that particular risk. It had occurred to her on more than one occasion that she'd arrived far too early, but the truth was, she had no place else to go.

She sighed and was about to push open the door, when a pair of brown eyes peeked at her from around the corner. The boy was about eleven, his hair black and shiny, his feet bare and his well-washed shirt sported a ragged hem. He summoned her with a crooked finger.

Curiosity being one of her weaknesses, she released the door and poked her head around the corner where he'd disappeared.

Standing several feet back from the sidewalk, he held out three perfect red roses. He smiled with all his teeth. "For you, *señorita,* three dollars."

Sunny grinned as she dug into her purse. "For one rose?" She smothered a laugh at his widening eyes over her "misunderstanding." "That's highway robbery." She handed him the three bills and took one of the flowers. She hoped he profited as well with the remaining two.

"I'll give you these other two for only five," he stepped forward eagerly, pushing the roses at her.

She laughed out loud, shaking her head, and ruffled the top of his hair. "You're going to do just fine."

Shrugging, he scampered off to find another pigeon.

Sunny stepped back up on the sidewalk and snapped off the long stem. Finding her reflection in the store window, she tucked the blossom behind her ear.

She started to reenter the store, when she heard a wild shriek. It came from somewhere behind her. But when she turned around, no one was there. She shaded her eyes and searched the street.

Two stores down, stood a motionless figure in baggy white coveralls. If it hadn't been for the big floppy hat and curly red hair, she wouldn't even have been able to tell it was a woman.

Sunny shrugged and pushed through the creaking door.

Chapter Seven

It was almost dark by the time Rainy headed back to Violet's house. Her head and body ached and all she could think about was a long, warm soak in her new friend's claw-footed tub.

She stuck her face nearer the windshield and searched the sky for a full moon. Blocks of fast-moving clouds obscured her view. She hit the steering wheel with the heel of her hand and let loose an indelicate word.

What else could possibly account for the loony behavior back at the McCloud ranch? After having kissed her until her toes curled, Cash had maintained a stony silence their entire ride back to the house. Though he had been reasonably pleasant at dinner—polite was a better description—he'd spent the rest of the evening giving her the cold shoulder. That is, when he wasn't reminding his son not to treat her like public enemy number one, which was something else she didn't understand. Up until today, she and Josh had gotten along great. And if Smiley asked her one more time what Violet put in her chili . . .

Rainy gnashed her teeth as she applied the brakes, nearly missing the turn to Violet's driveway. The promise of that long, warm bath was the only thing keeping her sane, she realized as she pulled up in front of the rosebushes.

The porch light was a welcome sight, and Rainy smiled to herself. Violet wasn't at all crusty, as she tried to make people believe and it was on days like this that Rainy was especially grateful for the woman's easy friendship.

She pulled her laptop computer from the passenger seat and traipsed around the rows of roses, giving them the wide berth that she'd learned from day one would help keep her in her landlord's good graces.

She'd reached the first porch step when she saw the suitcases stacked haphazardly near the door—bags that looked suspiciously like hers.

She hopped up the last two stairs, set down the computer and crouched to inspect the heap.

"You get off my porch this instant." Violet's voice boomed through a crack at the door. "And take all your junk with you."

Rainy's head shot up. She lost her balance and landed hard on her fanny. "Violet? Wh-what's going on?" She tried to stand, but the sound of Violet's shotgun being pumped had her butt making contact with the wood again.

"You're already packed, now get." Violet's face—what little Rainy could see of it—was nearly as red as her hair as the woman shouted from the shadow of the door. The soft cultured tone that normally colored her voice was gone. "And don't even think of getting near my roses. I've got both eyes and both barrels on you."

Rainy scrambled to her feet. *The centerfold.* Her stomach rolled. "Violet, I can explain—"

The distinctive click of a gun sounded once more.

Rainy grabbed one suitcase and the laptop. She started to turn and ask if it was all right to make two trips, but hurried down the steps instead. She threw both items into the car and rushed back for the remaining bags, half carrying, half dragging them in a wide U around the roses.

As soon as she was in the driver's seat, she heard the front door slam. Rainy puffed out her cheeks, dropped her head back against the headrest and took deep breaths until her heart stopped pounding in her ears. She stared up at the blackening sky. Restless clouds raced by and, sure enough, a full moon made a brief appearance.

Swearing silently, she straightened. How had Violet found out about the centerfold? At least that's what Rainy assumed was the problem. What else could it be? And what else could possibly go wrong tonight?

And then she remembered she had no place to go.

She thought of Smiley's chili, Josh's scowling face, Cash's frigid shoulder... his sizzling kisses.

She crossed her wrists on the steering wheel, dropped her forehead on them and groaned.

"NO, YOU CAN'T GO into Houston with me tomorrow. You've got to stay here and study." Cash flipped to the next page of the magazine he'd been trying to read ever since Rainy left almost an hour ago. Between his son's interruptions and his own sick, deluded thoughts, he'd managed to cover three whole paragraphs.

"Does that mean Rainy will be here, too?" Josh dropped to the couch in his father's den.

Cash put down the magazine and took a deep breath. "Where else would she be on a Friday?"

"With you." Josh flicked his wrist back, about to spin a baseball into the air, caught his father's warning look and pushed it into his open palm instead. "In Houston."

"Why the devil would you think that?"

"Ah, no reason."

Cash lifted a brow at his son, but decided not to press any further. "Time you got ready for bed."

Mumbling, Josh pulled his lanky body off the couch just as the doorbell rang.

Cash glanced at the clock and frowned. "You get up-stairs," he said to Josh as the boy made a quick left out of the den. Sighing, Josh reluctantly reversed his steps toward the staircase.

Smiley had long since retired to the bunkhouse, so Cash made the trek to the door himself. He paused with his hand on the doorknob and lifted the curtain away from the window.

Rainy stood near the porch swing, gazing out into the darkness. The light that seeped from the windows outlined her silhouette, and Cash got that all-too-familiar, funny feeling he got every time he saw her. She turned when he opened the door.

"Forget something?" he asked, noticing at the same time the tote bag that lay at her feet.

She stepped out of the shadows. Her face drawn and pale, she spread her hands. "Violet kicked me out." A look of sheer defeat crossed her face.

"She what?" He noticed a small hive surfacing near her wrist. "I thought you two were such great buddies."

"So did I."

"What happened?"

"I have no idea." Her eyes darkened and she glanced away for a moment. "I went straight home from here. When I got there, all my bags were packed and sitting on the porch."

Cash looked down at her single tote, then back at her shell-shocked face. She batted at a moth, and he realized that he hadn't even invited her in. Without a word, he stepped toward her. Rainy's soft gasp whispered in the still air as he leaned close to pick up her bag. He straightened and gave her a furtive sideways glance while gesturing her inside. A frown etched deep creases between her tawny brows and her lips pursed in uncertainty. She swiped at a few stray tendrils of hair before trudging forward.

Automatically, his hand went to the small of her back as she preceded him. He dropped it before making contact and sucked in some air. Having her under the same roof was going to be murder.

Once again, she hesitated in the hall. Cash continued on to the staircase. "I'll set you up in the guest room," he said over his shoulder, taking two stairs at a time. "Then I'll get your other bags from the car."

She hurried after him. "That's not necessary. I have what I need for tonight."

"And tomorrow night?" He led her into the room next to his.

"I'll find someplace else."

"Good luck." He laid her bag on the bed.

"I'll try Colesville, if necessary."

"Not with the Swing Festival going on. It's a pretty big event around these parts. People come from all over central Texas." He stopped at the door and faced her. "Besides, it wouldn't make sense to travel all that way back and forth every day."

Rainy cast a glance heavenward, and he noticed the dark semicircles under her eyes. "Well, nothing seems to be making much sense at this point," she said glumly.

Cash leaned against the doorjamb, rubbing his jaw. "And you have no idea what's got Violet riled up?"

"No." She lifted a shoulder in a casual gesture, but he noticed that her hand shook . . . right before it curled into a fist. "I have no . . ." She relaxed her hand and said, "I don't know . . . I—I'll have to speak with her."

"I'm going to Houston to sign up for the livestock show tomorrow, but I can talk to her when—"

"No. This is my problem. I'll handle it."

"Okay . . ." He lightly hit the opposite doorjamb with his palm and straightened.

She'd moved closer to the bed, her fingers wrapped around one of the four posters, her eyes wary. Although she stood perfectly still, he could tell she was ready to jump out of her skin.

Hell, he didn't have to go to Houston tomorrow. Any business he had there could be dealt with over the phone or by mail. But he was getting that restless feeling again.

"Cash?"

He blinked.

"Thanks for putting me up."

"No problem," he said with a half grin.

But when she smiled back, he knew his problems had only just begun.

"WHY DID YOU SLEEP here last night?" Josh asked Rainy as soon as she appeared in the kitchen.

She headed straight for the coffeepot and poured herself a full mug before answering. It was bad enough that she'd had a horribly restless night. Now she had her student's accusing tone of voice to contend with.

"There was a problem at Violet's place," she replied, mentally rolling her eyes at the understatement.

Josh narrowed his gaze on her. "What kind of problem?"

"Do I ask about all your secretive phone calls to Seth and Jimmy Ray?"

He blushed a furious red.

Rainy had felt her patience give way a second before her mouth had taken over. She sighed and sat down at the table. "I'm sorry for snapping."

A fresh wave of color washed over his face. "Those are business calls," he mumbled, looking away.

Business calls. Monkey business, no doubt. "And last night at Violet's was business, too," she said in a light tone as he brought his eyes slowly back to her. "As in *my* business."

"Okay, okay." He let out an exasperated sound. "But are you staying here tonight, too?"

Good question. She attempted one more sip of the scalding coffee, then put it down. "I don't know."

"What about the dance?" He frowned. "Are you still going?"

"Look, Josh, you want to tell me what's bothering you?" She pushed the mug aside altogether and, resting her elbows on the table, leaned forward. She'd heard Cash and Smiley leave earlier and knew she and Josh were alone.

He finished the last of his cereal and hurried to the sink with his bowl. "Nothing. Wanna start on algebra first?"

Rainy watched him, irritation creeping along her nerve endings. Why had this kid been treating her like the plague ever since last night? It wasn't as if she was thrilled to be staying here. Or, at this point, about going to the dance.

She thought about last night, about Cash being in the next room, and about how badly she'd wanted to be there with him... and she thought about how close she had come to telling him about the centerfold.

But she wasn't quite ready to kiss her tutoring job and the Maybe High teaching position goodbye. Too bad she wasn't so set against kissing Cash.

Sighing, she topped off her coffee and followed Josh upstairs.

By the end of the morning, most of the tension between Rainy and Josh had vanished. They wrapped up for lunch and even joked a little while making their sandwiches. When Josh asked her if they could make an early day of it so he could go into town, she agreed. It had occurred to her that she didn't have a proper dress to wear to the dance the following evening. So not only did she have to brave a trip to Violet's today, but now she'd have to make her debut in town. Neither place held much appeal at the moment. Especially now that it seemed Violet knew about the centerfold. It made Rainy wonder if anyone else in Maybe knew, although she did feel some comfort in the fact that the reclusive woman rarely went to town.

Perhaps it was foolish hope—or just plain wishful thinking—but a part of Rainy fought the idea that Violet could have suddenly discovered the centerfold. It wasn't as if *Midnight Fantasy* would be her kind of reading material. And the woman was so focused on her chili and rose entries, it was possible something pertaining to them had set her off. In fact, what was it she'd said about her roses?

Rainy's mind went blank. Too much had happened last night. But for her own sanity, she clung to the hope that she was completely mistaken about Violet's flare-up.

Two hours after they'd returned to his lessons, Josh began glancing at the clock and fidgeting.

She closed her book. "That's it. We're outta here. Need a ride to town?"

Josh pushed his books and scratch pads into a precarious pile. "Nope. I'll take my bike. I'm gonna meet Seth and Jimmy Ray." He gave her a surprised glance. "Are you going into town, too?"

She nodded. "Be back in time for dinner." In Mrs. Parker's absence, except for the casseroles supplied by the local husband hunter's league, Rainy had gladly assumed most of the cooking chores and felt justified in expecting Josh to be on time.

"Sure." He hesitated at the doorway. "When did my dad say he'd be back?"

"He didn't." She continued to tidy up her things and asked in a casual voice, "Does he usually get back for dinner?"

He thought for a moment. "Actually, he normally takes care of his Houston business over the phone."

She blinked, then her eyes met Josh's bemused gaze.

"Yeah," he said, smirking and nodding, something suddenly and obviously pleasing him. "He hardly ever leaves Maybe." He gave her a swift head-to-toe perusal and, with another satisfied snort, headed down the stairs.

The way Josh had just eyed her, she felt like the evil witch of the north who had just been stripped of her powers. Not that she had any powers. If she had, she wouldn't be in this mess. Not only had she been chased out of the town's only lodgings, it looked as though she'd just chased Cash off his own ranch.

Rainy didn't have much hope for a reconciliation with Violet, and she didn't want to get stuck here another night. After last evening, it was no secret how the rest of the household felt about that. Besides, she wasn't up to another bout of hives.

Sighing, she flipped open the phone book. But six phone calls later, she was still homeless. Massaging the back of her neck, she glanced at her watch and decided to hit the road. If she only spent an hour groveling to Violet, she could still make it to town.

"I CAN'T BELIEVE you guys only got twenty-three issues. This is really pathetic." Josh scratched out several numbers in his notebook. "Seth, are all your *Midnight Fantasy* included in this amount?"

"Jeez." Seth threw down his baseball glove. "I've already blown my damn allowance until Thanksgiving to get this stuff. What more do you want?"

"You just don't see the big picture, do ya?" Josh grumbled, shaking his head. "Borrow it if you have to."

"Are you nuts?" Tom Martin leaned his bike against the gas-station wall. "My mom is already asking a million questions."

Josh's head shot up. "You tell her anything?"

"Hell, no." A look of disgust crossed Tom's face.

Josh thought for a moment as he gazed down Main Street. "Where are you keeping your copies?"

"Under my bed," Tom said. "My mom never cleans under there."

"What about the rest of you?"

"They're under my bed, too," Seth said.

"Mine are out in the garage," Jimmy Ray said. When Josh gave him a funny look, he added, "Nobody'll find 'em."

"When are we going to get her to sign them, anyway?" Tom asked. "I can't hold on to them forever. Besides, I need to start getting some cash in."

The others echoed their agreement, while Josh finished his calculations. He took his time so he wouldn't have to admit that he hadn't figured out how they were going to get the autographs yet.

Damn it. He'd been too busy worrying about his father. The poor guy was going to flip, if and when he found out about the centerfold. Josh figured it was up to him to keep the old guy from making a fool of himself, in the meantime. Thank God, Rainy at least was pretty low-key. And the fact that his dad had left for the day was a good sign. He'd been hanging around the house far too much since she had arrived. Maybe things were looking up...maybe Josh could relax now. Still, he'd seen too many of his dad's lovesick looks...

"Hey, you guys know if thirty-five is the right age for a mid-life crisis?" he asked.

Seth and Tom exchanged frowns. Jimmy Ray glanced up from the bike tire he was filling with air and shrugged.

Josh chewed his pencil and stared into space.

"Wow, isn't that your dad's truck?" Tom stood and Josh followed his gaze to the dark green pickup stopped at the town's only intersection. "Cool motorcycle. Whose is it?"

Josh's mouth hung open as he watched the flashy hunk of black and silver metal bounce along on the bed of the truck. He caught his father's wide grin just before he made a turn and disappeared from view. Was that why he'd been so hot to go to Houston?

"Really cool. When did he get that?" Seth's tone was reverent as he absently punched a rhythm into his baseball glove.

Dread filled every pore of Josh's body. "I knew it. I damn well knew it." He let out a whoosh of air, then paced between his friends and their collage of bikes. "He's going through the change."

Josh took several turns back and forth before he realized that his friends weren't paying him any attention. Before he could point that fact out to them, he caught Seth's stunned expression. His eyes were fastened somewhere over Josh's shoulder. Beside him, Tom and Jimmy Ray gaped in the same direction.

Jimmy Ray balled his fists. "Holy sh—"

"Jeez." Tom swallowed convulsively.

Josh spun around to see what the attraction was.

Half a block away, a woman raised herself on tiptoes and leaned into a semitruck's passenger window. Two long tanned thighs showed below her black leather miniskirt, her stretchy pink top hugging her in all the right places. Laughing, she tossed back her long blond hair and presented the boys with a perfect profile.

It was Rainy. Josh's heart raced in his ears. For a split second, he wondered why in the hell she'd never dressed like that to tutor him. He faintly heard his friend's mumblings, felt his feet take two involuntary steps forward. Pressing his fingertips to his closed eyes, he tried to erase the disturbing vision. But when he pulled them away, she was still there.

He tried with all his might to summon the image of the tutor with the baggy shirt and jeans he'd known for nearly two weeks. But the new Rainy stayed propped seductively before him, and his traitorous hormones were rapidly turning his knees to jelly.

He watched her push back a couple of feet from the truck, balancing daintily on her ridiculously high heels, while the truck driver left his seat and came around to meet her on the sidewalk. Laughing, pushing back her blond hair, she took the man's arm and they entered Harry's Diner.

"I think I'm in love." Seth put a hand to his heart, his jaw dropping nearly to his chest.

"Me, too." Tom had a goofy grin on his face.

Josh pointedly glared at each of his friends, then let out a sound of pure disgust. He glanced back over at the empty doorway and tried to slow down his own pulse.

He had to admit, she was pretty damn hot. She was also trouble.

He drew his eyes back to his weak-kneed, sappy-looking friends and shook his head. If she could do that to them, who knew what she could do to someone as old and gullible as his father.

Josh folded the paper that held his calculations and, sighing, tucked it into his shorts pocket. He supposed he'd have to wait a few more days to get rich.

He strode over to his bike, the wheels in his head approaching a frantic speed, when he noticed Mabel Simms leaving the hardware store. She was in charge of the Swing Festival dance and booths. He groaned just thinking about his dad and Rainy at the dance. Next thing he knew, they'd be moving in on Maybe's only decent make-out spot. The thought made him cringe.

He jerked his bike upright and adjusted the wobbly seat. He had to do something about that dance....

His head shot up. Quickly, he scanned Main Street until he saw Mrs. Simms approach her car. He hopped on his bike, ignoring the shouts from his friends, and pedaled as fast as he could.

The woman was just about to close her car door when Josh came to a screeching halt on the sidewalk beside her. She gave the skid marks he'd left a disapproving look before offering him her attention.

Josh gave her his best smile.

"Can I do something for you, Josh?" Mabel Simms smiled back.

"Yes, ma'am. Are you still in charge of the booths tomorrow?"

"Yes, I am."

"You still need a volunteer for the kissing booth?"

Frowning, Mrs. Simms nodded.

Josh's grin stretched to Dallas as he hopped off his bike. "Have I got the perfect person for you."

Chapter Eight

Della's Boutique was small and quiet, but the selection was good. Since she was the only customer, Rainy took only a few minutes to find three suitable dresses.

She ducked into the tiny dressing room in the back corner. She quickly shucked off her jeans and shirt, slipped on a white peasant dress, then stepped out to view herself in the full-length mirror near the cash register.

"That looks awesome." The short, blond teenage clerk cracked her bubble gum one last time before coming around the counter. She stood back for a few seconds, and Rainy felt the uncomfortable weight of a head-to-toe perusal. Then she heard the sigh. "I hope I grow some more."

"I sprouted two extra inches when I turned eighteen," Rainy offered, smiling at the wistful expression on the girl's face.

"I haven't budged in three years." The teenager leaned back to check out the dress, then pulled the elasticized neckline down to expose Rainy's shoulders. "It's definitely you."

Rainy scrunched up her face, tilting her head at her reflection. "You think so?" She brought the neckline up an inch.

The clerk slipped it down two. "Absolutely."

Rainy laughed. "I don't know about that."

"Why?" The young lady frowned. "It's too long, huh? You like 'em short," she added, nodding and ignoring Rainy's puzzled look. "Maybe you ought to go with the red."

Rainy went back to the changing room and dutifully tried on the red sundress, but it stopped several inches above her knees. She took it off without bothering to go out to the mirror. The pink dress didn't look as if it was much longer, so she draped the white one over her arm and took the other two back out to the racks.

"Actually, you probably would've looked gorgeous in any of them," the clerk said, casting a glance at the rejects. She carried the white dress to the register and grinned. "But this will look great with those long, dangly earrings."

Rainy brought a tentative hand to one bare lobe as the girl continued cracking her gum while she rang up the dress. Rainy shook her head. She was definitely going to quit drinking the water around here. First Violet and now this poor young thing.

Violet. The reminder produced a lump of dread in her throat. She was almost glad the woman hadn't been home when she'd stopped by earlier. But cowardice wasn't going to find her a place to stay, she acknowledged glumly, promising herself she'd try again on the way home.

She paid for her dress, thanked the clerk and headed for her car. Several older men strolling Main Street waved to her. She waved back at the smiling faces and relaxed. Such a nice friendly town. And here she was a perfect stranger. She smiled and settled down in her seat. With a little luck, she could be home free.

SMILEY NARROWED his beady black eyes on his boss. "A what?"

Cash ignored his foreman. He was too damn happy to let anyone spoil his fun. He hauled out a wood plank and toted it from the barn to his truck. After securing his makeshift ramp to the open tailgate, he hopped up on the truck bed and untied the motorcycle.

"She's a beauty, isn't she?" he asked Smiley, who had followed him out, shaking his head the entire time. Cash stroked the heavy metal handlebars, then wiped away the smudges he'd left. "Stand there at the bottom and make sure she doesn't get off track, will you?"

"What are you gonna name her? Sunny?" Smiley laughed at his own joke, then sobering, eyed his unamused boss. "Get it? Rainy Daye, sunny day?"

"Make sure it doesn't slide off." Cash noted the abruptness in his tone as he guided the motorcycle down the ramp. Why the devil would Smiley bring up Rainy? Hell, it had been a battle not to think about her all day.

As Cash barreled down with both handlebars in his grasp, Smiley jumped back just before the motorcycle's tires hit the dirt. He made sure the foreman was safely out of the way, then gave the stand a firm kick. He rocked the bike gently to test for stability before releasing it, then stepped back to admire his new toy.

"How long you been fixin' to get this?" Smiley asked as he poked his face near the bike's engine.

"Not long."

The older man nudged his hat back and regarded him curiously. "Ain't gonna be much help around a ranch."

"This has nothing to do with the ranch, Smiley." Cash opened the truck's passenger door and hauled out a black helmet. Just then, a car pulled into the driveway. He looked up to see Rainy's MG circle around to the front of the house.

He glanced at the matching helmet laying on the seat, but left it there and closed the door.

"Ain't that somethin'." Smiley ambled over and touched the helmet's shiny smooth surface. "Looks like one of them science-fiction gadgets."

Cash laughed.

"Yup. Pretty impressive if you ask me." The older man winked, then allowed his gaze to stray to the house. "But I ain't the one you wanna impress."

Cash gritted his teeth. Smiley chuckled and aimed his bowlegged gait toward the kitchen, leaving Cash to fiddle with the controls of his new motorcycle.

He had no idea why Smiley thought Rainy had anything to do with his latest purchase. Hell, he'd actually been thinking about it for some time. He just never figured he'd get around to going through with it.

He rubbed the back of his neck. But he should have known, no one in this town would understand.

"Where'd you get that?"

Josh's voice came from behind him and he turned in surprise. His son climbed off his bike and stared at the motorcycle with a mixture of dread and awe.

"Hope you kept your pedaling below the speed limit," Cash said when he noticed the boy's red face and sweaty shirt.

"Is it yours?" Josh let his bike fall to the dirt.

Cash frowned, but he said nothing, nodding instead.

"Why?"

"What kind of question is that? I thought you'd be excited."

"When did you decide to get this?" Josh circled the motorcycle, his gaze shooting back and forth between his father and the vehicle.

"What is this?" First Smiley and now Josh . . . Cash had just about enough of the twenty-question bit, especially now that his good mood had been shot to hell. He watched his son, who, despite his words, looked as if he was dying to ride the bike. "You wanna tell me what this attitude is all about?"

He heard the kitchen door slam behind him and figured Smiley had returned to gang up with Josh.

"Where did *that* come from?" Rainy's voice sliced through the mounting tension between Cash and his son.

Cash swung a glance her way. "Houston." Then he trained his eyes back on Josh for a moment, already regretting his sarcastic tone. He threw her another look, this one apologetic, and said, "I bought it from one of the guys I do business with down there."

He noticed that Josh had moved in closer and was eagerly checking out the gears and radials.

"Really?" she drawled and traced Josh's earlier path around the bike. "Interesting."

Really? Interesting? What kind of remarks were those? "Go change your shirt, Josh, and I'll take you for a spin." Cash tucked the helmet under his arm and, with his free hand, fished in his pocket for the keys.

"Be right back," his son called as he took off at a run. It was about time somebody showed some enthusiasm.

"The spaghetti and meatballs will be ready in half an hour," Rainy said. She'd stopped at the handlebars, and as he'd done earlier, she took the corner of her shirt and polished the chrome.

"Darlin', there are some things more important than dinner."

She looked up at his playful tone and blinked, a strange emotion flittering across her face. Taking one last dab at the metal, she smiled, fastened her chocolate brown eyes on him and said, "I know."

Cash's throat suddenly went dry. Something big was happening. Something really big. She understood him far too well. It was both exhilarating and frightening as hell. He rubbed his palm against his thigh to squash the itch—and to stop himself from doing something really stupid, like pulling her into his arms.

Instead, he stood there, drowning in her simple honest gaze, knowing she did understand. Knowing that, somehow, she'd looked into his soul and comprehended the fact that sometimes he wanted more than life offered.

And...she hadn't begrudged him that want.

"Well," she began, drawing a hand up her opposite arm and glancing toward the house. "I'll keep dinner warm."

He gave himself a mental shake. She already had him heated. He swung a leg over the bike and settled onto the seat. "Thanks."

"No problem." She took a step backward.

The screen door slammed and he noted Josh in his peripheral vision. "Rainy?" he called when she started to turn away. "After dinner—"

She grinned. "You'll take me for a spin, too?"

Slowly, Cash shook his head, his eyes darkening. "No, sweetheart, I'll take you for a ride."

RAINY COULDN'T FIGURE out how the meatballs ended up tasting like cardboard. She'd dumped half of Smiley's spices into the mixture, for heaven's sake, but as she wrapped up the leftovers to be refrigerated, she wondered if they were worth keeping. Of course, everyone else had raved about the meal and gobbled most of it up. Maybe she was coming down with something?

She'd just placed the last of the sauce in the fridge, when Cash reentered the kitchen. "You ready for that ride?"

As soon as he uttered those words, she knew she'd lied to herself. She was coming down with something all right, she thought as she swiveled toward him. It wasn't contagious and it wasn't going to be pretty.

"Sure." She lifted a nonchalant shoulder. "But I'd better give Violet a call first or you'll be stuck with me another night." Twice this afternoon her former landlord hadn't answered the door, and Rainy wondered if the woman was home and purposely ignoring her. At this point, she held little hope of sleeping in her old room tonight.

"Don't bother. I'll get Josh to unload your car and take your things upstairs," he said. When she started to shake her head, he added, "There's a perfectly good room here."

Right. Next to yours. "That same room was here when I arrived almost two weeks ago," she reminded him. "What's changed?"

"My good sense," he muttered. "Anyway, since Mrs. Parker left, you're here all the time...which reminds me, we'll talk about upping your salary for all the extra work you've been doing around here."

"No." Her tone was so sharp she surprised herself. She softened it with a faint smile. "Whatever I do, I do because I want to."

"And I appreciate that. It doesn't mean you shouldn't be paid for it."

Be paid for it? Rainy rarely felt the urge to hit someone, but right now she wanted to smack him so hard she had to steady her hands. She took a deep breath and silently counted to ten. How silly of her to have forgotten that this was only a job. She should probably thank him for calling it to her attention. She sniffed. So why did she still feel like smacking him?

"Rainy?"

She balled her fists one more time, then flexed her hands. "Thanks for your consideration." She lifted her chin. "I'm sure we'll come to mutually agreeable terms."

Cash stared at her a second, then drove his hand through his hair. "For chrissakes, Rainy, I only want to be fair to you."

"And I appreciate it."

He eyed her a moment longer, briefly closed his eyes, then grabbed her wrist. "I'll give you something to appreciate," he murmured and pulled her into his arms.

Her breath caught as his lips slanted over hers. He pressed a palm into her lower back, bringing her flush against him. Her hands lay on his chest between them, her fingers curling slightly as she told herself to push him away. She raised her eyes to his hooded ones, clutched the front of his shirt and offered her lips to him.

He kissed her hard and breathless, and just when she thought she'd have to pull away, he gentled his touch, nibbling and tasting, drawing her lower lip into his mouth, nipping at it lightly with his teeth.

She sighed and he seized the opportunity to sweep her parted mouth with his tongue.

The front door slammed.

Rainy immediately straightened. What had they been thinking? Josh had been upstairs. Smiley had been in the study. Anyone could have walked in on them. She shuddered.

Cash pulled back only slightly, a dazed look on his face. He slid a quick glance toward the hall, then swooped down for another brief kiss before letting her go.

"C'mon," he whispered, taking her hand and leading her through the back door.

She tried to slow him down. "Where are we going? Shouldn't we say something to someone?"

"They'll figure it out." He hurried them over to the motorcycle and helped her into a helmet. He secured the other one on himself, swung onto the bike and held out a hand to her.

She was crazy to do this, she thought, hiking up her jeans and hopping on the seat behind him. When she took too long to settle in, he reached back and pulled her arms around his waist.

He revved the engine a couple of times. Smiling at his enthusiasm, Rainy laid a cheek against his strong, broad back. The hot, sticky July weather had eased up some, and now with the sun setting a light breeze trickled through the air. She wrapped her arms more snugly around him. He squeezed one of her hands, then gunned the engine once more, and they shot down the driveway.

At least a dozen miles later, Cash veered them onto a side road. Not a house was in sight, and several head of cattle grazed across the way. The cattle looked up in sync at the sound of the engine, then lazily returned their snouts to the tall grass.

The dirt road was rocky, and Rainy had to hang on even tighter. Not that she minded. Cash's stomach was hard and lean, and the rough ride gave her ample opportunity to explore the muscular ridges without being discovered. She wondered what kind of exercise he did to keep his stomach that way, wondered when he had the time. And then she realized how little she knew about him.

She knew he was an excellent father, he was kind and responsible and he treated his ranch hands like family. According to Violet, the entire community of Maybe showered him with well-deserved respect. Yet Rainy knew he kissed like a sinner.

She swallowed hard—her pulse beginning to pound again—and wondered some more.

The ground evened out, and as they approached a small clearing where the grass was not quite so tall and the sage clustered, Cash cut the engine. He glided to a stop and held out his arm to balance her as she slid off.

She lifted off her helmet and what little was left of her ponytail fell over her shoulder. Long, flyaway tendrils scattered about her face in the light dusky breeze.

Cash removed his helmet, cast it aside and positioned himself in front of her. Slowly, he lifted a hand and gently combed the loose strands of hair back with his fingers. She closed her eyes to the soothing touch against her scalp, enjoying his nearness.

When she opened them again, he was looking down at her, smiling, the sky streaked with pink and orange behind him. He pulled the elastic band from her hair and the remaining locks fell through his fingers. He spread them out over her shoulders, let his fingertips trail her jaw, then with the knuckle of his index finger, lifted her chin.

His smile slackened, but the lines bracketing his mouth remained. The muscle at his jaw tightened.

Rainy took a deep breath, hating the thought of stopping him. She wrapped a hand around the finger guiding her chin. "Guess what?"

He turned his hand until their palms met. He kissed the back of hers, then brought them down, clasped together. "We shouldn't be doing this," he guessed.

"No." She backed away. "I mean, yes, we probably shouldn't, but that's not what I was going to say."

He arched a brow—the scarred one—and Rainy, once again, wondered about him.

"It seems I always pick the worst time to bring this up, but I need to tell you that I applied for the teaching position today."

"I know."

"You do?" She pulled her hand back to join her other one. "You were in Houston."

"I stopped by Homer Simms's office on the way home." He brushed away some sage lint that had settled near her neck. "To recommend you."

"Oh, Cash." His word meant a lot in Maybe. Giving his word meant even more to him. "I can't tell you how much I appreciate your confidence in my teaching."

He grinned. "I have faith in the teacher."

She smiled back. "I won't let you down."

"I know."

His eyes were so serious, Rainy had to gulp back the knot forming in her throat. Had it only been four weeks ago that Richard, her long-standing boyfriend, had accused her of letting him down? And about something she'd had no control over?

She stared up into Cash's darkening emerald eyes and her senses swayed off kilter. She knew even less about him than she'd known about Richard. Was she setting herself up for a rebound fling that could get her in even deeper water?

"Where did you get that scar?" She put a fingertip to his brow and lightly traced the small half-moon.

All emotion fled his face. He angled away from her touch. "It happened a long time ago."

"But how?"

"Just kid stuff." He picked up the helmet he'd discarded earlier. "So what do you think of the bike?"

"Very liberating."

He jerked his face toward her as though her words had stung him. "Meaning?"

"Wind sailing through your hair." She spread her hands, lifted her face to the twilight and twirled around. "The miles flying under your feet, the sun setting behind you. I sound like a commercial." When she stopped and looked at him, she saw the beginnings of a smile again.

"Well put. Ever think of being a teacher? You'd be inspirational."

She laughed. "Why did you get it?"

He shrugged. "I always wanted one. But I never saw much use for a motorcycle in Maybe."

"If it gives you pleasure, that seems enough reason to me."

His turned his lazy grin on her and moved in a slow, stalking motion, circling behind her. "Are you trying to butter me up?"

She followed his movement with wary eyes. "Why would I do that?"

"So I'll teach you a few things."

"Like what?"

"Like dancing." He slid an arm around her waist, pulled her against him and swayed to silent music.

"I already know how," she whispered.

"You said you didn't."

"I lied."

"Me, too."

She tilted back to look at him.

He dipped his head down until his breath glided across her cheek. "That's not what I want to show you."

Rainy felt his hardness pressed against her belly. Her arms had found their way around his neck and she tightened her hold. "This is going too fast."

"We're just dancing, Rainy," he said in a voice so low she could barely hear him.

"Is that all?" she whispered back.

He didn't answer. Instead, in complete silence, in the middle of nowhere, they danced until the sun finally set.

Chapter Nine

The next day was perfect for a festival. Although the festivities had officially begun yesterday with the welcome reception for outside participants, the booths opened Saturday morning, the crafts and baked goods went on sale and the kiddie rides were operational.

More importantly, tonight was the dance.

Cash held little hope that it would come close to comparing with last night. Still, as he maneuvered his truck into the Maybe High parking lot near the festival entrance, his body tightened with the knowledge that in twelve hours he'd be holding Rainy again.

He climbed out of the truck, stretching his neck from side to side, trying to relieve the kinks caused by a poor night's sleep. By the time he and Rainy had gotten home from their motorcycle ride, five phone messages had stacked up, all requesting his presence at the welcome reception. He'd been so wrapped up in courting Rainy, he'd forgotten... hell, is that what he'd been doing? Courting Rainy? Yeah, he guessed it was.

Frowning, he gave his neck an extra stretch. Two little boys ran past him, laughing and sailing a Frisbee between them. He stood watching until they disappeared behind a tent.

He envied them. Life used to be uncomplicated. His priorities had always been clear. He had Josh to worry about, the ranch to run and hired hands to keep employed. And now there was Rainy... and lots of dangerous, unfamiliar and very exciting ground between them. The mere thought of her threw him off-balance.

She was the most caring, unpretentious, understanding woman he knew. She'd also had the common sense not to get carried away last night. All that, and a body that was about to put him into an early grave—a body she kept well under wraps. He felt a stirring south of his equator. Straightening, he glanced around, ran a finger inside the collar of his western shirt, then headed for the entrance.

Although the festivities were not scheduled to begin for another half hour, most of the booths were ready for business. Cash waved to some of his neighbors manning the baked-goods counter and spotted Smiley setting up his chili-making equipment. Each of the eight entrants had a stall they could decorate any way they chose. Cash noted that the person in charge had wisely assigned Smiley and Violet Pickford to opposite ends of the row.

Besides Smiley's, none of the other stalls were occupied yet, but colorful streamers, signs and other decorations established their individual territories. Smiley's banner, penned in sloppy felt-tipped letters, read, Smiley's Roadkill Chili—The One Everybody Is Dying To Taste.

Cash shook his head. And the man wondered why he never won. He glanced over at Violet's spot and noted that it sported the same decor she used every year—a pyramid of gaily wrapped, cylinder-shaped objects on a table behind her cooking station. Nothing special, but that hardly mattered. Her chili won every year.

As Cash approached, Smiley looked up. The foreman glared at him a moment, then whipped two wooden spoons out of a paper grocery sack with far too much force. Several cans of tomato sauce followed, each deliberately slammed to the plywood countertop.

When Cash said nothing, Smiley grumbled, "She's a doggone Benedict Arnold, that's what she is."

Cash crossed him arms over his chest and sighed. He wasn't quite up to another round of Violet bashing. "Who?"

"Don't act like you don't know." Smiley gave him a hostile, yet hurt look. "Cozyin' up to her like you been doin'."

Violet? He let out a brief snort.

"For all I know, you dropped her off at Jeb's Grocery." Smiley cursed under his breath as he pulled a knife out by the wrong end.

"What are you talking about?"

Smiley stopped setting out his equipment and glared at Cash once more. "Your houseguest, Josh's tutor, that's who I'm talkin' about." He gave him one final don't-act-like-you-don't-know look and went back to work.

"Rainy?" His disbelieving chuckle elicited another of Smiley's dirty looks. "You wanna start from the top?"

"I saw her last night. Probably thought I'd be home perfectin' my chili, but I saw her at Jeb's." The older man nodded smugly.

Cash figured that the poor guy had finally snorted too many spices. Then he remembered the woman in town the other day...the one who'd reminded him of Rainy. Granted the look had been brief, but maybe Smiley had made the same mistake. Cash frowned. Anyway, last night Rainy had been with him. The thought immediately sent his body into overdrive. And all they'd done was dance. God, he had it bad. "You're crazy."

"You're just coverin' for her." Smiley huffed. "I saw her buyin' them chili ingredients." He slapped his narrow thigh. "And all painted up like that. Ain't that the damnedest thing? Anyway, I'm warnin' you now, when she shows up for this here cook-off, I'm makin' the judges check her recipe. If she stole one thing from me..."

Cash wasn't listening anymore. Smiley wasn't making sense. She'd been with him last night...except after he'd been called to the reception. But she'd retreated to her room almost as soon as they'd gotten back from their ride. A fact that hadn't set very well with him at the time.

He rubbed his jaw. He supposed she could have gone back out again. All painted up? It had to be that other woman Smiley had seen. He watched Smiley jerking things around and mumbling under his breath. Well, he wasn't about to ask. Besides, it was more likely that Smiley had finally fried his brain with all his lethal chili experiments.

Cash's gaze drifted over the grounds, and he spotted Mabel Simms frantically waving him over to a row of booths. Gladly, he excused himself and headed in her direction.

Before reaching her, he saw Rainy and Josh approaching from the far side of a stretch of busy craft tables. He'd been disappointed when she'd decided to stay behind to run some errands this morning, but now, at the sight of her, his heart lurched in his chest. She wore only a slightly more reputable T-shirt than her normal baggy uniform, and he figured it was her going-out clothes. He smiled. To him, she'd look great in a burlap bag.

Their paths intersected just out of Mabel's hearing.

"Hi," Rainy said.

Cash's smile stretched even farther. Josh rolled his eyes, but Cash ignored him.

Mabel Simms gathered up her long, full, patchwork skirt and gingerly stepped over a section of grass to get closer. "You had me scared to death, Cash McCloud. I didn't think you'd get here in time for your shift."

Cash narrowed his gaze. "What shift?"

Mabel glanced at Josh, then back to Cash and smiled. "Don't you go teasing me like that, especially with all the excitement your volunteering has caused."

"I think I'll go help out with the pony rides," Josh said suddenly and sprinted off before anyone could comment.

"What shift?" Cash repeated.

Mabel drew her graying head back in surprise. "The kissing booth, of course."

He tried to open his mouth, but his jaw wouldn't work at first. "Uh, the kiss—"

Rainy burst out laughing.

"And thank you, dear," the woman said, turning to her, "for volunteering for the dunking booth."

Rainy stopped laughing. "The what booth?" Her eyes widened and looked from Mabel to Cash and back.

"It's for such a good cause," Mabel continued, oblivious to their stunned expressions.

"That's debatable," Cash said, "but also beside the point. Mabel, you must be mistaken. I did not volunteer for any... any kissing booth."

"But..." Mabel brought a fisted hand to her mouth and looked helplessly in the direction Josh had scampered.

"Did Josh have anything to do with this?" he demanded.

She returned her attention to him, her faded blue eyes pleading. "Please don't back out on me, Cash."

He kicked at a clump of dirt. Christ, if that kid had anything to do with this, he was going to be grounded until he was eighteen. Whatever the hell possessed him...

"Uh, excuse me." Rainy waved a hand. "What dunking booth?"

"Over there." Mabel gestured toward the far end of the grounds at a wooden contraption that resembled a giant hot tub.

"And how exactly does it work?" Rainy asked. Cash could hear the dread in her voice.

"Oh, it's very simple." Mabel pointed to something that looked like an oversize wooden spoon sticking out over the tub. "You sit there, and someone tries to dunk you in the water by throwing a ball at some mechanism that will release the seat. See?" Mabel beamed.

"Simple," Rainy repeated. She exhaled deeply, then slid Cash a bewildered look.

"Excuse us for a minute, will you?" he said to Mabel. Grabbing Rainy's arm, he pulled her several feet away.

"Don't be long," the older woman called out. "Your shift starts in ten minutes and Rainy's turn is in an hour."

Cash gritted his teeth. "Look, we don't have to do this," he said in a low voice. "I certainly didn't volunteer. Did you?"

"Of course not." She tugged her ponytail up higher. After looking heavenward for a moment, she cast a sympathetic glance toward Mabel Simms. "But it won't kill us, either." When Cash blinked disbelievingly, she added, "And she's right. It is for a good cause."

"To make money for participation in the cattle drive? You've got to be kidding."

"Actually, I've talked to a couple of people about the possibilities, and it sounds like a pretty good idea to me."

He shook his head. "You're as loony as the rest of them. But we can discuss that later."

"Well, you do what you want, but I'm going to do my dunking booth stint." She made a face. "I'll admit I'm not crazy about this, either, but really, what's a couple hours of our time?"

Cash gazed down into her sincere brown eyes and found he could think of at least one thing he'd rather be doing for a couple of hours. He pressed his lips together and willed his troublemaking thoughts away, while mentally adding the fact that she was a great sport to her list of admirable qualities.

"Okay," he said. "I'll do it."

"You're wonderful," she whispered as she turned toward Mabel. Then, grinning, she added, "Be sure to save me one of those kisses."

Cash watched her enticing backside lead the way until her words penetrated his stupor. Suddenly, he remembered precisely what type of booth he'd just agreed to man. And kissing was a far cry from dunking.

He groaned. If there was a way, he swore he'd ground Josh until he was twenty-five.

"THERE IS ONE small problem," Rainy said to Mabel. "I don't have a swimsuit with me in Maybe." Not that she'd be caught dead wearing one, but if that fact threw a wrench into the works, all the better. Despite her cheerleading attitude with Cash, she did not want to be a sitting duck.

"Oh, we'll take care of that." Mabel motioned to one of her assistants, then turned back to Rainy. "What size are you?"

"I—I, well, I don't know about a swimsuit. Maybe an eight?"

"I'm usually good at guessing." Mabel grabbed a handful of Rainy's extra-extra-large T-shirt and twisted it until the stretchy material hugged her body and deftly outlined every curve.

The older woman raised startled eyes to Rainy's face and blinked. "Oh, my..." A smile tugged at her thin lips. "I suspect dunking booth profits will be quite good this year." She whispered instructions to the young girl she'd summoned, before Rainy could ask her what she meant, then waved Rainy to follow as she set off at a clipped pace.

As they moved down the fairway, Rainy saw Josh walking a string of ponies in a circle, while youngsters bounced on their backs. He laughed and joked with them, and although he seemed to be giving them his full attention, she caught his gaze on her several times. This time his expression was more mischievous than malicious, but still, he was making her paranoid. Especially after the Violet incident . . .

She shrugged off the counterproductive feeling and forced herself to take note of the festival's many attractions. Food booths lined one side, offering everything from roasted corn to cotton candy. The smoke from several large, half-barrel barbecue pits spiraled into the still summer air.

The merry-go-round held center stage. A couple of toddlers in red-and-white striped sunsuits, their fingers stuck in their mouths, their necks arched back, looked on in awe. When the operator cranked up the music and set the fancy pastel horses in motion, more children flocked from the game and craft booths.

A man with a pipe stopped Mabel, and Rainy used the delay to check out a table half-full of turquoise-and-silver jewelry. The vendor looked up briefly from under her wide-brim straw hat and smiled before continuing to set out her inventory.

Rainy made a mental note to come back and choose a gift for her sister's birthday on Monday. Sunny would get a kick out of having some southwestern jewelry, she figured.

Maybe it was because their birthday was approaching or because they'd been apart so long, but Rainy had been thinking about her twin a lot the past few days, wondering what she was up to. With Sunny, there was no telling.

It was only a few minutes before noon but droves of people with long strips of yellow tickets were starting to flood onto the grounds. Rainy meandered back toward Mabel so she wouldn't lose her, although the thought was appealing. As she waited for the older woman to conclude her business, she noticed one of the booths already had a long line of customers—all women. She stepped up on tiptoe to get a better look.

Cash stood outside the booth, while two women inside frantically beckoned him to join them. A large banner above their heads offered a kiss for five dollars. Another, more amateurish sign appeared to be hastily tacked to one of the poles and announced that Cash McCloud would be featured from noon to two.

Her gaze drew back to the line of women, then to him. She could see him mumbling and she chuckled. He looked like a turkey the day before Thanksgiving.

Mabel called to her and, still chuckling, she started to turn away. Then she saw Della Witherspoon spilling out of a hot-pink sundress, sans casserole, second in line, blotting her lipstick. Bonnie stood behind her, and Kathleen and Kimberly Faye, number four and five behind them.

Rainy quit laughing. Her smile faded. What was she thinking? She didn't want Cash kissing all these women. And she certainly didn't want them kissing him. Hell, the cattle drive wasn't that good of a cause.

Mabel called her again and she took a couple of steps forward, swiveling in a full circle as she went, trying to catch one last glimpse of Cash hurdling over the booth's lower back counter. She was so preoccupied, she nearly ran into Mabel and the young assistant she'd sent in search of a swimsuit.

"Here you go," the girl singsonged. And waved two small strips of shiny black material.

CASH TOOK SEVERAL deep breaths. He signaled for a time-out and Sue Ellen, his assigned helper, hurried over with a large tumbler of water. He allowed the contents to glide very slowly down his throat, then passed the empty glass back to her.

"Don't tell me you want another one." She sighed in disgust. "It's your fourth one."

"Too bad." He arched a threatening brow at her, and the teenager scrambled over the ledge toward the food booths.

He hung back from the counter—and the ever-growing line of giggling women—and waited. He'd figured out early on that if he drank a glass of water every ten minutes, he could waste at least thirty minutes of his two-hour shift.

Parking himself in the far corner, he crossed his arms over his chest and ignored the catcalls from two of his male neighbors. He was going to be the laughingstock of the entire county. He gritted his teeth and vowed that this particular event would be banned from any future Maybe festivals. How the hell women had endured this humiliation for decades, he'd never understand. And to think he'd wholeheartedly encouraged this very event because of the hefty profit it generated. But no more, he vowed again, then looked up and groaned.

Della Witherspoon had gotten in line for the third time. His nose and eyes itched at the memory of her heavy perfume. Shy, quiet Kathleen stood behind her. A rush of heat climbed Cash's face as he recalled the smacker she'd already laid on him.

He tried to keep his eyes downcast while he checked out the rest of the line with sidelong glances. Thankfully, most of them he didn't know. He had no idea why these strangers would pay good money to embarrass the hell out of him, except he'd heard the laughter and whispers earlier about the shoe finally being on the other foot.

Sue Ellen threw a gangly leg over the counter, trying not to spill the two full glasses she held. He'd just have to "accidentally" spill one of them. Silently apologizing in advance, he took a long guzzle of the one she passed him, wiped his mouth with the back of his hand and took another fearful look at the waiting ladies. Slightly past them, down the midway, a dark blond head caught his eye. The woman's hair was long and full, hiding most of her profile.

Absently, he handed the empty glass back to Sue Ellen and moved forward, keeping sight of the mystery woman. She was at least a half a head taller than the other women, and when she stepped away from a cluster of people, he saw why.

Her legs were long and sleek and shot up to heaven. Short denim cutoffs rode high on her thighs, and with each step she took, a hint of her well-rounded buttocks peeked out.

Cash swallowed. There was no tan line.

Several men formed a fan club behind her. Cash looked away, immediately thinking of Rainy and feeling guilty.

Acknowledging the feeling, he swallowed again. Where had that come from? Hell, he wasn't married and he wasn't dead. He forced himself to take one last look.

Her back was partially to him as she shaded her eyes and looked first one way down the midway, then the other. She shifted from one foot to the other. Her shorts rode up another fraction. Cash tried to keep his eyes at chest level.

A big mistake, he found, when she turned toward him. Her sleeveless blouse was only partially buttoned. There was really nothing indecent about the way she wore it. Della was showing off more cleavage. But on this woman, it looked different, more provocative.

Cash raised his gaze to her face.

Rainy?

He blinked several times. Irrational relief galloped through him. It was Rainy. He didn't have to feel guilty.

Rainy? Relief turned to shock. A young boy walking past the booth gave her a double take and whistled. Cash's shock slid into anger.

Why was she dressed this way? Did Mabel Simms have something to do with this? Was this the dunking booth's new uniform?

He shook his head, thinking about Rainy's unlimited assortment of oversize T-shirts. It was hard to believe she'd allow anyone to dress her this way, but of course, two hours ago he wouldn't have believed he'd be standing here kissing half the women of Maybe.

His attention gravitated back to the impatient line of women and he dutifully stepped back into position.

Sue Ellen took Polly Posey's money and elbowed him to pucker. He was about to oblige, when he saw Rainy get in line.

He gaped. Polly's eyes widened, then she grinned and leaned closer. Cash closed his mouth and gave her a quick peck.

Peripherally, he heard Polly and the next three kissees complain about his performance. But he didn't care. He merely kept his eyes on Rainy and wondered why she was suddenly wearing makeup.

After two more customers, it occurred to him that he shouldn't be concentrating on her so hard. Tension twisted his gut with every step she took closer to him. And when Martha Wallbanger fanned herself after he'd done his deed, he realized that his excitement was spilling over into his work.

He took a calming breath and met Rainy's laughing eyes over several heads. He gave her a smile, anxious to claim one of hers. But when the woman blocking Rainy moved her head, the smile he saw stretched across her face was wrong. All wrong. It wasn't *his* smile. The special one she gave only him.

Panic, a country-mile wide, plowed through him. What was wrong with him? What was wrong with this picture? The clothes, for one thing. But surely he wasn't so shallow that he'd judge her for... for what? She hadn't done anything wrong.

But she also wasn't doing anything for him, either. That funny feeling wasn't quite there.

A baby, just beginning to walk, broke away from his mother and toddled toward Rainy. She bent down and scooped the little boy up in her arms, laughing and tickling the child.

Cash relaxed. Vintage Rainy. It was just this strange situation, he assured himself, and disposed of two more customers. Immediately, his body tightened again. Just four more to go and he'd be kissing Rainy.

He looked up to give her a wink, but she was gone. Searching the crowd, he spotted her absently wandering toward the merry-go-round, without even giving him a backward glance.

And Della Witherspoon took full advantage of his open-mouthed surprise.

Chapter Ten

Rainy gripped the side of her makeshift seat and closed her eyes. The baseball sped through the air and hit the dunking tank's canvas backdrop. After she heard the ball make contact with the fabric, assured that she'd received another short respite from dropping into the cool water, she opened her eyes.

Another customer stepped up, took the ball, aimed and threw. Bang! Right on the bull's-eye. She dropped into the water like two tons of chocolate.

She popped to the surface, swiped the moisture off her face and hopped back up on the seat. After nearly an hour of this, she knew the drill.

A line of at least two dozen boys and men waited to take their crack at her. She peeled the wet T-shirt away from her body, gazing over their heads and hoping like crazy that her replacement was in sight.

No such luck. She wrung out a wad of wet shirt, then draped it back around her as best she could. At this point, she wasn't sure what was worse, the skimpy swimsuit Mabel had given her or the white T-shirt that now clung to her breasts and belly. Wearing the black bikini underneath had seemed like the best solution, but the bra barely covered her breasts and being sopping wet made that perfectly obvious.

Stupid. Stupid. Stupid. She couldn't believe she was doing this. What had she been thinking? In her own feeble defense, she'd never witnessed anything quite like this dunking business before and had no idea it'd turn out to be a wet T-shirt contest.

She noticed one freckle-faced teenager openly ogling her near the edge of the tank and she dropped back into the water of her own accord. A wave splashed his face and glasses and Rainy chuckled. For her trouble, she got a mouthful of water and came up sputtering.

Hopping back up into position, she crossed her arms over her chest and waited for the next pitcher.

Several minutes later, she noticed Josh standing on the outskirts of the dunking area, his hands planted on his hips, his expression sullen. She recognized two of his friends standing a few yards in front of him, staring at her as if she might be lunch. When she glanced back at Josh, he shuttered a look he had no business giving his tutor. His expression darkened back to the more preferable, sullen one.

She plucked the T-shirt away from her skin and, groaning to herself, nonchalantly bunched it up as best she could. Where was Sunny when she needed her? Her twin could have pulled this off without batting an eye. She was the outgoing one, the one who'd have tossed her hair back and enjoyed the attention. She would have laughed at the ogling, returned the catcalls, told them to put their money where their minds were. Sunny was the one everyone expected to be fun. Not Rainy. And sitting here like a lamb waiting for slaughter, Rainy had never been so cognizant of that fact as she was right now.

Was she the one who'd convinced Cash that this was for charity? God, she felt like a twit.

She let out a soft, humorless snort. She was actually more like Sunny than she thought...jumping in with both feet before thinking things through. Hell, if anyone was going

to recognize her from *Midnight Fantasy*, they certainly
would now. And, Cash...oh, hell, she had to tell Cash...

Almost as if her thoughts had summoned him, Cash appeared in the distance. Rainy craned her neck to see past the
next customer, who was warming up to take his best shot at
the bull's-eye. Cash was still too far away for her to see his
face, but he was heading her way.

Bang!

Rainy hit the water again. She shot back up to the surface and wiped her face. But this time she didn't hop back
up on her seat. She struggled toward the edge of the pool
until she had the money taker's attention.

"Where's my replacement?" she asked in a loud whisper.

"Dunno." He shrugged and looked at his watch. "Mabel should be around shortly. Anyway, we can't stop now.
Business is too good." He grinned and gestured to the long
line of boys and men who'd started grumbling about the
interruption.

Groaning, she took deep breaths all the way back to her
station, repositioned herself and kept one eye out for Cash
and the other for Mabel.

Unfortunately, Cash approached first.

He hung back, behind Josh and his friends, and stared.

Cash hadn't meant to sneak up on his son. In fact, the
truth was, he hadn't even known the boy and his friends
were there. Not after he'd caught a glimpse of Rainy.

He made a great show of shading his eyes and looking in
the opposite direction from her, then he reached into his
breast pocket and pulled out a pair of sunglasses.

Behind the safety of the dark lenses, he stared straight at
Rainy.

He'd already touched her. Seen a bit under those monstrous T-shirts she wore, but nothing had prepared him for
Rainy in the flesh. Not exactly in the flesh, but damn close.

The white T-shirt might as well have been painted on. It clung to her body, outlining the tiny black strips she wore beneath it. Her legs, long and golden, dangled over the water and, if at all possible, looked even better than they had in shorts.

She crossed her arms and hugged herself, and Cash figured it had little to do with the ninety-five-degree temperature. But if she thought she was covering herself any... the way the wet material sank into her cleavage...

Cash shivered, the hot weather be damned.

He shoved his hands into his pockets to help stretch out the front of his jeans. It was starting to feel a little cramped down there.

Involuntarily, he took another step forward. He heard his son's loud snort of disgust and remembered that Josh and his friends were standing several feet in front of him. And the boys' gazes were glued to Rainy.

When Seth Johnson let out a swooning sound, Cash stopped in his tracks and, with a grain of guilt, made no attempt to let them know he was behind them.

"I think I've died and gone to heaven," Seth said and comically clutched his heart. "Maybe I'll try flunking this September and my mama will hire her."

"Shut up, toad brain." Josh gave his friend a shove, not once taking his eyes off Rainy. "This isn't the way it was supposed to work."

"Looks like it's working pretty well to me." Jimmy Ray gave Josh a dazed look, then let his mouth drop back open and returned his attention to the dunking tank.

"Yeah, that's because you guys don't have anything to worry about," Josh grumbled.

Seth laughed. "Huh, and you looked real worried while you were droolin' all over the place." Laughing again, he slammed a high five into Jimmy Ray's waiting hand.

Cash couldn't listen anymore. He moved in closer and cleared his throat.

Josh started guiltily. "Hey, Dad."

Seth and Jimmy Ray exchanged quick glances. "Hey, Mr. McCloud."

Cash nodded to the boys. "If you fellows don't have anything to do, I'd bet Mrs. Simms could use some help."

Josh darted a panicked look at his friends, and if Cash weren't so steamed, he would have laughed. Mrs. Simms could be a drill sergeant. "Sorry, we got plans."

His friends agreed and shuffled off.

"See ya, Dad," Josh called as he hurried to join them.

Cash watched his son sulk along, while the other two laughed and pushed their way across the grounds, then he turned back to Rainy.

It was bad enough hearing the boys make cracks about her, and as compelling a sight as she made, his attention drew sharply to two men, elbowing each other and noticeably gawking.

Until today, Cash had never known a single moment of jealousy. But right now, his fists ached to drop the two men where they stood. When one of his ranch hands stepped up to purchase a chance at dunking Rainy, Cash lost all ability to reason and lunged forward.

The younger man had already handed over his money, his hand angled back, ready to throw. Cash tapped him on the shoulder.

"I don't think you want to do that, Chet." He plucked the ball out of the man's hand. "The lady is through for today."

The younger man started to complain, but Cash fixed him with a deadly glare.

The money taker frowned, but he silently passed some bills back to his would-be customer.

Cash poked his hat back with his index finger and strode toward Rainy. She sat with her arms wrapped around herself, her eyes wide.

"You're done," he said, snatching up a folded towel from the tank's steps. "Where are your clothes?"

She hitched a thumb over her shoulder. Immediately, his gaze drew to the T-shirted breast her arm exposed with the motion. Good Lord, the wet fabric molded to her, and the scant piece of bikini material did nothing to help contain her.

He threw her the towel. It caught her unprepared and sank dismally below the surface of the water.

"Cash? I hope you aren't interrupting my prize attraction." The voice came from behind, and he turned to see Mabel Simms marching as fast as she could toward him. Fanning her heated face, she installed herself beside him. "Rainy? Would you mind dunking another half hour, dear?"

"I—I don't..." Rainy began helplessly.

Her face was pink and he couldn't tell if it was from embarrassment or the midday sun. The Rainy he knew would be embarrassed. A burn would account for the Rainy he'd seen in the kissing booth line earlier.

"She minds," he said and offered his arms to her.

She smiled shyly. "I can use the steps."

He watched her slide off the seat and slip into the water. His heart flip-flopped. He glanced out the corner of his eye. It looked as if half of Maybe was in attendance.

"Do you have a dry towel?" he asked Mabel, who had hurried over to where Rainy was climbing out of the tank.

"But, dear, we're doing so well," she said to Rainy, ignoring him.

"Exactly," he interjected. "So I think you owe her a big thanks."

Mabel blushed. "So I'm a pushy old lady, sue me." She winked at Rainy and tossed her a towel that had been stashed under the tank steps. "We sure do appreciate what you did."

And then, to his utter amazement, Mabel patted her graying beehive hairdo, then stripped off her patchwork skirt and denim blouse. She adjusted the straps of her old-fashioned, cherry red swimsuit, tugged the skirt down over her ample hips and trudged up the tank steps. She grinned at the groans coming from the onlookers and hopped into the water.

Rainy burst out laughing.

Cash switched his gaze to her. She had pulled the towel around her shoulders but a tantalizing slice of cleavage still showed and her legs were long, silky looking and hopelessly bare. He took off his hat and wondered foolishly how much it could cover.

"Here," he said, setting it atop her head. "You'd better wear this. Your nose is beginning to burn."

She raised a hand to feel her cheeks, and he wondered which of the two Rainys had sat up there on display. "I can feel it. I hadn't thought to bring sunscreen."

Then she moved her hand to his hair and, at his surprised look, she said, "Your hat left a ridge."

He felt her touch clear down to the toes of his boots. Grabbing her wrist, he pulled her behind the tank, behind the canvas backdrop, away from everyone, and faced her.

"Are you cold?" he asked under the hot July sun, holding both ends of the towel, drawing her closer.

A slow smile curved her lips and she nodded.

God, she was a beautiful liar. He circled his arms around her, urging her against him by the small of her back, then touched his lips lightly to hers. She tilted her head back farther and the hat slipped to the ground, rolling to a stop against the chain-link fence.

He ignored it. Her exposed throat looked far too tempting and he trailed a parade of tiny kisses down to her collarbone. She stretched up to him and his hands filled with her firm, half-exposed buttocks. Her fingers dug into his shoulders and he hardened.

The squawk of children reached his ears and he remembered where they were—not twenty feet from a dozen or so Maybe residents. He brushed a kiss against each closed eyelid and shifted slightly away. She blinked, then stared back with such trusting brown eyes that he very nearly lost all control.

He pulled the towel more snugly around her shoulders until the top two corners met, then bent down to retrieve his hat. He returned it to the top of her head and got a good whiff of lavender in the bargain.

"I need my clothes," she said.

"What? Oh, yeah. Where did you leave them?"

"At the information booth. Would you get them for me?"

"Sure. After you change I'll buy you lunch."

She studied her peach-tipped toes and shook her head. "Thanks, anyway."

"Rainy?" He hated the discomfort she was telegraphing. "Nobody saw us."

"Oh, it's not that." She gave him a brilliant smile. "I thought I'd head home." She made a face. "Besides, I think we already missed lunch."

"You're kidding."

Grinning, she shook her head. "I never kid about food."

"I mean about going home. This festival happens only once a year."

"So does the dance." Pink flooded her face and she turned to go. "I want to be ready."

Grinning, Cash followed without giving lunch another thought.

THE BAND BARELY FINISHED one song and slid into another. This was not at all what Cash had in mind. He backed up to lean against the wall, arms crossed, partially hiding his face among the shadows, so no one could see the darts spitting from his gaze. It would be an added bonus if Della Witherspoon overlooked him way back here in the corner. If she tried hauling him onto the dance floor one more time with the mood he was in, no telling what he was likely to do.

He edged deeper into the shadows and watched Rainy out on the dance floor with yet another one of his ranch hands. Her legs, long, tan and bare, beneath the hem of a pristine white dress, seemed to glide across the floor. She'd left her hair loose and it swung back and forth to the music, while the rest of her slipped back into Chet Custer's arms. Seeing her all dressed up like this reminded him that he hadn't asked her about standing in line at the kissing booth today. But right now, he had more important things to worry about.

He and Rainy had been here nearly two hours and Cash had managed to rope her for only three dances. One after another, men from at least five counties had asked her to dance. And each time she'd looked shyly at him, and each time, fool that he was, he'd encouraged her to go.

Hell, he was done being nice. He pushed off the wall, strode over and tapped Chet's shoulder. When Chet reluctantly looked at him without taking his arm from her, Cash leaned over and whispered to the young ranch hand, "This is not multiple choice, son."

Son? Damn it all to hell. He could shoot himself for saying that. He felt old enough watching all these young pups with Rainy. His left knee creaked and he muttered a curse.

"I'll see you later, Chet." Rainy patted the younger man's shoulder.

"Not if I can help it," Cash said as he circled his arms around her.

She darted a glance toward Chet, who had moved toward the edge of the dance floor and continued to glare at his boss. "What did you say?"

"I've hardly seen you all night." He pressed his cheek to her soft hair and breathed in the lavender.

"You haven't exactly been a wallflower. I thought Kimberly Faye was going to have to arm wrestle Kathleen for that last dance with you."

Cash laughed, happy that she'd noticed him at all.

She grinned up at him. Her normally untouched lips were tinted a pale rose, her cheeks pink from the afternoon sun. A light plum color edged lashes that seemed a little thicker and darker than usual, and although he liked her either way, his heart pounded knowing that she'd done it all for him.

Briefly, she closed her eyes and rested her forehead on his chin. And he was equally glad that, for her, he'd shaved twice today.

The music stopped and the band's lead singer announced they would be taking a twenty-minute break.

Reluctantly, Cash let his arms trail off her, but he kept her hand in his as he led her toward the door. They got as far as the refreshment counter when Susie, the short blond teenager who worked at Della's Boutique, approached them.

She made a clucking sound with her tongue, reached up and yanked the neckline of Rainy's peasant dress down around her shoulders, until an expanse of satiny skin showed from one end to the other. "Much better," the girl said, admiring her handiwork.

Rainy chuckled. "I don't think so." She started to pull one side back up, but the girl put a restraining hand on hers and asked, "What do you think, Mr. McCloud?"

Cash took a deep breath. "I think we need some air." He grabbed Rainy's free hand and hauled her out the door.

She glanced over her shoulder at the teenager standing with her hands on her hips, a put-out expression on her face. "I don't know if I should thank you or scold you."

"They both sound pretty good to me." He pulled her around a dark corner, and she came up flush against him.

Rainy happily sank against him and breathed in his musky scent. Her hands glided up his blue chambray shirt, until they curled around the back of his neck, her fingers buried deep in his hair. She lifted up on her toes and brushed a kiss on his smiling lips. "Thank you."

"I was thinking more along these lines." He settled back against the wall, bringing her with him between his slightly spread legs. Fitting his mouth to hers, he teased her lips apart with his tongue.

She opened to him, welcoming him, her breasts pressed against his chest, feeling the steady pounding of his heart. He deepened the kiss until she thought her knees could no longer support her.

Laughter and voices echoed from nearby, and they pulled apart just as two couples strolled around the corner.

"Evening, Cash...ma'am," one of the men said.

"Good evening," Cash responded. His voice came out raspy, and Rainy nibbled her lower lip to keep from laughing.

"They're goin' to be announcin' the chili winner in five minutes," the other man said as the group passed them. "Y'all don't want to miss that."

Cash groaned. "Right." He cupped her bare shoulders with his warm palms and gave her a quick peck. Then he adjusted his shirt, while she smoothed down his hair, which she'd managed to muss up considerably.

"You're going to get us in big trouble." He grabbed her wrists and pulled her hand away. She saw his Adam's apple work convulsively.

"Me?" She focused in on his mouth where a beam of light hit and laughed. "You're the one with the telltale sign."

He looked down at his straining fly and grinned. "Yeah? Well, that's your fault, too."

Rainy's laughter subsided to a feeble cough. And she brushed a quick thumb across the lipstick smudges at the corners of his mouth. "That's not what I meant."

She twisted her wrist out of his grasp and headed back inside. She heard him mumble a rather earthy word, and she chuckled with the knowledge of why he had to hang back.

Hovering at the doorway, she waited for him to catch up to her and watched Mabel Simms and two men, who Rainy didn't recognize, take their places on the stage.

"Would all you chili entrants please gather around the stage?" Mabel's voice bellowed forth without benefit of the microphone. "We'll be announcing the winner in two minutes."

Rainy's heart sank. How could she have been so stupid as to forget? She took an automatic step back while scanning the crowd for Violet. When Rainy hadn't been stuck in the dunking booth, she'd purposely avoided the area where the chili contestants had been assigned—for more reasons than one. Smiley had all but bit her head off this morning. She'd chalked that up to precontest nerves.

Violet, however, was the more serious problem. She knew she had to finally face the woman and explain about the centerfold, but she certainly had no intention of making it a public spectacle. She also had decided it might be better to tell Cash first.

Cash... She had definitely made up her mind to tell him. No ifs, ands or buts about it. Come hell or high water, she'd tell him tomorrow evening after the festival was officially over. There was no sense ruining his weekend.

"Why don't we go inside?" Cash placed his large, reassuring hand at the small of her back. "So we can see better."

"What's there to see?" She laughed nervously. "I thought Violet wins every year."

"She does. But believe me, the show will be worth seeing."

She sent him a quizzical look, but he merely winked and guided her deeper into the room. She shivered and, realizing the state of her dress, started to pull the fabric back over her shoulder. Cash stopped her, stroking her bare skin for a second, then took her hand.

"Okay, everyone, listen up," one of the men on stage commanded. "Mabel, will you do the honors?"

Mabel Simms patted her upswept hair, stepped forward and tapped the microphone. A screech vibrated throughout the hall.

Among a chorus of irritated mumblings, someone yelled, "Doggone it, Mabel, with your set of tonsils, you don't need the darn thing."

She lifted her chin and sniffed. "Third runner-up..."

Rainy let Mabel's voice drown into the background while she continued to search for Violet. With the woman's bright red hair, she couldn't understand why she was having so much trouble finding her.

A round of applause for the second runner-up made Rainy start. She hadn't paid one bit of attention to the names of the winners, not that any of them would mean anything...unless, of course, Smiley was named. She shifted to get a better look at the stage. She recognized Bonnie Brown, but not the other runner-up.

"And first runner-up is...Smiley Ferguson." Mabel led the crowd in frantic hand clapping. Hoots and howls accompanied a frowning Smiley up the two steps to the stage to receive his small trophy. He nodded, his eyes narrowing, and moved over next to the other two.

Cash clapped as loud as anyone. He bent his head near her ear. "This is the first year he's even placed. You must've brought him luck."

"And now, will everyone bring their hands together for this year's winner." Mabel took a long dramatic pause, until someone sailed a wadded-up paper napkin past her shoulder. "The winner is . . . Violet Pickford."

The response was a mixture of groans and applause, while people began looking around for her. A few who obviously were accustomed to her M.O. turned and looked pointedly toward the back.

She appeared through a rear door, one hand clutching her chest, the other fisted at her mouth, looking for all the world like she had never expected such an honor.

Her unruly hair was carefully arranged in a bun at her nape and multicolored sequins glittered about her person as she walked. But as she made her grand entrance through the parting crowd, Rainy realized that the patches of sparkle had been sewn onto a black sweatshirt and worn jeans.

Violet had made it to the foot of the stage, when Smiley cried out, "I protest." He plucked the hat off his head and slammed it to the floor. "She cheated and I can prove it."

"You darn fool." Violet bounded up the steps and met him nose to nose. "I don't have to cheat to whip your sorry hide."

"I know all about it, you ol' bat. All about it, ya hear?" He glanced down and realized he'd stepped on his hat.

"About what?"

"I ain't dumb enough to show all my cards. I'll be goin' through the proper appeal channels." Nearly everyone howled at that, but he ignored them all. He scooped up his misshapen hat, returned it to the top of his head and marched down the steps and out of the hall.

Violet watched him leave, her face scrunched up in irritation. Then, as if she'd suddenly remembered where she was, she turned and smiled at her audience. "I thank you all for this honor. And tomorrow, I'll do Maybe proud with another winning American Beauty entry."

She surveyed her court, grinning, until she spotted Rainy. Pleasure fled Violet's face and she pointed an unerring finger right at Rainy and said, "Provided that woman leaves town."

Chapter Eleven

Everyone turned to look at Rainy.

Cash exhaled loudly and made a move toward the stage. "Now, Violet, what the—"

"Please don't." Rainy cut him off and grabbed his arm.

It wasn't so much her request as it was the panic in her voice that made him stop and look at her.

"Can we go home?" Her eyes pleaded with him.

He sent a confused glance at Violet, but she was already surrounded by her old cronies, and the band members were beginning to reclaim their places on the stage. "Sure."

Several people lingered, their gazes swinging from Violet to Rainy. But most of Maybe knew the older woman didn't always play with a full deck, and they went about the business of having fun.

Cash tucked Rainy's cold hand in his and headed for the door. He stopped briefly to find out when the young people's dance next door would be over and to make sure Josh had a ride home, then he led her to the pickup.

The drive home was made in silence, and they no sooner coasted to a stop near the back door, when Rainy jumped out of the truck. She hurried around the pickup and put a hand on the doorknob, but she had no key and stood, toeing the welcome mat until Cash came up beside her. He put one gentle hand on her shoulder, and with the other he turned the knob.

"That's why I didn't give you a key." He smiled down at her anxious face and wondered what had happened between her and Violet. "It's pretty safe around here."

"Really?" Her tone was a strange combination of sarcasm and fear as she pushed ahead of him into the kitchen.

She didn't bother to flip on the light switch, so he did.

She blinked at the brightness, and he could see that even with the light sunburn she'd received earlier, her face had paled.

"Well..." She gave him a smile that was far too forced as she edged toward the hall. "Thanks for the nice evening."

"How about a glass of wine?" He reached into an upper cabinet and withdrew two stemmed glasses before she could say no. "Red or white?"

"I don't think so."

"Milk and cookies, then?" He grinned and was relieved to see her return his smile.

"You must be mistaking me for Mrs. Parker. You won't find your usual goodies in there." She cocked her head toward the cookie jar. "I don't do cookies."

"Sweetheart, I would never mistake you for Ida Parker." He opened the refrigerator and grabbed a bottle of chardonnay, then passed her the two glasses he held in his other hand.

After a brief look of indecision, she accepted them and held the glasses out for him to pour the wine.

He finished his task, grabbed one of the glasses of wine, returned the bottle to the refrigerator and peered inside for a moment. "How about some Brie and crackers with that? Or maybe some strawberries?" Food was the last thing on his mind right now, but he'd feed her anything that would keep her from retreating to her room.

Rainy chuckled. "Brie? Strawberries?"

"What's wrong with that?"

"You have mighty strange tastes for a cowboy," she drawled.

Smiling, he shut the refrigerator door and stalked her as she moved across the room. "Are you insinuating that cowboys don't have good taste?"

That made her giggle all the more and catching her was easy. He slipped an arm around her waist and swung her in a circle. She tried to protect her wine by raising it higher, but some of it sloshed out of her glass and landed on her bare shoulder.

He stopped, bowed his head and licked it off.

Rainy held her breath. When he raised his darkened eyes to hers, her knees buckled.

He tightened his arm around her and forced her against him. Carefully, he set his glass on the table, then took hers and placed it beside his. He turned back to her and hooked a finger under her chin.

Rainy swallowed. He was going to kiss her. And God only knew how much she wanted him to. She angled slightly away. "Cash?"

"Yeah?" He brushed his thumb across her lower lip.

Unable to keep from touching him, she lifted a hand to trace the small scar that bisected his eyebrow. "It's time we talked."

His thumb stilled. The wariness that glittered in his emerald eyes did nothing to boost her confidence.

She dropped her hand and straightened, reminding herself that she had done nothing wrong—except maybe having waited too long to set the record straight.

In what appeared to be an unconscious gesture, he transferred his touch from her to his scar. His finger remained there for only an instant, then he dropped his hand and pulled out two chairs.

They sat down at the same time and he asked, "What's on your mind?"

She didn't like his sudden change of mood. It was only a subtle change, one she couldn't quite pinpoint, but it was enough to discourage her from immediately telling him about the centerfold.

"Well, actually..." She injected just the right amount of teasing in her voice and managed to produce a smile. "I'm going crazy trying to figure out where you got that scar."

Her approach worked about as well as poking a pin at a balloon. His expression tightened, his shoulders sank back against the chair. Slowly, sadly, he shook his head. "You'd think they'd give it a rest by now."

She frowned in confusion. "Who?"

"Who have you been talking to?"

"I'm not following you."

He lifted a hand and fingered the scar before wrapping his palm around the back of his neck. "It happened almost twenty years ago. It amazes me that people still talk about it."

Rainy tugged at his arm until he brought it down and she laid her hand across his knuckles. "I really have no idea what you're talking about."

"You know nothing about how I got the scar?"

She shook her head, her gaze locking with his.

He let out a harsh breath, then a short humorless laugh. "And now that I've opened my big mouth, you're curious as hell."

She made a face and nodded.

He stared out the back window and laughed again. This time it wasn't so harsh. "Well, it's really no big deal. I was a kid when it happened...about seventeen. My friend Jesse and I decided we wanted to see the world, in spite of my parents raising holy hell over it." He looked back at her. "You sure you want to hear this?"

She gave him a serene smile. "Only if you want to tell me."

"I think so." He slipped his hand from under hers, clasped it with his other one and returned his stare to the window. "We knew we weren't actually going to see the world, but half of America would have been okay. Although I wouldn't have put it past Jesse to have made it." He smiled faintly at the memory. "But we only made it to the Texas-Oklahoma border.

"Jesse's motorcycle broke down halfway there and, instead of turning around, we decided to hitchhike. Damn fool kids that we were." He shook his head, laughing softly. "We were only four hours from Maybe. Anyway, we got one ride close to the Oklahoma border, then waited for two hours for the next one. We were happy to get that, and weren't real choosy about who picked us up. But like I said, we were kids."

He looked at her again with such emotion-filled eyes that she was about to reach out a comforting hand when he burst out laughing. "You know, if Josh ever did anything like that, I'd wring his damn neck."

Rainy grinned. "Remember when we said we'd never be as strict as our parents? I cringe every time I say something to him my mother would've said." She stopped and quickly looked down. She wasn't Josh's mother. This was not her family. For a moment, she'd forgotten that small detail. For a moment, she'd wished it could be true. Hesitantly, her gaze made contact with Cash.

He covered her hand and smiled. "Anyway, to make a long story short, we got picked up by the wrong people and got our butts thrown in an Oklahoma jail."

"What? Jail? You?"

"Yup. Accused of robbing a bank. The two guys who'd picked us up actually had. But there was no telling that police officer we had nothing to do with it."

Her brows rose in sympathy. He hadn't been much older than Josh. "And the scar?"

"He thought I was resisting arrest when I tried to tell him we were innocent. Figured I'd run, I guess, and he whacked me with his club. It didn't do any real damage besides the scar."

"So how did you get it all straightened out?"

His face darkened again. "With a whole lot of time and even more money."

"Your parents helped you?"

If it were at all possible, his face darkened even more. "Yeah, they helped me all right. It took every cent they had, plus another mortgage on the ranch, but they helped me."

"That's what parents do, Cash," she said softly.

"Yeah, I know. It just wasn't fair."

"What happened after that?"

"At the end of summer, I went off to college in Dallas for four years. After that I came back here. I paid off that second mortgage just last year."

Rainy drew in her lower lip and hoped she wasn't about to ask a hurtful question. But in the past few days, it had become crystal clear to her how much she cared about this man and how much she needed to know everything about him. "Where are your parents now?"

A wide grin spread across his face. "Living in Florida with my sister, enjoying their retirement."

Relief flooded her. "I didn't think ranchers or farmers ever retired."

"A lot of them don't, but my dad worked hard all his life, and since the ranch generates a decent enough profit, there's no reason he can't spend some of it in Florida."

Rainy studied the lines fanning out from his eyes, the tenseness in his jaw. She could tell he was genuinely happy about his parents' retirement, but something still bothered him. It troubled her, but also made her wonder if her close examination was a way of avoiding her own history.

One last question, she promised herself, then she would tell him about the centerfold. "Cash?"

"Hmm?" He stroked the inside of her wrist with his thumb.

"If it hadn't been for the mix-up, would you have come back here?"

His thumb stopped midstroke. He stared at her, as if trying to form his thoughts. "No."

"And you're sorry that you did."

He leaned back in his chair, his touch fading. "That's not an easy answer. I've got Josh now. I have to keep the ranch running. There's no room for regrets." He exhaled a loud sigh. "It's pointless to think about it. Besides, if I do, I might have to admit that Josh's mother is right."

He looked uncomfortable, as though he hadn't meant to reveal so much. Rainy didn't like the way his lips thinned in defeat, the way his eyes saddened.

"What are you saying?" she asked slowly.

"Maybe I have no business keeping Josh here. Maybe he'd be happier traveling with Maureen, going to school in the city. I doubt he'd come out and tell me if that were the case." He shrugged, as if the matter was inconsequential, only she knew better. "Hell," he added, "I'm probably being blind and selfish."

"Don't say that, Cash."

He smiled. It was a sad, tight smile. "Don't get me wrong. I know I've done the best I could. Maybe has a lot of faults, but it's crime-free and the people are basically good, hardworking folks. It's always been important to me that he know about that side of life before he has to make adult decisions. But now I don't know..." Wearily, he rubbed his eyes. "I'm wondering if I—"

Rainy stood suddenly. "Come here," she said, putting out her hand to him.

He frowned, confusion drawing his eyebrows together. But he wrapped his fingers around hers and followed her out of the kitchen, down the hall and up the stairs.

She led him to the study where she and Josh had been working. "I'm going to show you something," she said, "something I ordinarily wouldn't. But I think it's important you see this." She reached into a stack of papers and withdrew a single sheet of notebook paper, Josh's bold handwriting covering the page.

"The day I started here, I asked Josh to write me a short essay so that I could get a feel for his grammar. I told him to choose his own topic, that it could be the standard How-I-spent-my-summer-vacation stuff." She smiled. "He didn't write about visits with his mother. He wrote this." She handed him the paper.

Rainy watched him read the essay. He frowned in concentration at first, then his features began to relax. She knew the exact moment he'd reached the part where Josh explained why the ranch meant so much to him and why he thought his dad was the most honorable man on earth.

She watched as Cash tried to swallow the knot of emotion that had undoubtedly lodged itself in his throat, and she knew why she was falling in love with this man.

He was everything Josh had described and more. Yes, he was kind and honorable and caring. But even more, he was decent and sensitive enough to feel humbled by his son's admiration.

He cleared his throat. "Thanks," he said. "Thanks for showing this to me." His gaze slowly raised, then fastened on hers as he passed the testimonial to her. One side of his mouth lifted and he studied her face for several long seconds. "Guess I'll have to find something else to worry about."

Feeling the weight of his stare, Rainy's grin was faint. "I guess so."

Reaching out, he brushed a thumb across her lips. "Like how I'm going to keep my hands off you."

She felt her eyes automatically widen at first and then her grin deepened. "Sorry," she said, sliding her arms around his waist. "You'll have to think of something else."

Cash smiled back before bringing both his large hands up to cup her face. He kissed her mouth, her chin, her neck, her mouth again, teasing her lips open with his tongue, mimicking the rhythm his body longed for, making his intention perfectly clear. She stumbled back a little and put a hand to his chest to steady herself.

When he paused, his breathing labored, his heart pounding against her palm, Rainy knew he was giving her a chance to turn down his invitation.

"Are you sure?" he asked softly.

Slowly, she nodded, reaching up to cup his face with her trembling hands. She then gave him a kiss she hoped would affect him half as much as his had rocked her.

She felt his grin beneath her lips and happily settled for that. As he guided her backward toward the double doors to his room, he showered her jaw and neck with tiny kisses.

He opened one of the doors at her back and, once he'd managed to waltz them through without breaking physical contact, he slammed the door behind them. With the help of several moonbeams, he continued to propel her toward his bed.

As soon as the back of Rainy's legs connected with the mattress, she gave in to her weak knees and sank down onto the soft quilt. As Cash followed, the significance of the quilt they were sprawling on registered, and she had the deliciously nasty thought that the women of Maybe could eat their hearts out.

"What are you smiling about?" Cash asked, grinning himself as he flipped on a soft bedside lamp, then stretched out beside her, stroking her arm, then the side of her breast.

"You." She tunneled a hand through his hair and he brought his mouth to hers with renewed urgency. He kissed her lips, her chin, her jaw, her ear. He ran the tip of his tongue down the side of her neck and back up to her lobe. He nipped lightly at the fleshy part, before using his tongue once again to trace the shell.

Rainy let her hand trail away from his hair, down to the open collar of his shirt. Her fingers edged in to play with the soft, coarse hair blanketing his chest.

He angled back to rip the western snaps free from his shirt and, with his eyes still on her face, jerked out of it, throwing it over his shoulder to the floor.

He lowered himself back down, stretching out beside her, his head propped up by one hand, facing her, close, a breath away, slipping the fingers of his other hand under the hem of her dress, which had ridden up high on her thigh.

His hand skimmed her hip, her bare waist. He swirled his palms up, slowly, teasing her flesh until he cupped a breast. Her nipple, separated only by sheer silk, blossomed in his palm. One finger dipped in and out of her cleavage.

She shuddered and moved closer to him. His finger made contact with the front closure of her strapless bra and he quickly unhooked it. Pushing the cups to the side, he filled one hand with her naked breast. She heard his breath stall, felt his hardness near her belly.

Quickly, he levered himself to a sitting position and pulled up the hem of her dress. She rose, too, and helped him as he tugged the fabric free. Shrugging the bra off the rest of the way, she ignored the whisper of silk as it glided down her back. Instead, she concentrated on the thrilling darkness of Cash's eyes as he looked at her nakedness, while he touched her, gently, worshipfully.

He raised his gaze briefly to hers, then bowed his head to taste her breasts. His tongue circled one nipple, lightly, only the tip, over and over, until his tongue suddenly firmed and he flicked it hard and moist against her. Both her hands found his hair, and she reared her head back as he drew the sensitive nipple into his mouth and suckled.

He slid his hands down her body, his warm palms pressed to her skin, to the indention of her waist, over the curve of her silk-covered hips, down her restless thighs. Then he returned slowly, stopping at the waistband of her brief slip. He ran a finger inside of the band, teasing her belly, while his mouth continued to worship her breasts.

Overcome with sensation, Rainy didn't know the exact moment when he'd started sliding the slip down her hips, but he'd hooked a thumb in the elastic of her bikini panties and was bringing them down along with it.

She fell back on the bed and helped kick them off when he'd gotten them down to her ankles. He let the bundle fall to the floor and, smiling, crawled back over her. She ran her hands over his bare chest to his shoulders, then back down to his waist. Tentatively, she put a palm against the hardness beneath his fly.

Cash took a deep, shuddering breath. "Oh, no." He grabbed her wrist to stop her and, bringing her hand up, kissed her palm. "I don't think so. Or I just might make a fool of myself."

"Impossible," she whispered happily and tried to reach out for him again.

He stopped her. "Wanna bet?" He placed her arm around him instead and allowed his chest to make contact with her breasts. He groaned. "Oh, hell." He kissed her hard, and this time when she fumbled for his snap, he didn't interfere.

Nervous anticipation prevented her from making a quick, smooth job of it, but finally she got the last button undone. She'd have to speak to him about the miracle of zippers, she thought giddily as he finished the business of losing his jeans.

When her eager hands sought him once more, he gently pushed her shoulders back against the bed. He kissed each breast again, then her lips and slid into her.

Half out of surprise, half out of desire, she arched up to meet him. But he stilled his body and drew a finger up her cheek. "We've got to take this slow, baby," he said in a raspy voice. "Or I won't make it." He kissed the tip of her nose.

She felt the restraint vibrating in his chest and smiled. "Tough," she whispered and bucked up against him.

RAINY TRACED Cash's scar with her finger and thought of how nice it would be to spend the rest of the night in bed, instead of the scant hour they'd stolen—though they had managed to make love twice. But even as Cash kissed her again, she knew they'd have to get up before Smiley and Josh returned.

Although Cash had assured her that the two would never get home before midnight, and it was only eleven now, she was beginning to get nervous.

"Cash?" She stretched out like a contented cat as he massaged her breasts and nibbled her ear.

"Hmm?" His hand strayed down her belly to the tops of her thighs.

She shifted under his touch and, with a sigh of regret, said, "We have to get up."

"I know." The words were muffled against her skin as he licked a path under her jaw. His hand continued its journey, causing her to moisten all over again.

"I mean it, Cash," she insisted without an ounce of conviction. "As much as I hate for this to end."

"It doesn't have to." He kissed her on the lips, then, resting back on his elbow, he smiled. "We'll go to Colesville...no, too close. Hartsville. We'll go to Hartsville for dinner tomorrow night." He kissed her shoulder. "Maybe we'll make it room service."

"Tomorrow night? You've got to emcee the auction."

He groaned. "Oh, yeah."

She laughed. "I wonder if there'll be any interesting quilts this year?"

He gave her a suspicious look, but didn't ask what she knew about that part of the auction. "There'd better not be," he said. "I guess that leaves us with Monday. And I promise—" he picked up her hand and started kissing a path up her arm "—nothing will stop us."

Nothing? A sudden panic attack came out of nowhere, sending a shiver down Rainy's bare back. She pulled her hand away and tugged the sheet around her. She had to tell him about the centerfold.

"What's the matter? Are you cold?" Cash raised off his elbow to curve an arm around her.

"No." She scooted out of reach, across the bed, until she could swing her feet to the floor.

His eyebrows drew together. "What's wrong?"

She searched the floor for their clothes and began the job of untangling them. "Nothing." She stepped into her panties, skipped the bra. "I don't want Josh to catch us."

"The door is locked, Rainy, not that he'd ever come charging in here." He slid off the bed and accepted the clothes she handed him. "Besides, I doubt he's that anxious to hear from me. He knows he's in trouble over that volunteering business."

He made no attempt to put his jeans back on right away; instead, he watched her curiously. Rainy just couldn't help watching him back. The moonlight streamed in through the angled blinds and sent slender silver beams across his chest and midsection. Years of hard ranch work showed in each ridge of muscle, his flat belly, his lean thighs. He was beautiful.

"You keep looking at me like that and we won't be going anywhere." Cash grinned.

She blushed and pulled her dress on over her head. She wondered if he'd still feel that way once she told him about the centerfold. "Cash, I really need to talk to you."

He looked blankly at her and went perfectly still. When she started to speak again, he brought a silencing finger to his lips and frowned.

"What's—"

"That's Smiley's truck I hear."

"Oh, no." Rainy's eyes flew to her dress. She was put together...mostly. "The kitchen. How did we leave the kitchen?"

"I can't remember." Cash hopped on one foot, trying to get into his jeans.

"I'll go take care of it." She'd already made it to the door when she heard him mumbling something about being right there. She slowed long enough to fling her slip and bra into her room, then flew downstairs.

From outside the front window, she saw the truck's headlights switch off just as she raced down the hall to the kitchen. Two half-full glasses of wine sat on the table. Other than that, nothing looked out of the ordinary.

Rainy released a quick breath of relief and plopped down on a chair. She'd just settled into a casual pose, when Cash ducked his head in.

"Everything okay?" he asked.

Before she could answer, Smiley's high-pitched howl pierced the air. Josh's cracking voice responded, then the front door slammed.

Rainy put a hand to her heart. This had been too close a call for her.

Chuckling, Cash dropped into the opposite chair and casually picked up his glass of wine.

Fueled by an attack of nerves, she grabbed for her wine, as well, and took too big a sip. The liquid burned a path down her throat.

"Did you see the ol' bat's face when I told her I knew her little secret?" Smiley was asking Josh as he entered the kitchen.

Josh rounded the corner behind him, rolling his eyes. He slowed down when he spotted his father and Rainy, then looked suspiciously back and forth between the two of them.

Smiley eyed them on his way to the refrigerator. He opened it and moved aside a gigantic pot. "I don't suppose you two want chili for supper tomorrow?" He laughed heartily at his feeble joke and grabbed an apple. Then he frowned at Rainy. "You didn't show up at the cook-off."

"I was in the dunking booth, but I was cheering you on in spirit." She forced a smile, her arms crossed over her unbound breasts.

Smiley scratched his whiskered chin and sent his boss an odd look.

Cash raised his brows, appearing rather smug. Then he looked from Smiley to Josh. "Why are you back so early?"

"Ask him." Smiley nudged his chin in Josh's direction. "As soon as I told him y'all had left a while ago and he was riding with me, he got in an all-fired-up hurry to leave. I ain't got no understandin' of teenagers." He shook his head all the way out the kitchen door and headed toward the bunkhouse.

Cash set his narrowed gaze on his son.

Josh shrugged and pulled out a chair.

Cash gave Rainy a helpless glance before he turned to the boy. "So, Josh, care to explain how we got volunteered today?"

Josh didn't seem so anxious to stick around all of a sudden, and from the look Cash slid her, that was precisely the effect Cash'd had in mind. He gave her a wink as Josh made a point of looking everywhere but at them.

Then she noticed that the top button of Cash's shirt was still undone. Black curly hair, swirling toward his throat, had only minutes ago laid beneath her palm.

She couldn't believe what had developed between them, she thought, taking a deep, steadying breath. It had all happened so fast.

Rainy watched the hint of a smile roost at the corners of Cash's mouth, even as he tried to maintain his stern posture. His green eyes sparkled with banked amusement, a spray of fine lines etched at the sides from years of smiling, years of fatherly pride. He waited patiently for his son's answer.

She sighed inwardly. Nothing had happened fast at all. She'd seen it coming from the day she'd read Josh's essay, from the day Cash had given her her first riding lesson.

Yet she still hadn't told him about the centerfold.

And coward that she was, she wasn't going to tell him tonight, either. She couldn't. "I think I'll turn in," she said, careful not to look at Cash. "And give you two some privacy."

Before she made it to the door, she gave in and risked a quick glance.

Then hurried away, wishing she hadn't.

Chapter Twelve

Today at the festival, the sun seemed brighter, the sky bluer. Not that Rainy was one bit surprised. After last night with Cash, today had to be glorious. It would be nearly perfect, except she had to tell him about *Midnight Fantasy*.

She hated thinking about it, especially with the memories of their lovemaking still warm in her heart. And after what they'd shared, she had all the more reason to come clean with him tonight... after the festival was over.

No matter what happened, she swore she would tell Cash the truth. Then she remembered the auction this evening.

Tomorrow. She would definitely tell him tomorrow.

Coward.

She sighed, idly scanning the crowd. Waiting one night would make no difference. She wasn't trying to prolong the inevitable, she assured herself. She simply didn't want to ruin a perfectly good day.

Rainy took the last bite of her second hot dog, and was licking a ribbon of mustard off her thumb, when Cash returned with their colas.

He handed her one. "I hope you didn't eat so much you won't want to ride the tilt-a-whirl."

"The merry-go-round is definitely more my speed."

"What?" He laughed and she wondered when she'd decided that laughing could be so sexy. His open-neck, rose polo shirt was the perfect compliment to his green eyes and dark hair. "A city girl like you? I though you'd like it fast."

Her gaze riveted to his. What was wrong with her? She was acting like a hormone-raging teenager who boiled every comment down to sex. Then he winked and she wasn't so sure she hadn't been right.

"I told you already." She sniffed. "I'm no city girl."

He laughed and put an arm around her.

She started to snuggle in, then stiffened, looking around her at the crowded grounds. Stealing secret kisses and hugs at the dance in the dark was different from open affection in broad daylight.

"I think we're far enough into the courtship stage, don't you?" he whispered, grinning.

Heat blossomed in her cheeks and she darted another look around. This new level of their relationship was so fragile, so unfamiliar, it knocked her off kilter. "People will talk."

"Let them."

She tried to relax. There was no reason why two consenting adults couldn't be seeing each other. Well, maybe one small one, but she was going to take care of that tomorrow.

The mere thought of what she had to tell him made her start to protest again, until she caught sight of Mabel Simms barreling down on them. "Oh, no. I don't know about you, but I'm outta here." She ducked under his arm.

Cash followed her gaze. "I'm right behind you."

They both did an about-face, ready to race for the opposite corner of the grounds, when Mabel put two fingers between her lips and let out an ear-piercing whistle.

Everyone but them looked at the older woman. Finally, they looked at each other in defeat and turned around.

"Oh, dear." Mabel waddled the last few yards toward them, the wide brim of her shocking pink hat flopping wildly. "I hope I didn't startle you."

Rainy laughed. She just couldn't help it. The woman was a walking incongruity. Cash merely pursed his lips and waited for what Mabel had to say.

"I just wanted to tell you how fantastic our profits were yesterday." Mabel leaned her face toward them. "You know the dunking and kissing booths were a real hit. The two of them made over twice as much as all the other booths put together."

"Great." Cash didn't smile.

Rainy gave him a subtle elbow. "We were happy to help."

Mabel grinned. "And if today goes as well as we projected, we'll have enough to attract the attention of that cattle-drive committee."

"Oh, yes," Rainy said. "I was interested in hearing more about that."

Cash exhaled a cross between a sigh and a groan.

"Then you must come to our meeting next Thursday night. And, of course, you can always stop by my husband's office and get some information. Homer's the mayor, you know." Mabel looked directly at Cash. "We're still hoping you'll be our representative."

"I've already told you to count me out on this one, Mabel." Cash shook his head, affecting a disinterested look, which he let wander off toward the Ferris wheel.

"I have never seen him so stubborn," Mabel whispered to Rainy. "Maybe you can talk some sense into him." In a louder voice she added, "I'll see you Thursday night. You, too, Cash." Then she continued down the fairway.

"When hell freezes over," Cash muttered under his breath, watching Mabel's retreat through narrowed eyes. He turned to Rainy. "Are you ready for that ride?"

"Why are you so set against Maybe's involvement with the cattle drive?" She crossed her arms over her chest when he would have grabbed her hand.

"I've already told you. It'll take too much manpower and too many hours."

"But the return should be worth it. Violet's told me a lot about it. She says that national sponsors are interested in participating, so not only will it bring tourist dollars, but it—"

"Rainy." He placed his hands on her shoulders. "These people are ranchers, small store owners. They don't know how to negotiate for something of this magnitude. There's a great deal of money and a lot of blue suits behind that cattle drive, and I simply don't want my neighbors to get in over their heads. They don't have a clue how to deal with those Dallas and New York promoters."

"You do."

He dropped his hands. "Not interested."

Rainy looked at him curiously. Mabel was right, he was being stubborn. And although she thought he protested a tad too much, the hard set of his jaw told her she was fighting a losing battle. Whatever his reason—and she had no doubt he had one he wasn't sharing—he was not about to cave in to her.

"Oh, well, I don't know that much about it myself yet," she said breezily and started once again in the direction of the rides. "So why don't we take a spin on the merry-go-round?"

His frown softened, then eased into a lopsided grin. "Merry-go-round?"

"Don't you dare call me a wimp after my dunking tank duty," she warned.

"Never. You deserve a purple heart."

She laughed. "You, too. Although...I am a little upset with you." She tried her best to keep a straight face.

"Me?" His steps faltered.

She lifted her chin. "You didn't save me one of those kisses," she said, obviously ignoring the fact that she'd gotten far more than a mere kiss.

He stopped for a moment, his gaze roaming her pinkening face, then a slow, lazy smile curved his lips. "Wanna bet?" He grabbed her hand and raced toward the merry-go-round.

Only they bypassed it, skipped the tilt-a-whirl, flew by the ponies and didn't slow down until they arrived, breathless, at the Ferris wheel. Cash quickly turned in several scripts for two tickets, while Rainy clutched her side, laughing and trying to catch her breath.

"Um, I forgot to tell you," she began once Cash returned. Sobering, she tilted her head back, her eyes following the motion of the wheel. "I'm not crazy about Ferris wheels, either." An empty car came to a stop in front of them and the operator swung open the gate.

"Does the height bother you?" Cash asked, even as he urged her forward.

She nodded and wouldn't budge.

"Don't worry," he whispered, easing forward with a hand at the small of her back. "I plan on keeping your mind off it."

She tore her gaze from the looming car and shot him a quick look. His eyes twinkled with promise and his mouth... God, his mouth curved in a sensual guarantee.

Rainy blindly stepped up and sank into the seat. When Cash dropped down beside her, his weight caused the car to swing into motion. She grabbed the safety bar and one look at her white knuckles had him steadying the car with his foot on the platform.

The operator called out that he was about to start the ride. Cash gave her one last inquiring look and, when she nodded, he drew his leg back in and they slowly started to ascend.

"Okay?" He put an arm around her shoulders and pulled her close.

"As long as I don't look down and we don't rock." She leaned against him, enjoying the solid feel of his chest, the strong arm that held her.

"I think I may be able to help with that." He brought his other hand up to cup her cheek.

Automatically, her eyes met his. He winked before pressing a soft kiss to her lips.

The car lifted higher and Rainy's heart followed. She didn't look down, didn't even open her eyes. She did open her mouth, though, when in a seductive gesture, slowly, lightly, he ran his tongue over her lips.

She tasted the strawberry Sno-Kone they'd shared earlier, drank in his familiar musky scent and let the motion of the wheel free her from her worries.

As they swept back down within people range, she stirred away and tried to regain some semblance of a breathing pattern. Cash smiled his understanding, but the raw desire in his eyes was like a magnet for her body. She sighed and did a quick scan of the crowd to be sure they had no audience. That was when she noticed the tall blond woman.

Rainy squinted against the sun for a better look, and the flutter in her stomach had nothing to do with their car arching back up. The woman bore a remarkable resemblance...

"Hey, I thought you didn't like that," Cash said, and she suddenly realized that she'd leaned too far out and had caused the car to resume its rocking.

Her eyes widened and she clutched the safety bar with one hand and Cash's arm with the other. He shifted his weight backward and the motion began to even out. Rainy exhaled and looked out over the crowd, her gaze briefly snagging on every tall blonde in her path. But the woman was nowhere to be seen.

She returned her attention to Cash and his puzzled expression. No doubt he thought she was going bonkers. But she knew what the real problem was. Tomorrow was their birthday. That's why she was hallucinating about her twin. She'd been thinking a lot about Sunny lately, and how strange it was going to be to face their birthday apart for the first time.

Not to mention the other subject that came to mind when she thought of Sunny. Cash pressed his cheek to her hair and Rainy was sorely reminded of what she had to do tomorrow.

EARLY MONDAY MORNING Cash whistled his way down Main Street, the sound smothered by the roar of his motorcycle.

Jeb Haller was signing for a bread delivery outside his store and looked up in astonishment as Cash sped by. Mabel Simms was entering her husband's office when the unfamiliar revving of the bike's engine caused her to turn around. She lifted her hand in a halfhearted wave, her mouth hanging wide open. Grinning, Cash acknowledged her with a salute and resumed whistling.

But when Della Witherspoon poked her head out of her boutique, Cash nearly ran into Homer Simms's parked car. Remembering the unexpected smacker she'd laid on him at the kissing booth, his whistling died an abrupt death.

He guided the motorcycle to the nearest available space and parked it before he embarrassed himself by falling off the damn thing. He waved to Della, who was still gaping at him and the bike, and he promptly crossed the street, heading in the opposite direction.

Glancing at his watch, he saw that he had at least ten minutes before he had to be at the emergency PTA meeting called by Homer Simms. Curious as he was about what had the mayor fired up enough to call a meeting in July, he had something more urgent to handle.

He needed flowers for his date with Rainy tonight. It was a small detail that he hadn't yet asked her out. But she'd said this morning that she needed to speak with him, and he intended to have that quiet conversation over dinner... with candlelight... in Colesville... alone.

He smiled at the possibilities.

God, life was good. He couldn't remember the last time if felt so damn good just to get up in the morning. The only thing that could make it any better would be to wake up with Rainy. But with a fourteen-year-old lurking around and seeming to watch Cash's every move, it made that near impossible. For now, Cash was merely grateful she'd entered his life.

He looked down the strip of ancient, weathered buildings, at the chipping paint, the faded awnings. Hell, even Maybe was looking better these days. Now if he could just find some flowers. It'd been so long since he'd needed any, he wasn't sure where to look. Maybe had no florist and Jeb's Grocery was the only place he could think of to go. Of course, there would be the mandatory twenty questions from Jeb and anyone else who happened to be in the store, but he hadn't much choice.

Main Street appeared more crowded than usual for a Monday morning, and as he approached Jeb's Grocery, he was surprised to see Smiley's battered old '67 pickup. His hand on the grocer's door, Cash was about to enter the store when Seth's mother, Thelma Johnson, pulled her new sedan into an empty parking place on the street. He smiled at her, but she glared back. Then she got out of the car, went around to the trunk and withdrew a large, heavy-looking paper sack.

"Need some help with that, Thelma?" Cash let go of the door.

She ignored him.

John and Marian Hassett pulled up behind her with a very red-faced Jimmy Ray in tow. They yanked him out of the back seat along with another large paper sack. Marian ignored Cash, too, as she hurried to accompany Thelma toward the mayor's office. John Hassett mumbled a faint good-morning to Cash and followed his wife, taking with him Jimmy Ray and the mysterious bag.

Cash stared after the four of them, then, with inexplicable dread, started in their direction. He'd have to skip the flowers for now. Something very strange was happening in Maybe.

RAINY TRIED TO THINK biology. It was one of Josh's more difficult subjects and, with her mind on Cash and tonight, she was having her own problems. Not that her student's concentration was so hot, either.

His dark head was bowed close to the book, his guiding finger no longer moving. She furtively poked her face forward to see what page he was on. It had to be a record. No one took fifteen minutes to read one page.

She cleared her throat to rouse him, then leaned back and forced her attention to the quiz she was devising—a quiz that was sure to inspire a whole new attitude toward her.

He'd been looking at her funny all morning. In fact, ever since the festival, even his friends were acting peculiarly toward her. Enough so that it gave her a bad feeling. Had he discovered that she and Cash...

But that wasn't possible, she decided, sighing. Other than going to the festival together yesterday, she hadn't been alone with Cash for so much as a minute. She was just jumpy. It was going to be a relief to tell him about the centerfold this evening. Almost.

She checked her watch. The morning had gone on forever, but finally it was near lunchtime. She had two more questions to add to Josh's quiz, then she could rehearse her speech to Cash for the hundredth time since last night. And then, for two hundred more times, she would remind herself that she had done nothing wrong.

After Rainy added the final quiz question, the phone rang. Josh knew, and usually respected, the rules about interrupting his lessons, but this time he jumped up and ran down the hall before she could say boo.

He returned less than a minute later, his face red. "C-can we b-break for lunch now? I—I'll owe you an extra hour."

She knew he stuttered on occasion when he was nervous, but this was the worst lapse she'd experienced. "Okay, Josh." She eyed him a moment longer. "Is something wrong? Can I help?"

"N-no. I—I gotta go talk to Seth, that's all. I'll try to be back within an hour." He'd already made it to the door.

"Josh?" Her voice was soft but stern. He slowed down, but wouldn't look at her. "I'm not going to ask you any more questions, but I do expect you to get back here as soon as possible."

He nodded, his face still shuttered.

"I want to make sure that you understand we have some serious work to do. Starting tomorrow, we'll add another hour to our day."

"Tomorrow?" He looked at her then, a flash of panic in his eyes. "Yeah, tomorrow." Then he raced the length of the hall and down the stairs.

Rainy frowned and stared after him before straightening her paperwork. What else could go wrong today? She'd wanted to talk with Cash first thing this morning, but he had been unexpectedly called to town, and now this emergency with Josh. Strange day. It was a good thing she wasn't a big birthday person, like Sunny, or she'd be feeling mighty sorry for herself by now.

The thought of her sister cheered her a bit. She'd originally planned on calling Sunny to wish her a happy birthday this evening, hoping her sister was back from her promotional tour. But she couldn't stand the anticipation another minute. She walked quickly downstairs to use the kitchen phone to call home. She'd be horribly disappointed if Sunny weren't there.

Rainy had just punched in the area code, when the doorbell rang. For a moment she thought about ignoring it. No one ever called on a weekday morning, but it wasn't her house and it wasn't her decision to make. So she hung up the phone and answered the door.

"Surprise! Surprise!"

Rainy blinked several times. Then her eyes widened to the size of Frisbees. She had to be seeing things.

"Now I know you haven't forgotten what I look like." Laughing delightedly, Sunny stepped forward and hugged her. "Happy birthday, older sister."

"Only by two minutes," Rainy said automatically, then stood back, speechless, hoping she was seeing things.

"Aren't you going to wish me a happy birthday?" Sunny asked with her well-practiced pout.

"What are you doing here?"

"Jeez, Rain, you could at least ask me in."

Rainy's gaze traveled over Sunny's long, loosely curled hair, to her tight peach crop-top, down to her short spandex skirt. She swallowed hard as realization struck and she poked her head out the door, causing Sunny to stumble back. Rainy looked first right, then left. Without skipping a beat, she grabbed her sister, hauled her inside, slammed the door and sank against it.

"Well, at least I think you're happy to see me." Sunny's smile faltered.

"The question is, did anyone else see you?"

"Uh..." Sunny made a face. "You mean today?"

"I mean here . . . in Maybe."

"Well . . ."

Gosh, she looked great. Rainy unplastered herself from the door and stepped forward to embrace her sister. "I am happy to see you. I—I can't think of a nicer birthday surprise."

"Rain, I love you, but you are a horrible liar." Sunny laughed and handed her a brightly wrapped package.

Rainy accepted it with a sheepish smile and opened her mouth to defend herself.

Sunny held up a hand. "I know, I know. Where Sunny goes, trouble follows. But not this time." She smiled, clearly pleased with herself. "I haven't gotten into a jam for the whole four and a half days I've been here."

"Four days?" Rainy repeated faintly.

"And a half. And not an ounce of trouble. Must be a record, huh?"

"Oh, boy."

Sunny sobered suddenly. "Really, Sis, everything is fine. Let's not ruin our birthday." She took one of Rainy's hands and looked at her with such a heart-tugging, anxious expression that it made Rainy feel guilty.

"We won't." She hugged Sunny again. "We'll have a great day. I mean evening." She moved back with a small, regretful shake of her head . . . regretful for more than one reason. Was she destined to never tell Cash? "I have to work this afternoon," she explained. "It wouldn't be fair to cancel out at the last minute."

"No problem. I really didn't want to bother you so early, but I couldn't wait." Sunny broke into her award-winning smile. "Let's meet for dinner and you can catch me up on what you've been doing here."

"Yeah. And you can tell me what you've been up to for the past four and a half days." She frowned. "Where have you been staying, anyway? Why didn't you call me earlier?''

''A small town near here called Colesville. And I was waiting for our birthday.''

Relief resurrected Rainy's hope. Was it possible that quiet, conservative Maybe had been spared her twin's harmless but sometimes mischievous shenanigans? Still, it wasn't like Sunny to have waited four days. ''Maybe we should meet in Colesville for dinner.''

''I'll come pick you up at seven and we can decide then,'' Sunny said, walking to the door.

Rainy started to raise her hand in protest and brought up the package her sister had given her.

''And don't open that until we're together later. I can't wait to see your face.'' Sunny delivered one of her more devilish grins, then traipsed out the door.

Rainy stayed where she was, her brain scrambling for the best solution to this new development. Maybe if Cash met Sunny, it would be easier to tell him about the centerfold. Actually, the idea had great merit. She brought a finger to her lips. But then again, she thought, her stomach tightening...once Cash saw Sunny...

Disgusted with herself, Rainy let out a loud sigh. Sunny wasn't like that. It wasn't her fault all those little twerpy boys they'd gone to school with had dropped Rainy like a hot potato as soon as Sunny showed up. And besides, Cash wasn't like that...she hoped.

Slowly, she climbed the stairs to put the package in her room, and continued to ponder her best course of action, when she heard Cash's motorcycle pull up along the back side of the house.

As always, when she knew he was near, her pulse accelerated and she smiled that special smile that seemed to automatically blossom around him. Then, when she realized how close he'd come to running into Sunny, she about tripped over the last stair. Quickly, she put away her gift, hoping he'd have time for lunch.

She made it back downstairs just as he entered the kitchen. He hung his helmet on one of the pegs, careful to keep a paper sack tucked under his arm, and glanced at her without a smile.

Her own smile wavered. "I was about to make a sandwich," she said, her eyes taking in every tense move as he strode to the kitchen table. "Can I make you one?"

He didn't answer at first. An unfamiliar tick worked at his jaw. "I'm not hungry."

"Iced tea, maybe?" She jerked open the refrigerator door, her appetite suddenly gone, as well. When he didn't respond, she looked over her shoulder at him.

He'd taken a seat and was leaning back in his chair, his face still devoid of a smile. His gaze clearly and insolently aimed straight at her backside.

She stiffened and immediately tugged at her thigh-level T-shirt. She didn't know this man sitting here. This wasn't the man who had made such sweet, tender love to her. The dark hair, the tanned face, the full lips, they were all the same...but his eyes...they were sullen, thunderous looking. Today the scar made him look sardonic.

"Want some iced tea?" she asked again, her throat so dry the words barely creaked out.

He smiled then. But the salacious grin did nothing to ease the strain—it made her even more uncomfortable.

"Sure."

Rainy turned back to get the tea and glasses. Something was wrong. Very wrong. Had he talked to Violet? Had she told him about the centerfold?

Oh, heaven help her, had he seen *Midnight Fantasy?* She should have talked to him last night. She should have explained about Sunny more than two weeks ago. But the sad fact was, she hadn't.

She set the glasses on the table, her hands shaking so badly that the tumblers clanged together, the loud obnoxious sound disturbing the horrible silence.

She ordered herself to stop. There was no concrete reason to think his strange mood had anything to do with her.

At least a third of the tea missed the glass when she tipped the pitcher to it. Some of the liquid puddled on the table. A good deal of it splashed her light blue T-shirt.

"Something wrong?" Cash asked in a tone caught between casual and caustic. He watched Rainy's ashen face turn even paler as she surveyed the large brown splotches on the front of her T-shirt. When she pulled the fabric down to blot the stains with a napkin, he got a bird's-eye view of the generous curves of her breasts.

The scene both angered and aroused him, and the fact that he was aroused at all angered him even more. She had hurt him—she'd hurt his son.

As calmly as he could manage, he rose from the table and ripped off a length of paper towels from the rack near the sink. When he approached her with it, she held out her hand, but he ignored it and pressed the towel to her shirt, his palm over her breast, the cold liquid seeping through, moistening his hand.

She moved, a tiny, almost imperceptible, jerky movement and brought suddenly wide eyes to his. She stepped back a breath out of his reach. "I think I'll just change."

"Good idea." He wadded up the paper towel and threw it in the sink. "Why don't you try that little red number? You know, the one your sister packed for you?"

Hurt and fear settled in her eyes. She opened her mouth to speak, but her lower lip quivered and not a sound came out.

For an instant Cash absorbed her pain, remembering the Rainy he thought he knew, the one who had moaned softly in his arms just one night ago. Without thinking, he lifted a hand to her. But she flinched, anger and bitterness flashing across her face, and he was, once again, reminded that she was a fraud.

"You've seen it," she said simply.

He reached around the table to his seat and snatched the paper sack he'd brought with him. He pulled out a copy of *Midnight Fantasy* and sent it flying across the tabletop. It bounced off a chair back and landed on the table. "You mean this?"

Chapter Thirteen

She closed her eyes for a few moments. He saw her chest rise and fall with the two deep breaths she took. The action stirred his memory of her naked from the waist, her breasts high and proud, her nipples extended, the fake, surprised look on her face—in glossy color for all to see.

He balled his fists and took a couple of deep breaths of his own. How could he have been deceived like this? Why had he bought her girl-next-door act? She had played him for a fool from the very beginning.

He raised his eyes back to her saddened face, her shattered spirit. And damn it, he wondered most of all, how could he still want her?

Cash slammed his fist down on the table, causing her to jump. "Why did you do it, Rainy? Or should I call you Sunny?" She shook her head helplessly, spreading her hands, but he didn't give her a chance to speak. "Was it for money? Did they pay you a lot? Was that it? Or do you just like to show yourself off?"

"I can explain—"

He picked up the magazine and opened it to her picture. Out of his peripheral vision, he saw her flinch, but ignored the reaction. "I gotta admit..." He gave the page a long, deliberate perusal before looking up at her. "You are incredible. But of course . . ." He paused deliberately, cruelly. "I already knew that."

She stared back, her throat working convulsively. "You're a bastard."

Yeah, she was right. A foolish bastard for allowing sympathy and longing to still twist his gut. Moving a step back, he tried to calm himself. He needed to shut up. He didn't want to hurt anymore, didn't need to hurt her.

"Why so indignant? You took the pictures. You got paid for it. And for four bucks, we all get to see it. You did know it works that way, didn't you?"

"If you shut up for one minute, I can explain." She lifted her chin, anger darkening her once beautiful eyes.

"Really?" He held up the picture to her face and gave her a bland smile. "I don't think so."

Rainy slapped the magazine to the floor. "Maybe you're right. For you, maybe there is no explanation." A small strangled laugh escaped her as she turned to leave. "And I thought you were different."

"I think that's my line."

"I guess now you'll never know."

"Wait."

She stopped by the hall door and turned extraordinarily sad eyes on him. At that moment, he couldn't help nurturing the small seed of hope that embedded itself in his heart. He swallowed the bitter taste of disappointment and prayed for a miracle. "Tell me why you did it. And why I had to find out this way."

"I thought you had all the answers."

"If you won't explain for me, at least do it for Josh."

Her entire expression changed. "I never meant to hurt him or the potential custody hearing. You've got to believe that."

Cash crossed his arms over his chest. She looked devastated, and if he weren't so scared out of his mind that she had done exactly that, he'd believe just about anything she had to say.

The tension had been so thick between them that until the kitchen door swung open, he hadn't realized that Smiley had pulled up in his truck.

Cash followed Rainy's stricken eyes to the older man, who stepped through the door and turned three shades of red as soon as he looked at Rainy.

The foreman's gaze strayed to the battered magazine laying on the floor. He'd already removed his hat, but instead of hanging it on the peg, he set it back atop his head. "I guess y'all don't wanna be disturbed 'bout now."

Rainy's face fell. She turned her accusing stare on Cash. "What did you do, tell the whole town?"

He let out a short, malicious laugh. "That's priceless." He passed a hand over his face and brought it to rub his jaw. "No, Rainy, they all told me."

"Oh, God." Her shoulders sagged and she buried her face in her hands.

"That's okay, missy," Smiley piped up. "He had a whole lot more to say to them."

Her fingers gradually parted and one eye peeked between them.

"Yup. I was mighty proud of him. Told them you were a damn fine teacher and that they oughta keep their noses outta your personal business. Wouldn't let 'em say a thing bad about ya." Smiley beamed at his boss, then looked curiously back at Rainy with raised eyebrows. "Said you probably had a good reason for posin' for that magazine."

She lowered her hands altogether. "He did?"

Cash turned redder than Smiley had a moment ago. "Now's a real good time for you to go mend the south pasture fence." He jerked his head in the direction of the door and Smiley quickly complied.

As soon as the door slammed, Cash turned back to see a small lift to the corners of Rainy's mouth.

"You stuck up for me," she said, and he didn't understand how she could sound both grateful and accusing at the same time.

"Well, damn it, Rainy..." He reached to grab his hat and throw it down, but his head was bare. "I was so damn stunned. I still can't believe that's you."

She watched him mutter those last words in frustration, then happily said, "It's not."

"I've got Josh to think about, and all of Josh's friend's know... Hell, Rainy, if his..." He stopped. "What did you say?"

She was so overwhelmed with Smiley's information, she didn't answer right away. Cash had actually faced the town on her behalf. Richard hadn't been able to face his own peers, even though he'd known the truth. Her own school principal had shunned her, as well as some of her co-workers. But not Cash. He had stuck up for her.

Her heart constricted and she offered him a tentative smile. She wanted very badly to put her arms around him, but he still looked hurt and angry and she didn't blame him. Her thoughts immediately filled with Josh and she drew in her lip. That was where her error in judgment had been. In view of the custody problem, she had owed Cash the truth. Instead, she may have delivered ammunition to his ex-wife.

"Cash," she began, "that isn't me in that magazine." When his face tensed and he started to speak, she held up a hand, trying to spare them any more hurtful words. "I have a twin sister. Her name is Sunny."

"A twin?" He put a hand up to massage his temple. He said nothing more for almost a minute, and then as her words sank in, his scowl transformed itself to a look of shocked relief. "You have a twin."

She nodded. "I should have told you about the center-fold."

He exhaled a long, steady breath and bent down to pick up the magazine. It looked as if it had been through a war. It looked like Rainy felt. He ran a hand to smooth back the battered cover, staring at it in awe, and said, "This isn't you."

"No." She took an uncertain step forward. She hadn't deserved the verbal lashing he'd given her, just as he hadn't deserved the lies she'd delivered with her silence.

And then she stopped, her momentary elation fading. One of the traits she admired most about him was his fierce dedication to his son. It was for that reason she could for-give his harsh presumption, but it was also for that reason he might be unable to forgive her.

Maybe it was too late for them, but she wanted it clear that omission had been her only sin. "No," she repeated sadly, "I did not pose for those pictures." She searched his wary face. "And if you don't believe me—"

He moved forward and put a finger to her lips. "I do," he said softly. "I believe in you."

Cash caught sight of the moisture in her eyes before she blinked it away. His finger trailed from her lips to her chin and he nudged it up until she looked at him. He smiled, hoping to chase away the residual sadness he saw lurking in her eyes.

A small answering smile lifted her mouth from total de-spair. "I wouldn't blame you for still being angry."

"I still am, a little," he admitted gently. "But I'm also damned happy that isn't your picture."

Her head angled in a wry tilt. "Almost a moot point though, isn't it?"

He dropped his hand from her chin. "Well . . . yeah . . . I mean you really are identical, aren't you?" He glanced at the glossy cover of *Midnight Fantasy* he'd placed on the table and, remembering the erotic pictures, his body tightened. Without thinking, his eyes raked a path up Rainy.

She blushed. "I meant, it was irresponsible of me not to tell you about it from the beginning."

He reddened, too. "I'm sorry...I—"

"That's okay." She lifted a shoulder. "I mean that's part of the problem. We really are identical."

"Yeah, but more to the point—" he hitched a thumb toward the magazine "—that isn't you. You didn't do anything wrong."

A flash of gratitude sparkled from her eyes and then she looked away with a stubborn lift to her chin. "Neither did Sunny," she said, jumping to her twin's defense. "I may not approve of what she did, but it was her choice to make."

Cash nodded. He guessed it was true what they said about twins and how they bonded. He admired her loyalty. "I agree. But I can't ignore the problem her choice...and yours...leaves us."

She looked prayerfully to the heavens. "I know I should have told you from the beginning, but I was afraid you wouldn't give me the job."

He sighed. She was right about that. "Why don't you go get out of that wet T-shirt? I'll make us some more iced tea, then we'll talk."

She hesitated at first, then nodded, her expression so forlorn that as she started to turn, he grabbed her hand and tugged her back to him. She raised her surprised face and he kissed her lightly on the lips. And then he let her go.

The shy smile she gave him before disappearing around the corner was more than he deserved. Cringing at the memory of the things he'd said to her, he ignored the half pitcher of tea and headed straight for the cupboard. He removed a short tumbler, then reached up to the top shelf and pulled out a full bottle of Scotch.

Although he appreciated fine whiskey as much as the next man, he didn't drink hard liquor very often. But he figured today was as good a day as any to open the eighteen-year-old, single-malt Scotch he'd been saving for a special occasion. And at this point, the fact that Rainy had a twin sister was good enough reason for him.

After unscrewing it, he poured two fingers' worth and downed half of it in one swallow.

He withdrew another glass and brought it along with him to the table. Sinking into a chair, he slid the clean glass to a place across the table, then with his booted foot, he pushed out a corresponding chair for Rainy.

Better to have her sit away from him, he decided, and took another swallow of his drink. They had several issues to discuss and he had trouble thinking with her near. And as much as he'd grown to care about her, he had to deal with the fact that her poor judgment could affect custody of his son.

Josh. Cash shook his head. The kid had one hell of an imagination, that was for sure. He wondered how the boy had figured he could get her to autograph those pictures. Although Cash hadn't actually had words with him yet, Jimmy Ray had spilled the beans about the entire plan. Cash knew Josh was at Seth's right now. The only reason he hadn't hauled his butt home was because letting him stew a little longer would be a greater justice.

He tipped the glass up to his lips again. Right now, he needed to straighten some things out with Rainy. Even knowing the truth, his anger hadn't totally subsided. She still had a lot of questions to answer, and she'd been wrong in not telling him about the centerfold from the start.

The only reason he could maintain some semblance of calm at this point was out of relief for the truth, and the misery he'd witnessed in her face... her lovely, sweet, familiar face. His gaze strayed to the closed copy of *Midnight Fantasy* still laying on the table.

He cocked his head to make sure she wasn't approaching and slowly dragged the magazine toward him. His pulse hammered with the vivid image he recalled—the long, sleek legs, the full, rounded breasts, which had so recently filled his palms...

A fresh surge of anger erupted in him as he recanted the scene of Homer Simms spreading the pages before him, God and everyone else in the meeting. Even as stunned as he'd been, spears of jealousy had pierced his heart. He'd wanted to rip the magazine from Homer's hands. His fists had ached to connect with every male face in the room. No one should have seen her like that. No one...but him.

He toyed with a corner, tracing a finger over the glossy cover, contemplating one last inspection of the centerfold.

He jerked himself upright and slammed his palm down, disgusted with himself. What the hell did he think he was doing? That wasn't Rainy. Hell, looking at it would be like cheating on her.

Cheating? His fingers shook as he reached for his glass. He wasn't sure if it was from frustration or the sudden realization that had just penetrated his addled brain. Rainy was more than his son's tutor, she was more than a friend...she was more than his lover. Somewhere, somehow, she'd carved out a place for herself in his heart. And now he wanted more.

Taking an unsteady breath, he grabbed the bottle of Scotch. It was going to be hell sending her away.

RAINY TOOK MORE TIME selecting a simple T-shirt than she had choosing a dress for the dance.

The dance. She pushed the pile of shirts aside and sank to the bed. What she wouldn't give to turn back time, when she'd been full of hope and anticipation, when she'd found contentment in Cash's arms... when she should have been more responsible and told him the whole story.

She fell back on the bed and stared at the ceiling. Beating herself up now over her horrible lapse in judgment wasn't going to get her anywhere, she knew, but the self-pity felt good for the moment. And then she thought about the sweet, reassuring kiss he'd given her, and she sighed.

Reluctantly, she picked herself up and pulled a yellow shirt over her head. Her jeans had sustained only small dots of tea and they were mostly dry by now. Besides, she didn't want to procrastinate going back downstairs any longer. Kiss or no kiss, she and Cash still had a lot to talk about, and she certainly didn't want to be in the middle of a discussion over this when Josh returned.

She padded softly down the stairs, slowly continued down the hall and listened to make sure there were no voices before she entered the kitchen.

The half pitcher of iced tea sat on the counter where she'd left it. So did the glass that had shared the serving of iced tea with her shirt. Cash sat at the table with a bottle of Scotch.

She'd never seen him drink hard liquor before. He did keep beer in the fridge, which he had on occasion, and they'd shared a glass of wine once—the night they had made love.

He looked up when he heard her approach, then ran his gaze over her. "Do you have stock in some T-shirt company or something?"

She gave him a wry grin and sat in the chair opposite his— the one he'd obviously designated for her... the one farthest away from him. A trickle of apprehension slivered down her dry throat.

He leaned forward and poured some of the amber liquid into the glass in front of her. She wasn't keen on Scotch, but she picked it up and took a small sip. It burned all the way down, but was preferable to the nervous dryness.

"Obviously, we need to straighten this entire story out so we know where we stand." He recapped the bottle. "I suppose you ought to go first."

She gripped her drink tighter and looked down at her free hand. Surprisingly, it was relatively steady. She raised her eyes to his. "As nervy as this is going to sound, I'd really like you to tell me about who... well, about how... Did Violet...?" A soft sound of exasperation escaped her. "Cash, you've got to tell me what happened in town today. I'm going to be a basket case until you do."

He nodded slowly. "I can understand that. But I don't know anything about Violet..." He paused, his eyebrows furrowed, and she could tell he was pondering her unexplained eviction and how it may be tied in. "Though it seems my son is quite an entrepreneur."

Her mouth dropped open. "He knows?"

"Are you kidding? The little sucker started it all."

Any small hope she had of smoothing things over enough to resume her nice, quiet life here in Maybe shriveled up like an aged prune. And as Cash explained about Josh's get-rich scheme and the reaction of his friends' parents when they'd discovered how their little darlings were spending the summer, the old feelings of shame Rainy had managed to suppress in the past few weeks hit her with the force of a tornado.

"Rainy?" Cash tapped the table to get her attention, a worried frown on his face.

A large whoosh of air deserted her lungs as she looked at him.

"I meant what I said about you being a good teacher. And you're a good person. When people hear about the mix-up, they'll understand. Nothing will change."

"It will for me," she said in a soft, resigned voice.

"Only if you let it."

"You don't understand. We're identical. Most people can't get past that. They see one of us and they've seen us both."

Cash sipped his drink in silence for a few moments, while the reality of what she'd just pointed out appeared to sink in. She saw the hint of anger tensing his mouth and thought about running upstairs to pack.

Finally, he said, "Why don't you tell me what happened and we'll work on a plan of action from there?"

We'll work... Sappy tears burned the back of Rainy's eyes. She supposed Cash would never know how much those few words meant to her. "Some months ago, Sunny posed for a photographer who talked her into doing this layout. The story is a little fuzzy. Sunny wasn't clear on how it all happened." She frowned. "In fact, she was downright evasive. Not that it matters. The result was that they decided to sell the pictures to *Midnight Fantasy.*"

"Didn't she think about how something like that would affect you?" His irritation broadcasted itself in the tight clench of his jaw, the hard set of his mouth.

"Sunny generally doesn't think. Period." She stiffened at her own sour tone and added, "It's not that she's bad or inconsiderate. Most of the time she acts first and thinks later. But she's a wonderful, fun person. You'll really like her. Everyone does."

"Well, fortunately, I'll be spared having to make that judgment."

Oh, boy. Rainy bit her lip. Obviously, now wasn't the time to tell him her latest surprise regarding Sunny.

"Did you ever try talking her out of it?"

"Of course I would have..." Annoyance took a nasty bite out of her earlier, gentler tone. "Had I known about it beforehand."

"You mean she never told you?"

She sighed. It seemed as though she were indicting her sister at every turn. "Not until a week before it hit the stands." She looked down and briefly studied her cuticles.

He cursed. "What happened then?"

"Most people who knew us figured it had to be Sunny. But like I said, we're identical, so it didn't end there."

"Is that why you left your job?"

"I didn't exactly leave it." She grimaced. "I was asked to leave."

He shook his head. "But they knew the pictures were of Sunny?"

"It didn't matter. I counseled teenaged boys, and their parents wanted them concentrating on what I was saying and not what was under my clothes."

He cringed, and Rainy knew without a doubt that the same thought had crossed his mind about Josh.

"I didn't blame them at all," she hurried on to say, "but it was still hard not to take it personally. I was a good counselor and teacher. I had always received perfect evaluations."

"For what it's worth, your recommendation was impeccable."

She tried not to seem bitter.

"So you packed up and left." He still looked somewhat confused. "But you still have family and friends there?"

"I couldn't stay. The stares, whispers... I wasn't kidding when I told you Boon's a small town. My parents have been totally supportive. As far as friends..." She returned her attention to her cuticles, thinking about Richard and how he'd cared more about his university's board of regent's reaction than he had about her. "Well, Sunny has always been my best friend."

"And she screwed you."

Rainy's face came up and she pinned him with a warning glare. "Don't say that about her."

Cash pressed his lips together. "I'm sorry, but she's not who I care about."

She swallowed. Did he? Could he still care about her? Dare she hope?

"I do care about you. You do know that?" He reached across the table and took her hand, his pensive green eyes gently studying her face, then gripping her gaze. "Maybe too much."

She pulled back her hand. She didn't like the sudden change in his tone, the way his face saddened. Fear clutched her heart. He was going to send her away.

The sudden and irrational urge to laugh erupted, as life's irony closed in on her. One of the reasons she'd left Boon was because Richard hadn't cared enough. And now she'd leave Maybe because Cash cared too much—for her and for his son.

When he lightly stroked her hand, Rainy realized that she hadn't left Boon because of how Richard felt, she'd left because she hadn't cared enough about him to make it work. If it hadn't been the centerfold, it would have been something else. Richard was nothing more than a part of her history and she laid him to rest there in her mind.

She refolded her hands in front of her and stared at Cash's puzzled but earnest expression. This time it wasn't going to be so easy. This time she'd leave a piece of her heart.

"Rainy?" Cash glanced down at her tightly clasped hands, but made no further attempt to touch her. Various scenarios flew so fast through his head, he could barely formulate a thought...except the obvious one. "We'll have to make it work."

She dipped her head as if she hadn't heard correctly. "Make it work?"

"We both know damn well you're not going to escape the stares and whispers here, either..." He lifted a hand in a helpless gesture. "Once we let people know the true circumstances, we'll have to give them some time to let it all die down."

"But they won't want me to teach their kids." Hope began to replace her initial shock at his suggestion. "Will they?"

"I've already told them I'd vouch for your ability. That was never in question. And if they want to look at those pictures out of their own nosiness..."

She made a face. "You know they will."

"But they won't want to admit it." Cash grinned. "We have some pretty reasonable members on the hiring committee, and if parents complain about the pictures, we'll call them on it."

The beginnings of a smile tugged at her lips. "You're going to get a lot of flak."

"I can take it."

Before the smile could take complete hold, it faded and her tongue darted out to moisten her lips. "What about Josh?"

"He's in enough trouble right now." Cash knew what she meant, but he hadn't figured that part out yet. It was possible Cash could end up in trouble with his ex-wife. She'd use anything she could to get her way.

Rainy gave him a wry smile. "Let's put it this way, what about the custody hearing?"

"It's not really about custody. It's about Josh's education." Although he knew his ex-wife would make it about more than that, if necessary. But Rainy had enough to worry about and she didn't need the burden of that possibility.

"We both know better, Cash." Sadly, she shook her head. "It'll be about character if his mother finds out. The truth won't matter to a good lawyer. Everything will be twisted around. It'll be far too risky for you to be associated with me."

He stared at her for a moment, digesting what she'd said, then asked, "Whose character, Rainy? Mine?" He didn't wait for her response. The answer was suddenly clear to him. He couldn't send her away. That would make him as narrow-minded as the rest of the town . . . and make his ex-wife right. Worst of all, sending Rainy away would make him miserable.

"You're right," he began, "my character will be in question. That's why I have to stand by what I believe in, be honorable and be the best role model I can for Josh. That's why I won't sacrifice my relationship with you." He stood and took the few necessary steps around the table to pull her up to him.

He slipped his arms around her and kissed the corner of her surprised mouth. "I won't turn my back on someone I care about just because the road gets a little rocky. That's what I hope my son, or anyone else, sees in my character."

Her weight sagged slightly against him and a small whimper escaped her. He hugged her tighter for a moment, then urged her gently back so he could look at her face.

Her eyes were moist and thankful, and he felt renewed anger about the whole damn mess.

She was a good, loving person who gave her loyalty and enthusiasm to those around her. Even though it hurt her, she'd defended her sister, worried about his son . . . about him.

He nudged up her chin and pressed a gentle kiss to her quivering mouth. He felt her lips soften beneath his, her warm breath slip out on a sigh.

He stepped back, studying her weary face for a moment, then, pulling her around the table, he reclaimed his seat and settled her onto his lap. He brought both arms around her, cuddling her, soothing her. She snuggled against his chest and sighed.

"I'll be all right, baby," he said softly. "We're gonna make it all right."

"I want to believe that," she whispered.

So did he, he thought glumly, so did he. He stroked her hair and rocked her against him.

Chapter Fourteen

Rainy could gladly spend the rest of the day sitting here on Cash's lap. She loved the feel of his strong, soothing arms around her, allowing her to temporarily shut out the cold reality of the centerfold and all its attendant problems. He'd been kind and gentle, whispering words of encouragement and asking for nothing in return.

But she knew there was a lot more music to face and she shuddered just thinking about the townspeople's reactions.

"You okay?" Cash asked, rubbing his warm palm up her arm.

"Sure." She kissed the side of his jaw. "But I think it's time we get a move on. Josh should be home soon."

"I don't expect he'll be in any hurry to get here." He shook his head. "But after he does, and I've grounded him until he's thirty-five, he can make his own dinner. I'm taking you out."

"Dinner? Tonight?" She straightened. She'd almost forgotten about Sunny.

"Yeah. You'd said you wanted to talk to me." He trailed a finger down her cheek. "So I planned on taking you to dinner. I don't see any reason to change plans now."

Yeah, she'd wanted to talk to him all right. God, what a mess she'd made. She sighed. "About dinner—"

He cut in before she could finish. "It'll have to be after I get some chores done. Then we'll head out to Colesville."

"I can't go tonight." The words came out in a rush. She wanted to say it before she chickened out. Before he gave her one of those heart-stopping smiles that would have her making a further mess of her life.

Confusion and wariness crept into his gaze. Calmly, he adjusted his shirt collar, then tugged at it as if it were too tight. "You have plans?"

She nodded, her eyes miserably meeting his. "With Sunny."

His hand fell to his side. "Your sister?"

"She stopped by this morning."

"Stopped by?"

She nodded again and stood. "Apparently, she's been staying in Colesville. She came so we could spend our birthday together."

Cash took a long time to smooth out the front of his shirt. "When is that?"

"Today."

"Well . . ." He stood, too, and stretched out his back, an unreadable expression on his face. "Happy birthday."

"You're angry."

"Should I be?"

"She's my sister, Cash. My twin. She knows me better than anyone on this earth."

"Then how could she have hurt you like this?"

Rainy turned away. "I'm not discussing her shortcomings with you."

He sighed. Then she felt his hands on her shoulders. "I'm sorry." He urged her around to face him. "You're right. It's none of my business. I just hate to see you hurt." He brushed her forehead with a kiss. "Can we celebrate your birthday after your plans with Sunny?"

She tilted her head back in time to catch the twinkle in his eye. She smiled and said, "I think that can be arranged."

"I'm counting on it," he said, then covered her mouth with his.

CASH RODE UP to the barn and dismounted his horse in time to see the red convertible pull up the driveway.

It had to be Sunny.

No one in Maybe drove a flashy red convertible. No one else had a motorcycle, either. Not since his friend—and Maybe's most undesirable citizen—Jesse Logan had left town nineteen years ago.

Now Cash had a motorcycle and a centerfold. He snorted. Although that wasn't quite accurate, he knew that's the way the rest of Maybe would see it.

He swung his saddle off Montoya and watched out of the corner of his eye, waiting for Rainy's sister to exit the car.

Rainy. Merely thinking her name got his heart up to a healthy rate. He'd wanted to keep her in his arms all day. He took a couple of deep breaths to regulate his breathing, wondering at which exact moment he'd crossed the line. She was more than a friend and a lover to him. That was as clear as the sun dipping toward the horizon. And for that reason, he'd fight tooth and nail for her to stay.

The car door slammed and his attention riveted back to their visitor.

Even though he already knew Sunny was Rainy's identical twin, their resemblance overwhelmed him. She was too far for him to get a good look, but the way she absently tossed her hair, took small dainty steps, the inherent grace with which she carried herself, was just like Rainy.

The leather miniskirt, however, was not.

He squinted for a better look and it suddenly dawned on him that she was the person he'd seen in town outside of Jeb's store last week. He brought his hand up to block the last of the waning sun as he realized that she was also the one who'd been in the kissing booth line.

"Close your mouth, son, them flies are nasty this time of year." Smiley strolled out of the barn and ambled up beside him, straining to get a look at Sunny himself. "What the dickens is she all dolled up for?"

Cash grinned. He could have some fun with this one. Plus, he did owe the guy for having to stomach several weeks of chili fumes. "The autographing."

Smiley slowly twisted his head around to skewer Cash with his beady stare. "What autographin'?"

"I decided to let Josh go ahead and make some extra money for college." He shrugged and tried to keep from laughing at Smiley's horrified look. "After all, the boy spent every last dime he had on those magazines."

When Smiley's eyes bugged out, Cash couldn't keep his composure any longer. "Take care of Montoya for me, will you?"

He left the older man gaping and headed for the house, trying to keep from laughing aloud. He felt punchy all of a sudden. A welcome relief from the tension of the day.

It hadn't given him any pleasure grounding Josh for the rest of the summer, after his son had finally dragged his frightened butt home two hours ago. He also hadn't been pleased to learn of Sunny's presence in Maybe. But as the afternoon had progressed, he'd convinced himself that having her here would probably end up being helpful. Even the more skeptical of Maybe's citizens couldn't dispute what they could see with their own eyes. And knowing his neighbors, he and Rainy would need all the help they could get.

He entered the house by way of the kitchen, wiping his boots on the welcome mat, letting the door slam in warning.

Rainy sat with her sister on the living room couch. They faced each other, their profiles so remarkably identical that

Cash stood speechless at the entryway. Rainy had put on a touch of makeup as she had for the dance, and unlike most days when she drowned in a T-shirt, she wore a pair of tailored, cream-colored slacks and a turquoise silk blouse.

Sunny, on the other hand, wore a skirt that was undoubtedly shorter than any skirt or dress that anyone in Maybe would dare to own. But she wasn't as heavily made up as she had been the other day and appeared more like Rainy. Watching them face each other was like having had one too many shots of tequila.

"Cash..." Rainy acknowledged him, then darted a quick look back to her sister. She seemed nervous, and he was sorry for having made her feel that way. He'd been a jerk when she had first told him about Sunny's arrival. But he'd had enough surprises for one day and, in all honesty, his initial thought had been that he didn't want to share Rainy. He only hoped that she'd accepted his later assurances that her sister was welcome in their home . . . his home. He took a deep breath and hoped this wasn't a mistake.

"Hi," he said, walking toward Sunny. "You must be related."

She giggled, rising to accept the hand he offered. "My gosh, Rainy, you're right. He is adorable."

He cocked a brow at Rainy, who blushed to her hairline.

"That's not exactly what I said." She rose, too, grimacing at her sister, while a fresh wave of color suffused her face.

Cash couldn't take his eyes off Rainy. God, but she was gorgeous. How had she possibly grown more beautiful since this afternoon? She had her hair down the way he liked it, all soft and fluffy looking. And her intelligent brown eyes sparkled with life and humor. The inevitable, gravity-defying tug curved the corners of his mouth.

Sunny cleared her throat. "Hmm..." she began as she brought a finger to her lips. "Cash, would you like to join us for dinner tonight?"

Rainy watched Cash blink in her sister's direction. He looked confused for a moment, almost as if he'd forgotten Sunny had been standing there.

An arrow of joy, unlike anything Rainy had ever felt, ricocheted through her body. Not once in her entire life had she ever upstaged Sunny. She chased away the tiny voice that called her silly and petty for feeling so triumphant. Instead, she flashed Cash a big smile and enjoyed the moment.

When he smiled back without responding to Sunny, her sister pressed, "Is that a yes on dinner?"

He still didn't answer, and Rainy happily considered how embarrassed he'd be if he realized his rudeness.

Finally, he returned a quick glance toward Sunny and said, "Thanks, but not tonight. You two probably have a lot to talk about."

Sunny exhaled loudly. "Yeah, I suppose so." She turned to Rainy. "Are you about ready?"

"Sure." She picked up her purse and the small wrapped package her sister had given her. She slid Cash a look, wondering if he'd be awake when she got home. She hadn't had a moment alone with him since Josh and Smiley had come home. And suddenly, inexplicably, a small germ of doubt infected her recent bliss.

"Ah, Rainy, could I see you a minute before you leave?" Cash asked, neither his tone nor his face giving anything away. He lifted a palm. "It's about Josh."

Rainy hoped her expression didn't betray her disappointment as she nodded, then looked at her sister.

"I'll meet you in the car," Sunny said and flipped her long hair exaggeratedly over her shoulder as she headed for the door.

Rainy recognized that move immediately and felt her blood pressure soar. If her sister thought she was getting within two feet of Cash . . .

"God, I thought I'd never get you alone." Cash grabbed her arm and pulled her to him almost before Sunny had disappeared from view. He kissed her hard and fast on the mouth, his hands moving up her back, stroking, caressing, pressing her to him.

Giddy with relief, she kissed him back, then asked, "Think you'll be up when I get home?"

He grinned. "In more ways than one."

When his meaning sank in and she opened her mouth in surprise, his lips and tongue took full advantage of hers. "Happy birthday, baby," he whispered.

Rainy doubted her knees would ever work the same again.

"SO TELL ME what's been happening with you." Sunny pushed aside the leather-bound menu and leaned forward. "I want to hear about everything." She paused, winking. "And everyone."

Rainy shook her head at her incorrigible twin and relaxed in the high-back tapestry chair. The restaurant Sunny had found was casually elegant with enticing aromas wafting from the kitchen. "I think you may have something a little more interesting to contribute to the conversation."

"Afraid not." Sunny straightened and reached for a pumpernickel roll. "Nothing going on with me."

"I thought you were on some kind of promotional tour." Rainy narrowed her gaze on the roll her sister was coating with butter, then raised her eyes to her twin's bland expression. Sunny hated pumpernickel. And she never ate butter.

"Oh, that." She waved a dismissive hand. "I was bored. So tell me about you."

Rainy watched her take a bite of the roll. Sunny was hiding something. She didn't believe her sister had simply got-

ten bored. And as flighty as her twin could be at times, she
certainly would never welsh on a commitment because of
mere disinterest. Besides, Sunny had never experienced a
dull moment in her life. "I don't have much to tell. I've been
tutoring Cash's fourteen-year-old son."

"And his father's been tutoring you." The old Sunny was
back, her eyes flashing, her teasing smile in place.

"Oh, please," Rainy drawled, rolling her eyes.

"Oh? Does that mean he's fair game?"

"Try it and you die."

Sunny laughed delightedly. "I knew it."

Rainy took a deep breath. She hadn't meant to let Sunny
bait her that way, but it was that one, challenging lift of her
sister's brow that had her blurting out their childhood taunt.
She sniffed. "Actually, he's quite nice."

"Really?" Sunny mimicked her suddenly stiff posture.
"If he's so nice, then why didn't he give you time to touch
up your lipstick after your little talk about Josh."

Rainy automatically brought a hand to her mouth, which
sent Sunny into hysterics.

"All right." A grudging smile curved Rainy's lips. "We
have a little bit of a thing for each other."

"A little, huh?" Sunny dabbed at her eyes and smothered her laughter. "Tell that to someone who doesn't know
you so well." She leaned back, taking a sip of her wine. Her
expression sobered. "Does he know about the centerfold?"

Rainy nodded. She hated the fact that it had to be brought
up, but she knew it was inevitable and explained everything
that had happened.

Sunny listened in gloomy silence, sad regret darkening her
eyes, and Rainy silently forgave her all over again.

"I sure screwed things up, didn't I?" Sunny took another sip of her wine, then tried to smile. "But look how
well it's turned out. You've met Cash."

"True." Rainy's attempt at a smile was far more success-ful, although she didn't fool herself. She and Cash weren't out of the woods yet. Their relationship was so young and fragile that reaction over the centerfold could still foul things up. And then there was the custody issue. But she didn't want to ruin their birthday by thinking about that. Glad she'd been remiss in not already having mailed Sunny's gift, she said, "Let's open our presents, shall we?"

Sunny readily agreed and she knew her twin wanted to salvage their good moods, as well.

Rainy was pleased that Sunny liked the southwestern jewelry she'd given her. Her sister immediately replaced the earrings she wore with the ones she'd opened, then slipped on the matching bracelet.

"Now open yours," Sunny urged.

Whereas Sunny had attacked her package with custom-ary zeal, Rainy slowly and methodically peeled back the bright pink paper until she got to the plain white box. She grinned at the rapid and impatient tapping of Sunny's long red nails on the table, then removed the lid.

"Well?" Sunny beamed at her.

Rainy peered at what looked like an oversize hood orna-ment of a pricey car tucked into a nest of tissue. "It—it's . . . what is it?"

"An installment."

"Oh." Her sister had really gone off the deep end.

Sunny laughed. "Remember when we were kids and you said you wanted a Mercedes?"

Rainy laughed, too. "That was before I knew how much they cost."

"Well, you don't have to worry about that. I'm going to get you one."

"Jeez, did they pay you that much for the centerfold?"

Sunny flinched. "This has nothing to do with that." She traced a pattern on the table. "No, that's not true. It does.

I owe you, Rain. I owe you big time for what I did to you."
When Rainy started to protest, Sunny held up her hand.
"I've caused you a lot of trouble. I can't change what's
done, but there's this car dealership in Los Angeles that
wants me to do some modeling work for them. If I do,
they've promised me a good deal on a two-door model—the
one you like."

"Liked," Rainy corrected, shaking her head. "I was
thirteen when I wanted that car. A lot has changed. I've
changed. Besides, you hate that kind of modeling."

Sunny was quiet for a while before she looked at Rainy
with sad eyes that clearly stated how she felt about change
in their lives. "You're going to stay here, aren't you?"

"I don't know." Rainy looked down. At this point, she
truly didn't. But she couldn't face her twin's fear without
feeling like a traitor for having flourished during their sep-
aration.

She swallowed hard. Until this moment, she hadn't realized that that was exactly what had happened. And not only
had she flourished, she'd stepped out of Sunny's shadow.
The discovery was heady. Only a small amount of guilt
dented the euphoric feeling.

"I wouldn't blame you," Sunny said in such a wistful
tone that Rainy looked up. "I've had a great time here."

She frowned. Was this her twin talking? Maybe was far
too calm and conservative for her. Besides, she was supposed to have had commitments as a result of the centerfold. "I still don't understand how you've had all this time
on your hands. Or why you didn't contact me earlier."

Sunny sighed, looking as though she were suddenly bored
with the topic. She twisted around and signaled the red-
vested waiter.

"So why did you arrive so early?" Rainy pressed. "I
thought you had a ton of promo appearances and model-

ing work." Or so she had said. They had even left Boon the same day.

The waiter appeared and, instead of answering, Sunny ordered another glass of wine and an artichoke appetizer for them to share.

Rainy declined another drink. Instead, she watched her sister perform her usual, harmless teasing and flirting with the eager waiter. Sunny was certainly going through the motions of the carefree, fun-loving person she generally was, but something was wrong.

"So," Rainy began once the young man left with their order, "you were going to tell me why you got here so early."

"Was I?" Sunny raised her eyebrows over the rim of her glass. "Sheesh, Rainy, since when did you get so pushy?" She issued a long, put-upon sigh. "I had to find you a birthday present, okay?"

"You could have found one anywhere."

"But I ended up getting the perfect gift here." The devilish twinkle was back in Sunny's eyes and Rainy considered dropping the subject, which her twin very obviously did not want to discuss. And then Sunny added with a great deal of smugness, "Didn't I?"

Rainy smiled and glanced back at the used ornament. "How did you manage to get it?"

"From a truck driver here in Maybe."

Rainy laughed. "You didn't . . ."

"Of course I did. He pried it right off his truck and all I had to do was buy him lunch at that little diner on Main Street." Sunny grinned, obviously pleased with herself.

Still laughing, Rainy shook her head. "Only you could get away with that." And then she sobered suddenly, remembering all the times in the past Sunny had impersonated her and had gotten them both in trouble. "Uh, you haven't done anything strange while you've been here, have you?"

Sunny wrinkled her perfect little nose. "I don't think so."

Rainy let her head drop back against her chair. Then she brought it up, shaking it from side to side. "Look who I'm asking." She laughed at the familiar phrase she'd used half her life, at the same conversation they'd had since they were kids.

Sunny didn't. She pressed her lips together and briefly bowed her head.

Rainy cringed. "Is there something I should know?"

Her sister smiled such a tiny, weary smile that it made Rainy feel bad even though she didn't understand it. "Uh-uh."

"Did I say something wrong?"

"No." Sunny sighed.

A chill raced through Rainy. Something was horribly wrong with her twin, and for the first time in her life, Rainy was at a loss to help her. And that fact scared the hell out of her. "Look, Sunny, if you don't have any place urgent to be, maybe you could spend some time here with me."

Her sister's face brightened. "Really?"

"Sure." Rainy felt the comforting tentacles of their bond tightening again. "It'll be fun."

After all, how much trouble could Sunny get into in just a few days?

Chapter Fifteen

Rainy got home much later than she had expected. She'd had a wonderful evening with her sister, even though she was certain something was troubling Sunny. But now, as Rainy slipped into the dark house with only the entry light to welcome her, her spirits sagged at the realization that Cash had not waited up.

She ascended the stairs with all the enthusiasm of an overcooked noodle, until she saw the soft flicker of light from a narrow crack in Cash's bedroom door. Reaching her own room first, she paused. Her hand wrapped uncertainly around the doorknob.

Cash's door opened wider and a warm glow seeped into the dark hall. Then he appeared, a slow, lazy smile lifting the corners of his mouth. He was shirtless, his jeans only partially buttoned. "The party's in here," he whispered.

A warm shiver of anticipation skittered across her nerve endings. "Am I invited?"

"Are you kidding?" One brow arched up. "You're the main course."

A delighted laugh rippled through her as she sauntered toward him. "Isn't that supposed to be guest of honor?"

"Oh, yeah." Grinning, he reached out and pulled her to him. Then, holding her against his awakened body, he gave her a long, thorough kiss. As he backed them into the room, he quietly toed the door shut with his bare foot.

A candle burned on the nightstand. The flame of another flickered near a fragrant spray of honeysuckle by the bed. Fresh cranberry-colored sheets had been turned back.

Rainy's gaze soaked in the little touches he'd added, while he continued to trail tiny kisses over her jaw and neck.

She pulled away slightly to look at him. His gaze swept her face and his brow puckered in sweet uncertainty at her action. "This is the best birthday I've ever had," she whispered.

His expression relaxed. "It's only just begun." He took her purse and slid it from her shoulder.

"Cash?" She needed to tell him about Sunny. Omission had gotten her in big trouble with him already. "My sister is going to stick around for a while."

His tone stiffened. "Here?"

"No. Colesville."

He nodded. "I hope you understand why I don't think it's a great idea for her to stay here at the ranch."

She wondered how well Josh had fared with his first night of grounding. "Of course I do. I wouldn't ask that. Besides, she's promised to keep a low profile."

He fell silent for a long moment. "I don't mind if she hangs out here, as long as it doesn't interfere with Josh's studies."

"I'm aware of my priorities."

"C'mon, Rainy." He cupped her face with his hands. "I'm walking a tightrope here. I want you to have time with your sister, but I don't want her choice of profession to antagonize Josh's mother, either."

Choice of profession? She straightened. Defending Sunny was too old a habit to ignore. Then she sighed and pressed her cheek to his palm. Hadn't she distanced herself from her sister over the centerfold problem? If she were totally honest with herself, she wasn't entirely comfortable having Sunny around, either. And Cash had every right to be worried about his son. "I'm sorry," she said, gazing up at him. "You're right."

He smoothed back her hair and lightly traced the shell of her ear with his fingertip. "Let's not allow this issue with your sister to come between us."

"We won't." She shook her head, praying she was right. "I know this is a difficult situation and I think you've been very patient."

"Right." He grinned and fitted her against him. Immediately, she felt his desire and smiled.

Apparently, he was *hardly* patient at all.

RAINY HAD JUST set up a biology test for Josh when he sheepishly entered the room. She'd seen little of him since he'd been grounded. Yesterday he'd spent most of the day studying in his room. The rest of the time he'd kept himself pretty scarce. He'd been extremely embarrassed about the trouble he'd caused her, especially when he found out about Sunny. Rainy watched him shuffle past and actually felt sorry for him.

He restacked a pile of books and lined up several more pencils than he needed, while avoiding her gaze. Finally, he looked at her. "Ah, Rainy..." He puffed out his cheeks, then blew. "I'm such a jerk."

She put a hand on his arm. "We settled this the other night. You apologized, and I accepted. It's history, Josh." She smiled. "Speaking of which...ready to get to work?"

He grinned and nodded vigorously. Rainy had to keep from laughing at his sudden enthusiasm and wasn't at all sorry the doorbell pealed an interruption. She steered him toward the test and hurried downstairs.

"You and me need to have a talk, young lady." Violet Pickford stomped through the front door as soon as Rainy opened it. The woman continued to march past her toward the kitchen, poking her head into the living room and scanning the area as she walked by.

Rainy scrambled after her. Violet didn't know about Sunny yet. It had only been two days since her twin had showed up at the ranch—the same day Cash had made his untimely discovery. And Violet had been off celebrating her festival victories in Dallas. With Cash's help, news that Rainy had a twin was spreading fast, but obviously Violet was still out of the loop.

When Rainy got to the kitchen, she found Violet riffling through the large bunch of flowers Sunny had bought and arranged in a brass urn earlier today.

"Ah-ha." Violet plucked out a particularly beautiful, scarlet rose. She spun around and speared Rainy with a venomous glare. "You must think I'm a damn fool. I had half a mind to bring my shotgun with me. And if my American Beauties hadn't won first place last Sunday, you can bet your fanny I would have."

"Violet, you're right. We do need to talk. But about that..." She pointed to the flower. "I have no idea."

The woman's hand flew up in impatience. "Are you telling me I can't see what's right in front of me?"

"No, I'm trying to tell you that I can explain about the centerfold."

"The what?" Violet slapped a wave of unruly red hair away from her puzzled eyes.

"That's not me in that centerfold."

Violet frowned. "I don't know about any darn centerfold. But I do know as plain as the nose on your face that I told you these roses were off-limits."

"The roses?" It was Rainy's turn to be confused.

Then Sunny bopped down the hall, slowing at the door. "Hi," she said cheerfully to Violet. "Sorry, Sis, I didn't know you had company."

Standing in the doorway, Sunny never looked more like her twin than she did right now, dressed in a pair of Rainy's baggy jeans and a very large white T-shirt, no makeup, her hair pulled into a ponytail at her crown.

Her mouth wide open, Violet clutched the rose, pricked herself with a thorn and let out something quite colorful.

"Uh, Violet Pickford, this is my sister, Sunny." A smile teased Rainy's lips as it always did when some unsuspecting person came face to face with the two of them.

The older woman looked from her to her twin with narrowed eyes. "Is this one of Smiley's tricks?"

"No," Sunny assured her with a matter-of-fact shake of her head. "One of nature's."

Rainy laughed at her sister's earnestness and at Violet's once-suspicious, now-baffled look. "Let's all sit down, shall we?" she suggested and reached for the coffeepot.

By the time Sunny had explained about her two innocent flower purchases from the little boy in town, the three of them had fit the rest of the pieces of the puzzle together and had a hearty laugh. Violet insisted that this was the most excitement Maybe'd had in years. And Rainy only hoped that tonight's meeting to discuss her teaching application would be as easy to fix as her relationship with Violet.

"Well, I best be getting back," Violet said, rising from the table and wiping away the last mirthful tear from her eye. The woman made it to the hall before she turned toward Sunny. "You know, Rainy, you're welcome back at my place."

Her twin aimed an impish grin at Rainy, and Rainy spoke up. "Thanks, Violet, but I'm pretty settled here." Rainy grinned, too, when the older woman quickly did a double-take.

"You two are remarkable. Makes my head spin."

"Yeah. It still happens with our parents, too," Sunny admitted cheerfully.

"I'm not surprised," Violet mumbled and, shaking her head, waved goodbye. As soon as she left, Rainy ran up to check on Josh. By the time she came back downstairs, Cash was coming in the back door.

His work jeans were tight and faded. His T-shirt fit snugly at his biceps. He removed his hat and hung it on the wall peg, then looked unerringly at Rainy and smiled. "Hi."

One small word out of him and Rainy's insides were a quivering mass of Jell-O. His tone was soft, raspy. His smile downright lethal. "Hi, yourself," she said.

"You're all out of breath."

"I just came down from checking on Josh. Major test today."

His smile deepened for a moment. So did the color of his eyes as he stayed focused on her, then he tossed a quick look at Sunny. "Morning."

He walked to the refrigerator and allowed his fingers to furtively brush Rainy's thighs as he passed by.

She swallowed a deep sigh of satisfaction. From the first moment he'd seen them together, despite Sunny's playful efforts at sabotage, Cash could always tell them apart. She didn't know how he did it. No one ever had the success ratio he'd had. Not their parents, not their brother. Not even Richard.

"Don't worry about dinner tonight." Cash pulled a carton of orange juice from the fridge. "Josh can fend for himself and the three of us can eat at the diner before going over to the meeting."

"That'll make Josh real happy." Sunny glanced at the ceiling and pulled out a chair.

"Tough." Cash took a long swallow of the juice he'd poured. "He's lucky I'm leaving him with anything but bread and water."

Sunny covered her face with her hands.

Rainy frowned. "You don't have to go tonight," she said to her sister. "Cash thinks having you there could make the decision go either way. We're just hoping it'll be in my favor. So don't feel like you have to."

"Oh, no." Her twin looked up. "It's not that. I *will* be there. I just can't believe what a mess I've made of things. And all for a lousy joke." Absently, she shook her head. "Now even Josh is getting flak because of me."

A joke? Rainy stared at her. That centerfold could hardly be classified as a joke. She curiously noted her sister's miserable expression over Josh's dilemma. Sunny had never actually shirked responsibility before, but she hadn't ever been so quick to grab it, either.

Cash darted Sunny a look and shook his head. "Josh knew better than to do what he did. He's got no one to blame but himself. I'm more concerned about tonight."

For the first time, oblivious to Sunny's appraising gaze, Cash openly reached for Rainy. He circled an arm around her shoulders and pulled her to his side. When she looked up at him, he brushed his lips against hers.

"We have to make sure everyone in Maybe knows what a wonderful teacher you are," he said, smiling. She smiled, too. She couldn't help it. And he added, "If not, we'll just have to convince them."

"Yes." Sunny slapped her palm on the table.

When they both turned to her, she stared back, smiling widely. "Yes," she repeated more calmly, "we certainly will."

SUNNY WAITED UNTIL Cash returned to the barn and Rainy had headed upstairs to correct Josh's test before she began to put her plan into action.

As soon as she heard the study door click shut, she grabbed her tote bag and began applying her makeup. Being bare faced and glamour-free had been sort of fun while it lasted, she admitted, but it was time to prepare for battle.

Having the experience of a dozen beauty pageants under her belt, it took her no time at all to complete her ritual and put together a suitable ensemble from an assortment of clothes she'd brought in from her car.

She checked to make sure she had no runs in her red-tinted hose, which was no small feat with the sizable amount of leg showing under her ultrashort skirt. After enjoying the comfort of Rainy's baggy jeans for two days, she tugged at the small piece of spandex and wondered why in the heck she wore something so darn impractical.

She didn't wonder long, though. She knew damn well why she did it. To counter the small-town narrow-mindedness that had driven her crazy most of her life. The same myopic view that, unless she did something about, could ruin her sister's chance at happiness.

She quickly scribbled Rainy a note and hopped in her rented car. Having only four hours to accomplish her mission, she sped toward town and didn't ease off the accelerator until she hit Main Street.

She pulled into the first parking stall she could find and slid one leg out of the car. When she heard a whistle come from a group of young skateboarders, she tossed back her long, freshly curled tresses.

An older woman, her hair rolled in pink sponge curlers, stopped on the sidewalk to give her a once-over and, in a clipped, disapproving tone, said, "Mornin', Rainy."

Sunny exposed a disarming amount of thigh as she brought out her other leg. "Oh, I'm not Rainy." She flashed the woman a brilliant smile. "I'm Sunny...her evil twin."

"I SUPPOSE WE COULD leave her a message with Josh." Standing at the window, Rainy stretched up on her toes to look out for Sunny's car. The driveway was clear.

She held her breath and turned to Cash, who had just come down the stairs. She'd never seen him so dressed up. His navy blazer had to have been tailor-made, it accentuated his broad shoulders so well. The white shirt beneath it, he left open at his throat. And the taupe slacks fit perfectly around his lean hips, his muscled thighs.

"You look gorgeous," she said, surprising herself as much as she did him.

A flush climbed his face and he ran a finger inside the collar of his open shirt. He gave her a faint grin. "I'm supposed to look authoritarian."

"I'd listen to you," she teased.

"Yeah?" He lifted a brow and crooked a finger at her.

Rainy obeyed.

A long, thorough kiss was her reward.

"Two-second warning," they heard Josh announce his approach from the second floor and, to her amazement, Cash kept her in his arms even as his son bounded down the stairs.

Josh gave them a quick, curious look as he passed them on his way to the kitchen. "I'm gonna make a sandwich," he mumbled in passing.

"Okay." Cash nodded to him. "We'll be leaving soon." Then he looked back at Rainy's stunned expression and smiled. "He might as well get used to the idea."

"What idea?" she asked cautiously, hopefully.

"About us."

"And what about tonight?"

"Whatever happens tonight won't change how I feel." He issued the words like a statement, only Rainy heard the question in them. In fact, she had her own question about how he felt. Only she didn't have the guts to ask it.

Although they hadn't discussed it, Josh's custody hearing hung between them like a dense fog. And right now, it looked as though Cash's ex-wife held all the cards.

She turned back toward the window. "Sunny's note said she'd be back in time. I have no idea what's keeping her."

"If she's not here in ten minutes, we'll have Josh tell her to meet us at the diner. Then we'll go over our strategy."

"Our strategy?" She tried to laugh, but only a small nervous squeak came out. Tonight was nothing official, but if the town members turned on her, it was a sure sign she wouldn't be hired. "All we can do is tell them the truth and hope for the best."

Cash shrugged. "I'm still hoping the shock of seeing Sunny will quiet the naysayers." Then he frowned. "What do you suppose she'll wear?"

She groaned and looked down at her own conservative tan camp shirt and black skirt. "No telling, although I would hope—"

The sound of a car engine interrupted her and she pushed aside the curtain. Cash ducked a look over her shoulder and they both groaned.

Sunny teetered precariously in her spiked heels as she moved over the gravel toward the house. She had her hand up, ready to knock, when Rainy opened the door. She wiggled two fingers in greeting instead. "I hope I'm not late."

Rainy stole a glance at her sister's short red skirt, her red-tinted hose, down to her red spiked heels. She sighed.

"This could work," Cash whispered and he herded both her and Sunny out the door to his truck.

Other than the odd looks Sunny attracted, dinner at Harry's Diner was uneventful. They quickly decided that showing the two sisters as total opposites might not be a bad thing. Sunny seemed strangely quiet and terribly smug, which worried Rainy no end. Her twin's appetite seemed entirely unaffected, while Rainy barely touched her food. And still, Rainy's stomach rebelled all the way to Maybe High.

By the time they finally entered the tiny school gymnasium, which served as Saturday's dance hall and today's town hall, Rainy's nerves were totally shot. Cash'd already explained to her that the position she'd applied for was only one of several issues to be discussed tonight and that meant a full house. Suddenly, facing all these people, who could influence her future here in Maybe, seemed more than daunting.

She took her place on one of the folding chairs beside Cash, and Sunny sat beside her. Several of the people she'd met at the festival waved; equally as many snubbed her. But everyone stared at Sunny.

Mayor Simms rose to open the meeting and the murmurs began to subside. Cash nudged Rainy's shoulder with his and she followed his gaze to see Smiley standing at the entrance to the gym. He gave her a thumbs-up sign when he caught her eye. She smiled her gratitude, then nearly fell off her chair when she saw Violet sidle up beside him.

Cash chuckled at her expression. "They called a truce for tonight."

"Why?"

"They're joining forces to support you."

Rainy blinked, a suspicious moisture collecting in her eyes.

He squeezed her hand. "They think you're special, too."

She turned so he couldn't see her holding back tears and saw Sunny giving Homer Simms one of her two-finger greetings behind her other hand. Rainy leaned toward her. "Do you know him?"

Sunny winked at Mayor Simms, and he cleared his throat and called the meeting to order. "We had lunch today."

"What?" Rainy leaned closer and didn't even try to keep the dread from seeping into her tone. "Sunny..."

"Don't worry about it, Rainy." She waved to Martha Wallbanger, who owned the town's only newspaper. Martha enthusiastically waved back. "It was a very nice lunch. He likes a little nip of gin now and again, you know."

Rainy rolled her eyes and wilted back against her seat. "Don't even tell me how you know Mrs. Wallbanger."

Sunny shrugged. "Okay."

Mayor Simms's secretary had already begun reviewing the minutes of the last quarterly meeting and Rainy listened with only half an ear, wondering what her twin had been up to, until Homer took over the podium. He immediately began ticking off a list of impressive numbers relating to the festival's profit.

"The bottom line is," he announced, puffing his chest out with pride, "we now have enough in the treasury to spruce ourselves up to be seriously considered for the cattle drive's kickoff town."

Several people grumbled that they didn't want to spend the money on fixing up the town to attract only one venture, but the overwhelming majority sided with the mayor. Rainy knew Cash was dying to say something. But she figured that he was saving up to speak his piece on her behalf.

She reached over and gave his forearm a squeeze. He sent her a devastating smile and winked.

It didn't take long for the subject of the high school teacher's position to come up. When several pairs of eyes automatically turned in her direction, Rainy felt her heart slide to her toes.

"Now, although this won't be our decision to make," the mayor reminded them, "we do have some say, and y'all should know we have a fine candidate right here in Maybe..."

Sunny crossed her arms over her chest and smugly leaned back in her seat.

Mabel Simms stepped up beside her husband and elbowed him out of the way. "Yes, we do. Bonnie Brown." She sent a pointed and baneful look past Rainy to Sunny.

"Bonnie ain't taught school since her kindergarten class committed mutiny seven years ago," someone called out from the back. Everyone laughed and Bonnie, who'd been sitting in the first row, blushed and tried to slink away.

Martha Wallbanger hurried up to the podium to defend her friend, Mabel, and said she supported Bonnie, too.

Sunny straightened, narrowed her gaze and started to rise from her seat. "Why that two-faced, conniving little—"

Rainy grabbed her sister's arm and pinched it. Whatever her twin's plan had been, it'd obviously backfired. Sunny's squeal was drowned out by the crowd's preoccupation with teasing Bonnie Brown.

While Homer Simms tried to wrestle his position back from his wife, Cash rose from his chair. Rainy heard his irritated sigh just before his deep voice called for order.

"Can we be civil here?" he asked. "I bet the high school kids who usually use this gymnasium behave better than this."

Several people gave him a sheepish look, then hung their heads. Della Witherspoon stood, giving him a bright smile, and clapped. But her only response was silence and several pairs of raised eyebrows, so she calmly reclaimed her seat.

Rainy was pretty sure she was the only one who heard Cash's low groan.

"I'm surprised at you, Mabel," he continued. "We all know Bonnie has no interest in teaching. But more to the point, like Homer said, most of us know who our next teacher should be." He glanced down at Rainy and smiled. "And for the rest of you, I'd like to introduce Ms. Rainette Daye."

Certain her legs wouldn't work, Rainy accepted the hand Cash extended to her and stood.

"We already had this conversation the other day, Cash McCloud. And there is no room for the likes of her in this town." Mabel planted both hands on her generous hips, but when it came time to meet Rainy's eyes, she couldn't.

"Excuse me, Mabel." Cash's voice grew dangerously low. "But are we talking about the same person who you roped into that dunking booth of yours, and who graciously accepted the task when no one else would? The same person you dressed in that skimpy bikini?" Mabel blushed and Cash went in for the kill. "And whose booth made more money than any other booth in the history of the festival? You didn't seem to mind her kind then."

"That was before we knew about her," Mabel mumbled, inspecting her manicure.

"And what do you know? I can assure you it's nothing more than I do. And that is that she's the best teacher this entire county could ever hope to have."

Rainy gazed at the strong set of his jaw, his determined and sincere eyes. The corners of his mouth were bracketed with restraint in wanting to defend her in the best possible way, and she knew deep in her heart it was because he cared for her more than anyone else ever had...or ever could. Her knees got weak all over again.

"And what about this?" Mabel jerked out a copy of *Midnight Fantasy* from her handbag. A murmur rippled through the crowd.

Out of the corner of her eye, Rainy saw Violet and Smiley lunge from their seats.

Cash held a hand up to his two friends. "You know damn well that's her twin." He pointed to Sunny, who blanched, then slowly lifted her chin and stood beside Rainy.

"I need to say something here," Sunny said. "I'm the responsible party." She made a face. "Or irresponsible as the case may be. And I realize now that when I tried to remedy the situation earlier today, I made things worse." She glanced at Mabel and Martha. "But it's not fair for you to take it out on my sister. Besides, you'd be cheating your-selves out of a damn good teacher."

"You ever heard the saying about the apple not falling far from the tree?" Mabel haughtily addressed the crowd.

"Is that why that son of yours can't even keep a job washin' toilets?" Smiley bellowed.

Laughter vibrated throughout the gym.

Violet delivered an elbow to Smiley's ribs. He glared at her, but she laid a gentle hand on his, keeping her eyes on the crowd. "I don't think this meeting ought to get per-sonal," she said, giving a wary-looking Mabel and her friends pointed looks. "We all know it'd get pretty ugly if it did."

Mabel blinked and looked away.

Rainy sighed. In her opinion, it was already getting ugly. She reached for Sunny's hand, held it tight, then took a deep breath and put her other hand on Cash's shoulder. When he looked at her, she gave him a sanguine smile that indicated she was far braver than she actually felt.

"Everyone..." Rainy had to clear her clogged throat and start again. "You all don't know me. Although in the short time I've been here, I've come to know a few of you. Some of you I met at the festival, some at the dance. Had coffee with a couple of you." She glanced over at Mabel and Mar-tha, who both quickly looked away.

"I know that doesn't have anything to do with my cre-dentials, which I'm confident you'll find in order, but it does impact your view of my character. And apparently, some of you are disappointed...in me...because you've judged me for something over which I had no control. But you've disappointed me, too. I had thought Maybe might be the kind of town I could be proud to call my new home."

Heads bowed, and when Rainy started to finish, she found that her voice was no longer working. Cash slipped an arm around her and pressed a kiss to her temple in front of the entire assembly.

"You ain't the only one disappointed." Smiley's voice rose above the murmurings. "I'm downright disgusted with all y'all." Shaking his head, his gaze canvassed the crowd, some heads still bowed, some tongues wagging, most folks nodding in agreement. After a minute, people started rising from their chairs, having heard enough.

"When you find your backbone, Homer," Violet said, slipping an arm through Smiley's, "I hope you tell Mabel and the rest of her cronies what a bunch of jackasses they are."

Smiley gave her an approving grin and they walked toward the door together.

Cash suspected the crowd's surprise had more to do with the older couple's civility than their well-aimed words. He glanced from Rainy to Sunny. He was proud of both of them tonight, but as his gaze drew to the twin's tightly joined hands, a disturbing feeling settled over him.

He wondered how they could be so different. Sunny lived life in the fast lane—no doubt about that—and until recently, she had been a major part of Rainy's life. How could Rainy accept a life without her twin's excitement?

Cash started ushering the pair toward the door, anxious to get out of here, when he heard pounding and saw Homer wearily lowering the wooden butcher's mallet he sometimes used as a gavel. "Folks, before you start leaving, I want to remind you that this was an unofficial meeting. But I want it known publicly that I fully support Ms. Daye."

Mabel said nothing. She picked up her handbag and hurried for the door. Several paces ahead of them, she turned with a smile. It wasn't a pleasant one.

"By the way, Cash, your ex-wife says hi."

Chapter Sixteen

Although Cash and Rainy had both known it would be only a matter of time before they'd hear from Josh's mother, Rainy still felt the sting when the phone call came two days later.

Her hands shook as she turned the sizzling bacon over in the pan, waiting for Cash to return from his study. He'd already been on the phone with Maureen for fifteen minutes.

"Hmm...something smells good." He surprised her from behind and wound his arms around her. Turning her around in his arms, he ran the tip of his tongue across her lower lip.

The bacon hissed behind her, and when she tried to grab the pan off the burner, her hand was so shaky the bacon almost slipped to the floor.

"Hey. What's the matter?" Frowning, he sandwiched her hand between his. "Where's Josh?"

"Studying. We've added an extra hour to our day."

"Is he starting to worry about the test?"

"No. He's actually doing much better now that he's not worrying about how he's supposed to get my autograph." She made a wry face, pulled away and got the eggs out.

He shook his head and the tightness forming around his mouth had her sorry she'd brought it up.

"He's really doing very well," she assured him. "I'm not a bit worried about the exam." She started to turn back to making breakfast, then spun on him instead. "Damn it, Cash. Are you going to tell me about Maureen?"

His smile was grim, his answer reluctant. "She arrives tomorrow."

"Tomorrow?" She wasn't prepared for that. "And she knows..."

He nodded.

"Oh, God. I'm so sorry." She leaned heavily against the counter. This wasn't news. The smug look on Mabel's face the other night made it perfectly clear that Josh's mother had indeed heard every sordid detail. But it was still hard to take.

"Take it easy. We knew she'd show up eventually." Cash rubbed a palm up her arm. "We'll handle it, just like we did the town meeting. You know, I've heard in town that most everyone hopes you get the teaching position."

"I'm not worried about that right now."

"I know." He sighed. "Where's Sunny?"

"Packing. She's leaving today."

"I'm sorry." He grimaced in apology. "But I gotta admit, the timing is right."

"I agree, regardless of Maureen." She pulled away, reached for the eggs and started cracking them into a bowl.

Cash narrowed his gaze on her, but said nothing.

"Sunny and I have set an unhealthy pattern. She gets in trouble and I bail her out. Ever since we were kids it went that way. I had never questioned it until recently."

"What brought on this sudden realization?" he asked quietly.

"I think she's in trouble again." She rinsed and wiped her hands, then started beating the eggs with a vengeance. "But that's not my problem. We need to worry about Maureen."

"Look, Rainy, if you need to do something with Sunny, I'll handle my ex-wife."

Something in his tone made her head jerk up. He almost sounded anxious... like maybe he wanted her to leave, too. She studied his face a moment, but she saw nothing in his caring smile to support her theory.

"No. I'm done being Sunny's keeper. Part of our problem has been that I loved fixing things for her. I wasn't a victim, like everyone teased. I was a volunteer. It made me feel important to be her guardian."

"You're a loyal, giving person. There's nothing wrong with that."

She shook her head. "There's more to it. I liked being in her shadow, living her life vicariously without having to personally face the consequences... until the centerfold." She thought about Richard, the stares and whispers of her neighbors. "Then I faced those consequences, too. And I'm realizing that I haven't done Sunny any favors by bailing her out. To some degree it was selfish."

Cash took her hand, stroked the inside of her wrist. "I think you're being too hard on yourself. I'm sure you never wanted to see your sister hurt. You don't have a selfish bone in your body."

Smiling, he cupped her cheek and she felt her heart lighten. "Now," he said, dropping his hand, his smile faltering. "How would you like to move back in with Violet?"

RAINY WAITED GLUMLY in the living room while Sunny said her goodbyes to Cash, Smiley and Josh in the kitchen. She knew Cash was right. Even if he hadn't asked her to return to Violet's, she would have done so herself. But the distance she felt growing between them still hurt.

"Well," Sunny said, tossing back her hair as she entered the room. "I guess it's time to blow off this small-town dust." She grinned, but not before Rainy saw the brief wistful look.

Rainy mentally counted to three before she took Sunny's hand and pulled her to the couch. Rainy had sworn to herself she wouldn't do this. "Sit with me for a minute."

Sunny hesitated at first, then warily she nodded.

Once they had taken their seats, Rainy asked in a quiet voice, "Will you please tell me what's going on?"

"What are you talking about?" Sunny laughed. "Surely you didn't expect me to stick around this—"

"Knock it off, Sunny. I'm talking about whatever it is that's been bothering you since the first day you got here."

Sunny flapped a hand and started to laugh.

"You're supposed to be on some kind of promotional tour. You were in such a hurry to leave Boon for it. Then you show up here? And frankly, you haven't been yourself."

Sunny frowned and started to rise, but Rainy caught her arm.

"This isn't like you. You don't keep things from me."

Her twin shrugged, her flippant smile valiantly trying to return. "As they'd say out here in the sticks, it's water under the bridge."

"Then it won't matter if you tell me, will it?"

Sunny's eyes grew sad and wary all at once. "I hope not." She settled back down on the couch and flicked at the tip of a scarlet fingernail. "It was supposed to be a joke."

Rainy allowed a brief silence, then said, "You lost me."

"Those pictures of me." Sunny looked up, a helpless, pained expression on her face, which Rainy had never seen before. "They weren't suppose to end up in the magazine."

"But you posed for them . . ." Rainy shook her head in confusion.

"Yeah, but not for *Midnight Fantasy*. It was supposed to be one of those lingerie shoots women do for their husbands. I was going to pretend they were of you and send them to Richard as a joke. I thought it would be funny."

Rainy digested the information about the same way she would a triple chocolate cake. Her stomach lurched and her head spun with more questions. She asked the most obvious one. "Then how did this happen?"

"The photographer I used was supposed to be reputable." Sunny threw her hands up in supplication. "I checked him out. I swear I did. A friend had used him to take photos for a Valentine's present for her husband. And everything went fine during the session. Then, when I was changing behind the screen, he snuck up on me and snapped a picture."

Rainy recalled the series of pictures. They had indeed all been of Sunny in lingerie—a provocative selection, but, nevertheless, lingerie had covered key areas...except in the one. "That centerfold with you topless?"

Sunny blushed. Rainy could count on one hand the number of times her sister had done that. "That's the one," Sunny said, nodding, then added bitterly, "Said he loved the surprised look I gave him. Made it more salable."

Rainy remembered the expression well. It was probably the one that had made her resent what her twin had done the most. Now she felt horrible over it. She put her arms around her sister. "Why didn't you tell me what had happened?"

"I was embarrassed. I thought I could stop him before he'd actually sell the pictures. But I had signed away my rights when I agreed to do some modeling in exchange for the fee." Sunny sat back, her normally teasing eyes flat and dull. "I even hired an attorney. He tried until the last minute... and then before I knew it, the issues were hitting the newsstands." She looked down, lifting a shoulder, the movement labored. "No one seemed overly surprised that I'd do anything so stupid, so I let it go."

Rainy felt the stab of guilt somewhere near her heart. She'd been one of those people. But in her own defense, she reminded herself that Sunny'd always shunned convention. That fact helped little.

"You still should have told us."

"The damage had already been done."

"So there is no promotional tour," Rainy said.

"God, no." Sunny looked horrified. "The sooner people forget about this fiasco, the better." She grimaced. "I didn't mean to leave you holding the bag. You're so rational and sensible and smart. I mean, you have it so together all the time... We're so different I... Sometimes I forget how people can mistake you for me."

Rainy smiled. "You're all those things and more."

Sunny shook her head, but she smiled back. "You're the best sister I could have."

Rainy didn't feel like a good sister at the moment. She hadn't believed in Sunny as she should have. Deep down she knew her sister could not have purposely done anything so foolish as posing for a men's magazine, but Rainy had been too panicked and self-absorbed to have even asked questions.

She met her sister's expectant gaze and said, "Ditto." They both laughed at the familiar saying.

"You know..." Leaving the couch, Sunny dabbed at the corner of her eye. "I feel better already." She tossed back her hair. "But what would really make my day is if you and Cash set a wedding date." At Rainy's dumbstruck expression, she added, "Something good has to come from all this."

Rainy shook her head in an indulgent manner, trying hard not to buy into Sunny's tempting fantasy. And thinking about the packed bags that Cash had already delivered to Violet's, pretty much took care of that.

CASH PEEKED IN on Rainy and Josh. His son braced his chin with one hand, while his other hand fidgeted with the pages of the open book at which he peered so intensely. Rainy sat across the table from him, leaning slightly forward. Cash knew she was waiting for some kind of answer from Josh. He could tell by the way she worried her lower lip, the way she gripped the edge of her chair, almost willing Josh to know the correct answer. The McClouds' very own cheerleader.

Cash smiled. She was far more than that, of course; she'd become their salvation—and their biggest problem.

Rainy looked up, her beautiful brown eyes touching him, caressing him, and she smiled. God, how he'd missed her last night. He didn't know how much more he could take of her staying at Violet's, but it couldn't be any other way. He had Josh to consider, and although the boy was consistently scoring high on every test Rainy gave him, Cash knew he'd be wise to worry about Maureen and her knowledge of the centerfold. He gave Rainy the sign that lunch would be ready in ten minutes and quietly closed the door.

It still stunned him at times to think he'd found someone like Rainy, especially here in Maybe. She was kind and beautiful and accepting. It was obvious she cared a great deal for Josh. And somehow, life was different, more exciting, since she'd come to the ranch.

Although Cash was not a pessimist by nature, he was realistic enough to acknowledge that they had a lot working against them. In fact, between Josh's mother and the monotony of Maybe, he had nothing going for him at all, he admitted bleakly as he scrubbed the grime from his hands.

Even five hours of mending fences hadn't tamped down the restless energy he was feeling today. Maybe he was just reacting to the arrival of his ex-wife, or it could be because Rainy hadn't yet been officially offered the teaching position. Maybe he was just waiting for the bottom to fall out of their lives. Hell, maybe he was a damned pessimist, after all.

Cash retrieved some leftover ham from the refrigerator and had sliced it for sandwiches when the doorbell rang. Before he could get to it, Josh came bouncing down the stairs and flung open the door.

"Hey, Mayor Simms." Josh stepped aside and the older man entered.

Homer nodded to the boy and then looked past him to Rainy as she descended the stairs and smiled. He gave Cash a quick glance and hello before returning his gaze to her.

"Ms. Daye, how nice to see you again."

Rainy blinked and Cash knew she was wondering the same thing he was. What the hell was Homer sucking up for? They hadn't seen the man since the town meeting and, although he was probably slightly embarrassed over the spectacle his wife had made, it wasn't like Homer to be so patronizing unless it was to his advantage.

"It's nice to see you, Mayor Simms." She left the last step and came to stand next to Cash. The simple gesture made his heart sing and he no longer cared why the man was here.

"You're just in time for lunch, Homer." He put a hand at Rainy's lower back and started to turn toward the kitchen. "It's only sandwiches."

"Actually, I have some business with Ms. Daye," Homer said. "I know I should have called first..."

"Can I go eat?" Josh asked, shifting from one foot to the other. "I'm starved."

Cash cocked his head toward the kitchen, indicating his approval. He should probably join his son. Homer's business was with Rainy, but he'd be damned if...

Rainy slipped her hand in his. "Shall we go to the living room?" she asked.

Homer gave Cash a look that clearly spoke his mixed feelings over Cash's presence, but he nodded.

Once they were seated Simms wasted no time in getting to his point. "I've come to ask you to represent Maybe to the cattle drive committee in Dallas." When she opened her mouth in surprise, Homer quickly added, "This may seem sudden, but since you're about to become an official member of this community..." He winked. "Everyone on the town council feels you'd be the best person." He glanced over at Cash, who tried like hell to keep his temper in check. "Except maybe Cash, of course. He's already made his feelings plain on the subject."

"I don't know what to say." Rainy's astonishment dwindled to a grin. "I'm very flattered." She looked from Homer to Cash. "I—I just don't think I have the time."

Homer embarked on several more persuasive arguments, shrewdly playing up how much the entire community would appreciate the efforts of their newest member.

Cash did everything but sit on his hands to keep from punching Homer in the nose. He didn't want Rainy involved in the drive. He wanted her here with him, not chasing projects that would remind her of how boring life in Maybe really was. Selfish, he knew, but that didn't change how he felt.

He continued to sit silently, stomaching as much as he could, and was about to tactfully suggest that Homer give her some time to think about it, when the mayor turned to him.

"By the way, McCloud, thought you'd be interested in knowing who'll be heading the drive." Homer stalled, brushing some lint off his pant leg. "Jesse," he said finally, shaking his head. "Jesse Logan. Now who'd have thought that boy would've amounted to anything?"

Jesse? Heading the cattle drive? Cash stared coldly at the mayor. "There was never a doubt in my mind."

Homer shrugged. "Thought you'd want to know." He returned his attention to Rainy. "Give it some thought, young lady. We'd all sure appreciate it."

Rainy had been darting curious looks from Cash to Homer but she settled her gaze on the mayor and lifted a shoulder, an apologetic smile on her lips. "I'm afraid there isn't much to think about. I simply don't have the time."

Jesse Logan. Cash cleared his throat. "Yeah, you do." Both pairs of eyes magnetized to him, one pair cagey, one pair startled. "Because I'm going to help you."

RAINY LOADED the dishwasher while Cash and Josh prepared the guest room for Maureen. She felt out of sorts knowing another woman would be taking her place here at the ranch—even if the woman was Josh's mother, she thought flatly.

"Everything is in order upstairs." Cash startled her from behind and she jerked. "I'm sorry for making you jump." He pushed her ponytail away from her neck and nipped her lightly on her nape.

"Maureen is going to be here any minute and you're acting like a . . . like a . . ."

"Lovesick fool?" he supplied, grinning.

Lovesick? Her heart skipped a beat. He'd never mentioned that word in any way, shape or form before. He'd hinted at permanency a couple of times, mainly in conjunction with the teaching position. But he'd never mentioned the word love . . . or marriage.

Rainy wanted to scream. It was Sunny's damned phone calls that were getting to her. Since she'd left, her sister had called every day to ask if they'd set a wedding date.

"I need to get back to Violet's," she snapped.

"Meeting Maureen is inevitable."

"She has nothing to do with it," she lied. "I wanted to spend some time reading up on the cattle drive."

Cash frowned. "You'll have to spend time in Dallas."

"You mean, if I decide to take this on?"

"Sounds like you've already decided."

Rainy saw his jaw tense, but she didn't understand why. "I haven't really. But it could be fun if you'd go with me to Dallas sometimes," she said, warming to the idea.

"I have responsibilities here."

Now Rainy frowned. He looked so stern. "I know that."

He sighed and put a hand out to her. "Come here."

She went to him, slipping her arms around his waist and tilting her head back. "Why did you change your mind about the drive? Is it because of Jesse?"

Cash grimaced, but he hugged her closer. "I haven't changed my mind. I merely said I'd help."

"But it is because of Jesse?"

"And you." When she sent him a skeptical look, he kissed the tip of her nose and added, "Jesse's a good guy who didn't deserve the bad breaks he got or the way this town treated him. If I can help him in any way, I will."

"Even by sending him your girl?" she asked, teasing.

Cash's eyes registered surprise, as if she'd brought up something he hadn't considered, then he narrowed them on her. "Don't even think about it." He dipped her backward as she clung to him, laughing.

"On second thought, maybe I'll send Sunny," she said.

"Jesse and Sunny?" He straightened, a funny look on his face, then burst out laughing. "I don't think so."

She was about to ask what the joke was, when she heard the sound of a car pulling up near the house. They looked at each other, then Cash took a deep breath. "Show time."

Rainy hung back near the kitchen door as he headed down the hall. He caught a glimpse of Maureen's silver Mercedes out the window before he opened the door.

"I hope you have the air conditioner turned up," Maureen said, stepping up onto the porch and fanning herself. Her sable brown hair was rolled into a fashionable twist. "This place is even hotter and dustier than I remember."

Cash held the door open with one hand, the thumb of his other was hooked in his belt loop. "It's July, Maureen. It's hot all over Texas."

She looked past him toward the stairs, down the hall and smack dab at Rainy. "Yes." Her brows arched. "So I hear."

Chapter Seventeen

Josh flew down the stairs within minutes of his mother's arrival. After several hugs, he gladly helped her unload the car of the many extravagant gifts she'd brought for him.

Cash watched each of Josh's trips upstairs to stash his loot with growing irritation. Maureen'd had their son with her for the first three weeks of summer and had already spoiled him plenty. Besides, Josh was supposed to be in his punishment stage.

Cash glanced over his shoulder to look for Rainy. He knew she had slunk back into the kitchen as soon as Maureen had deflected his crack about it being hot in Texas toward Rainy. As much as that had ticked him off, what was more disturbing was the old resentment Maureen's presence had suddenly stirred up. He'd long ago rid himself of any hard feelings, but today, seeing her, reminded him that their relationship—that he—hadn't been enough to keep her in Maybe.

By the time Cash returned to the kitchen, Rainy had scrubbed the sink and chrome spigot until she could clearly see her reflection. Faint spots of blood appeared near her cuticles from rubbing so hard, but she ignored them and started to tackle the stovetop.

"What are you doing?" Cash took the scouring pad from her. He smiled, but it didn't reach his eyes. "You don't want to show up Mrs. Parker. You know she returns tomorrow."

"I want her to come home to a clean house." Rainy swiped nervously at her hair. "Or she might quit and I'll get stuck doing this permanently."

Cash's smile brightened. "I like the sound of that."

"What? Making me a permanent housekeeper?"

"No, just the permanent part."

Rainy swallowed. He was doing it again. "I'd ask you to expand on that, but I think this may be the wrong time." She could hear Josh and his mother approaching the kitchen.

Cash glanced toward the door. "Yeah." He moved away from her, and although she realized why he'd done that, his action bothered her.

"Josh tells me you may have some leftovers." Maureen walked in just ahead of her son and immediately switched her sky blue gaze from Cash to Rainy. "I didn't have a chance to eat anything along the way."

Cash tossed the scouring pad he held into the sink and introduced Rainy to Maureen.

"So..." Maureen drawled, obviously sizing Rainy up. "You're my son's favorite teacher and cook extraordinaire."

"I'm not sure about that." She pasted on a smile for the woman. Maureen was stunningly beautiful, petite, too. She made Rainy feel like an amazon. "But there's meat loaf and scalloped potatoes, if you're interested."

"Hmm, meat loaf and potatoes. How Maybish." Maureen walked unerringly to the cabinet with the dinner plates and brought one out. "Anyone care to join me?" They shook their heads and she continued to get out eating utensils, not once searching the wrong drawer or cabinet.

Rainy felt more like an outsider than she ever had before, as she fumbled in her pocket for her car keys. It didn't help that Cash remained silent. His gaze followed Maureen's movements, his eyes strangely sad. Did he still have feelings for her?

Surely not after ten years. Rainy was reading too much into his sullen mood. He had every reason to be tense, Rainy told herself, his future with Josh was at stake.

She was foolish to be taking any of this personally, she knew, but it didn't stop her from looking for some small sign of reassurance—a wink, a look . . . anything.

But as she excused herself to return to Violet's place, he barely gave her a nod.

CASH WASN'T A BIT surprised that as soon as Rainy left and Josh went upstairs to inventory his goodies, Maureen brought up the centerfold. He watched her put the last of her dishes in the dishwasher before returning to join him at the table.

"So," she said with obvious amusement after they'd recounted some of the story. "How are the squeaky-clean people of Maybe taking the scandal?"

"Rainy's about to be offered a job at the high school," he told her, not much caring for her tone.

"Really?" She lifted both perfectly arched brows. "Things apparently have changed around here."

He declined comment. It'd be useless to point out that wasn't true. She simply hadn't given the place a chance.

"I hope her twin didn't leave on my account." She pulled a cigarette case out of her purse. When Cash frowned, she laid it on the table. "How's *she* doing with Josh?"

"*Her name* is Rainy. And Josh is doing great. I wouldn't be surprised if he aced the exam."

"Really?" Maureen drawled, leaning back in her chair and piercing him with her icy blue stare. "So when are you going to make an honest woman out of her?"

Cash choked back a grunt. "For chrissakes, she's Josh's tutor."

"Uh-huh. And I'm Mother Teresa."

"Maureen," he warned.

"You're worrying that I'll make an issue out of your relationship, of course." She pursed her lips, tapping a long pink nail on the table. "I haven't decided yet, though I have to admit she may be good for this Podunk town and Josh . . . if she stays."

Cash shook his head. Why, after all these years, was she getting to him now? *Because she makes me feel inadequate, that's why.* He shoved a hand through his hair. "Okay, I'll bite. Why would she be good for this town?"

She shrugged. "With a sister like hers, I figure she's gotta be open-minded."

Cash didn't appreciate the reminder. Life with Sunny was interesting. Life with him in Maybe could be boring, to which Maureen would surely attest. "She is, and she cares about Josh," he finally said, staring meaningfully at her. "I care about Josh."

"I know that, Cash." Maureen sighed and yanked out a cigarette. "You were always the better parent."

"That wasn't what I was getting at. I just don't want you using this centerfold misunderstanding to uproot Josh. It wouldn't be fair."

"You've already decided I don't play fair."

"This isn't about you and me, Maureen." Cash blinked. Uneasiness nudged him. He'd do well to remember that himself.

She lit the cigarette. He pulled out an ashtray and slid it across the table to her. She put up five perfectly manicured pink nails and the ashtray stopped against her palm. "Give me some credit, will you? We may not agree on most things, but I do care about my son."

He ran a weary hand down his face. "I know."

"And that includes wanting him to have the best education he can. With Rainy around, Josh benefits both ways. He's exposed to new ideas and someone in tune with how important an education is. On the other hand, there's this centerfold issue."

Cash stared back at his ex-wife. Why did she have to always rub his face in it? That he was from a nowhere town, going nowhere. When it came to Josh, he was all those things she'd just mentioned, but because he was from Maybe, to Maureen it didn't count.

Worst of all, she'd reminded him that sometimes he thought she was right.

VIOLET WAS OUT working in her shed when Rainy got home. Rainy was glad to be alone with her thoughts, even as morose as they were. When the phone rang, she thought seriously about not answering it, but on the slim chance that it was Cash, she made a dash for it.

"Hi, Sis." It was Sunny. "You sound funny."

"Josh's mother is here," she blurted at the familiar sound of her sister's voice.

"Oh, no." Sunny sighed heavily. "Is this visit routine... or centerfold related?"

"Well..." She thought about sugarcoating the situation, but she was too tired, too depressed. "Custody related."

Sunny was quiet a long time. "Bad news, huh?"

"Nah." Rainy tried to laugh, but her voice caught. "So is this a pester-Rainy call?" she asked teasingly.

"Only if he hasn't popped the question yet."

Rainy choked out a small laugh. That was pretty much the last thing she expected from Cash right now, but she went along with her sister's usual game until the words ran out.

Silence stretched across the line and Rainy congratulated herself for totally messing up her sister's good mood. "Sunny? Are you there?"

Her twin cleared her throat. "Yeah, I'm here." Another long pause. "Uh, listen, Rainy, with Josh's mother there, you won't be working this weekend, will you?"

"I hadn't thought about it. Why?"

"Well...I, um, you see, I've got this problem..."

Oh, no. Rainy dropped her head back and closed her eyes for a moment. Here it comes.

"Let's put it this way," Sunny said. "How would you like an all-expense-paid weekend in Las Vegas?"

"Sunny?"

"I mean plane fare and everything. All I need are two teensy little hours of your time and—"

"No."

"You can have the rest..." Sunny stopped. "No?"

Rainy braced herself. Denying her sister anything at all was an alien experience. "No, Sunny. I can't help you."

In the ensuing silence, Rainy clung to every ounce of resolve she possessed.

Finally, Sunny said, "You haven't even heard me out yet."

"I know," she replied quietly, earning her several more moments of unnerving silence.

"You're still mad about the centerfold."

"No, I'm not."

"Then why won't you help me? You always have before." Sunny's voice quavered.

"And I was wrong to do it. If I keep bailing you out, I won't really be helping you. Do you understand that?"

"Just this one last time?"

"I can't."

"Will you at least listen to what my problem is?"

Rainy knew she shouldn't. She could get sucked into Sunny's game if she did. Besides, it was a tempting diversion from her own problems. "Go ahead. But I'm warning you, I'm not budging on my decision."

"You're forcing me to reform cold turkey, you know?" her sister complained. "That isn't very fair."

"Sunny," she warned, but smiled at her twin's logic.

"Okay, okay." Sunny sighed. "I accepted two modeling assignments on the same day. Problem is, one's in San Antonio and the other is in Las Vegas."

Rainy rolled her eyes. "Postpone one."

"I can't. The one in San Antonio is on a strict deadline and the Las Vegas job is for a convention."

She groaned. "You know I hate those convention deals."

"It's only for two hours." Sunny sounded hopeful.

Rainy instantly realized her mistake and said more firmly, "It doesn't matter. The answer is still no."

"Look, Rain, I understand what you're doing. And you're right. I need to grow up."

Rainy briefly pulled the receiver away and narrowed her gaze at it, then fitted it near her mouth again. "Nice try."

"Please, Sis. I swear this will be the last time."

It was Rainy's turn to dole out the silence.

Sunny sniffed. "You're right. After the centerfold stunt, I had no right to ask." Before Rainy could correct her, Sunny added, "But it was my chance to get some legitimate work and I had to try."

"What do you mean?" she asked cautiously.

"The offers haven't exactly been rolling in since the magazine's publication. Not decent ones, anyway," she said wryly. "So when I received two good offers, I got overanxious. Figured they might put me back on the right track."

Rainy bit her lip. Why did Sunny have to put it that way just when Rainy'd had the courage to take a stand? God, she hated losing ground. But how could she let her twin down with so much at stake? Sunny needed to get back on her feet. Rainy of all people understood that. Besides, getting out of Maybe while Maureen was here sounded like a pretty good idea right about now. She sighed and reached for a pencil and paper. "When do I have to be there?"

HE HAD TO SEE Rainy. It was late and Cash knew Violet turned in early, but after restlessly pacing for an hour after Josh and Maureen had gone to bed, he couldn't stand it anymore. He needed to see her, to hold her. He needed reassurance that she was still in his life. After scribbling a note in case Josh woke up, he grabbed his keys.

Only one light was on when he knocked softly at Violet's door ten minutes later—obviously *too* softly. He knocked again.

The door creaked open and Rainy peeked sideways through the narrow crack at him. The way her eyes lit up when she saw him was like a balm to his wounded spirit and he realized how much he needed her. Smiling, she swung the door open.

He grabbed her around the waist, hauled her up against him and buried his face in her hair, breathing in the clean, reassuring scent of lavender.

"Hey, we can't do this." Laughing quietly, she briefly looked back over her shoulder into the house.

"You mean this." He ran his tongue over her lips before drawing the lower one into his mouth. "And this." His tongue dove in to seek out the source of her sigh.

Finally, she straightened. "Knock it off." She nibbled at his mouth a second longer. "I mean it."

"Okay. But only until I can get you into—"

Her eyes widened. "Not here you aren't."

"Wanna neck in my truck?" he asked, grinning.

"I don't think it's a good idea." She ducked from his gaze. "What happened with Maureen?"

"The usual. We're at a stalemate. Although she's being pretty reasonable," he admitted, then nudged her chin up and looked into her beautiful, troubled face—a face in which he found comfort and joy. Without a doubt, he knew what he had to do. Tonight he'd have to take the chance. He'd ask her to stay, ask her to marry him. "Is that what's wrong? Are you worried about her visit?"

"Of course I'm worried." She tried to duck from him again, but he wouldn't let her. Staring up at him, she sighed. "Besides, I have to pack."

Cash slowly angled his head farther back to get a better look at her face. Her expression was bland. He swallowed. "Do what?"

"I'll only be gone overnight," she said quickly. "And Josh was going to take the day off to be with his mother..."

"Where?"

"Las Vegas."

He blinked. "Does this have to do with Sunny?"

She averted her eyes. "Yes. She took two modeling jobs on the same day by mistake. She's got a written contract on both. One's in Las Vegas and the other is in San Antonio."

Out of the blue, Maureen's cigarettes popped into his mind. Although he'd beat the habit more than ten years ago, the sudden urge to light up was overwhelming. "I thought you were through bailing her out."

"I was." She shook her head. "I am. I told her this is the last time."

"How many times have you told her that?"

Rainy's chin went up. "This was the first time."

Cash didn't say anything. His thoughts drifted to the cigarettes. Maybe Maureen was right. Neither he nor Maybe were worth sticking around for. The idea shook his confidence to the core.

"It's different this time, Cash," she began. "I told you about how Sunny was tricked. Now good jobs have been few and far between. I've got to help her out."

"What happened to her having to face her own consequences?" Was she really going for Sunny, he wondered. Or was this just an excuse to get away?

"I still believe that. But I need to help her back on track."

He shook his head. "You'll always feel that way. Every time she gets into a scrape."

"That's not true. And she knows that."

"But you don't." Wearily, he rubbed his eyes. "You'll always run to her."

"And even if I did?" Rainy frowned. "How would that be different from you running to help with the cattle drive just because your friend Jesse is involved?" He frowned back at her and she added, "Or the fact that you'd put me out on my butt if I'd truly jeopardized your custody of Josh."

This time he looked away.

"It's okay, Cash." She moved closer and laid a hand on his arm. "I wouldn't blame you at all. Your first concern should be your son and it is. That's just one of the many things I admire about you. But I want you to see that your loyalty is no different from mine."

Cash closed his eyes. He felt like a jerk when she put it that way. Still, it wasn't quite the same. Josh was his responsibility...

"In fact, I think you should come with me."

The excitement in her voice—more than her actual words—brought him around. Her eyes sparkled, her smile was wide, her cheeks nearly glowed.

"It was Sunny's idea, actually," she said. "I didn't think it was a good one, at first, but it could be a blast. I've never been to Las Vegas before. Have you?"

He watched her growing excitement as dread multiplied in his heart. It wasn't Sunny she was running to. It was the dazzling melodrama that surrounded her twin. It was the thrill of the unknown. He knew the feeling well. Too well. Except he'd already made his choice. He had a son to raise in Maybe. Numbly, he shook his head.

"No. You haven't been there?" Her eyes grew wary.

"I'm not going."

"Oh." Rainy withdrew her hand from his arm. She didn't like the look on his face. Didn't like the finality of his tone. "I hope you don't mind that I'll be gone overnight. Josh won't miss any tutoring time." She stopped. "Cash? What's wrong?"

He backed away. "Go ahead and pack."

"You don't want me to go."

He didn't say anything. He didn't have to. His expression said it all. If she left tomorrow, it would never be the same between them. And she didn't understand why.

"I'm coming right back."

"And what about the next time?"

"There won't be a next time." She stared at the skepticism darkening his eyes. "Cash? Is that what's bothering you? You think I'll always be flying off at the drop of a hat. That's not true. Please understand why I have to do this."

Cash smiled a small, sad smile. "I do understand," he said and urged her toward the door.

But Rainy knew otherwise. No one could possibly understand how important the independence she'd found in the past few weeks had become to her. She barely understood it herself. Being separated from Sunny had made everything clear. So much of Rainy's life had been in reaction to her twin. But from the moment she'd decided to leave

Boon, Rainy had consciously made all of her own decisions.

Just like she'd decided to help Sunny one last time. Just like she couldn't not do it for Cash.

For the first time in her life, Rainy felt free. And she had to hang on to the feeling for all she was worth.

IT HAD SEEMED a long time until dawn. He should have stayed last night, Cash thought as he put on some coffee. He should have snuck into her room and made love to her one last time. Didn't he have enough regrets in his life? Did he have to add another? Why couldn't he have been happy with some nice woman from around Maybe?

Why couldn't Rainy have signed the one-year contract for the teaching position? It was going to be offered any day now. Everyone knew that. It would have given them a little more time.

Pulling out some mugs, he laughed humorlessly. More time for what? For her to decide that Maybe wasn't exciting enough? That he wasn't worth staying for?

Cash went to the refrigerator for milk. Only, after he opened the door, he'd forgotten what he was looking for and peered in for several moments.

"I finally figured out what the ol' bat's been doin'," Smiley said, coming through the back door.

Cash snapped out of his daze and turned to him. "What?"

"She's been bribin' the judges." Smiley reached around him, withdrew the milk, then shut the refrigerator door.

"Who?"

"Who? Violet. That's who." Smiley frowned. "What's the matter with you?" Then he took another look at Cash's white cotton shirt, his tan slacks. "Ain't this a workday?"

"I'm taking Rainy to the airport," Cash said.

"Airport? You finally chased her outta town." Smiley laughed until he saw the dismal look on his boss's face. "Where's she goin'?"

"Las Vegas—something to do with her sister."

"She's coming back, ain't she?"

"Who knows?" Cash turned away to pour his coffee.

Smiley moved to peer at him. "Did she say she is?"

"Yeah."

"Well, doggone it, then she is."

"Yeah."

Smiley shook his head. "Don't go bein' a damn fool. Not everyone is as hot to git outta this town as you."

Cash slid him a warning look.

"Don't go eyein' me like that. You spend all those hours readin' them travel magazines, but you don't do a doggone thing about it. Thinkin' is better than doin', if you know what I mean."

Cash felt his irritation waffle as he watched Smiley root around for his favorite chipped mug. He had no idea anyone suspected his wanderlust. But what did that have to do with anything?

The cattle drive came to mind and how adamantly he'd lobbied against acting on the town's behalf. The uncomfortable weight of self-discovery settled on his shoulders.

Smiley had been off base. Cash hadn't been afraid of doing, he'd been afraid of wanting more. As long as he stuck around Maybe, he wasn't reminded of how much more life offered. But Rainy had snuck in and upset the balance. And deep down, he resented that. Then he'd transferred his own frustration on to her.

"Now let me tell you about the ol' bat," Smiley said after he found what he was looking for. "You know all those wrapped packages she decorates her chili booth with. It's moonshine. She uses it to bribe those snivelin' jackass judges. Now I figure if I . . ."

Cash stared at Smiley while the man continued to drone on. Except Cash heard nothing. Looking at Smiley was like looking at himself in twenty-five years. He'd be fishing around for the same mug, drinking exactly two cups of coffee before breakfast, one more at lunch. And just like Smiley pined for Violet, Cash'd be longing for Rainy. Because he'd been too worried about all the wrong things.

It wasn't about custody hearings, or where they lived. It was about having the guts to take a chance . . . it was about loving Rainy.

"Thanks, buddy." Cash wiped his hands on the dish towel, then threw it at Smiley, who narrowed his confused black eyes on him. "Hold down the fort for a couple of days, will you?"

"WHAT DO YOU MEAN she's gone?"

"Sorry, Cash." Violet shrugged. "I thought you knew. She left for the airport an hour ago."

He swore violently under his breath, then glanced apologetically at Violet.

She chuckled. "But I know where she'll be." When he looked suspiciously at her, she said, "Sunny called after she left, wanted to know if you were with her."

He wondered why Sunny would have done that? But he didn't have time to analyze it now. He had a plane to catch. After taking the information from Violet, he hopped in his truck and floored the accelerator through three counties.

ON TOP OF HAVING a horrible night's sleep, Rainy was having a dreadful day. She tried to steady her compact mirror as the cab bounced over the Las Vegas streets, which had surely not seen new pavement in two decades.

Since her first flight had been late, she'd missed her connection in Phoenix. Now she was fifteen minutes away from missing Sunny's appointment.

And she looked like hell. Her eyes were puffy from crying half the night and her nose was red. She didn't want to be here at all. She wanted to be back in Maybe. With Cash. But right now she didn't even know if he wanted her back. The thought made her tear again.

This was all Sunny's fault, she decided, for having bugged her about the "M" word every day. Because of her twin's teasing, Rainy had made the mistake of fantasizing about staying with Cash, marrying him, having babies...

The driver slowed down and, drying her eyes, Rainy squinted at the row of odd buildings. "Is this the right address?" she asked. He verified that it was and she paid him, then stepped out of the car with her small bag.

It was a strange area of town, she decided, turning in a circle. Not only were there no hotels in sight, but she wouldn't have expected to find one, either. She was about to confer with the cabdriver, when he took off into traffic.

Muttering to herself, she raised a hand to flag another cab. When one pulled up in front of her, the back door opened and she moved back to make room.

Cash stepped out of the car. His smile reached clear to his green eyes. His dark hair was slightly mussed. "Hi."

Rainy's hand flew to her chest as if she could slow the pounding of her heart. "Hi? What are you—"

"I changed my mind." His smile was a tad uncertain. But he looked so achingly good to her, it squeezed her heart. She wondered what would have happened if he'd tried to deny her independence. Except he hadn't. "Where's the hotel?" he asked, looking around.

She shook her head, not trusting herself to speak, then turned when she heard a clicking sound.

Sunny stepped out of the shadow of a large, gaudily painted building. "Surprise!" She clasped her hands together delightedly. "Whew. Am I glad you're here, too,

Cash." She hurried over to them as fast as her stiletto, fuchsia heels and skintight white leather skirt would allow.

Rainy gaped at her crazy sister. "You're supposed to be in San Antonio."

"I lied," Sunny said cheerfully.

Cash slowly tilted his head back and looked up at the top of the building. Rainy followed his incredulous gaze. A light flashed, died, then flickered to life again. In neon, the King's Wedding Chapel was announced.

Rainy swung her attention back to her sister. "Sunny?"

She shrugged. "I had to do something. You two are so slow."

Rainy turned stricken eyes to Cash. What if he thought she was in on this? What if he thought this was a trap?

He grinned. "I always did like your sister."

"But..."

"All you have to say is yes."

"You haven't had time to think about this. We..."

Smiling, Cash reached into his pocket and withdrew a small velvet box. He flipped it open to display an antique emerald ring. "It belonged to my grandmother."

Rainy glanced at Sunny, who held a hand to her mouth. This wasn't easy for her sister. Their lives were about to change once again. And Rainy loved her for her selflessness. Rainy smiled at her before looking back to Cash's anxious eyes. "What about Josh? The custody—"

"This is about us, Rainy. I love you." His jaw tightened.

"I love you." A tear slipped down her cheek.

"Can you believe the rest will follow? Together we'll fight to keep Josh. He belongs with us. We'll make it right. I know we can."

She nodded. He slipped the ring on her finger, then slid both arms around her.

"Hey, hey. You gotta wait for the king," a familiar, husky voice said from the doorway.

When Rainy looked up, she realized why it sounded so familiar. Complete with white rhinestone jumpsuit, the man with jet black hair hurried down the three stone steps.

Cash laughed.

Sunny sighed.

Rainy shook her head. Only her sister would think of an Elvis-impersonating minister. She turned helpless eyes to Cash, feeling the heat rise to her cheeks. "I swear I don't know anything about this. Sunny has a very kooky sense of humor sometimes. Of course we don't—"

"Rainy?" Cash hooked a finger under her chin and tilted her face up. His lips twitched with amusement.

She stared up at him and watched his eyes darken with desire as his face descended upon hers. "Yes?"

"The only words I want to hear from you are 'I do.'" Then he covered her mouth with his.

Sunny Daye tells her side of the story...

If you enjoyed Rainy's story, turn the page for a
bonus look at what's in store for you next month in
the sequel to *The Cowboy and the Centerfold*:

THE OUTLAW AND THE CITY SLICKER

by Debbi Rawlins

March 1996

Chapter One

"Tell me that isn't her." Jesse Logan watched the taxi driver unload the fifth, sixth and seventh piece of matching designer luggage. He hadn't actually seen the passenger yet, but taxis in the small west Texas town of Maybe were unheard of, and Sunny Daye was expected at any moment.

A pair of long, shapely, tanned legs swung from the back seat of the cab. The feet were covered in short, pink leather boots, studded with rhinestones.

Jesse's friend Cash cleared his throat. "That's her, all right."

Jesse slowly turned to his longtime buddy. This was going to be a really bad trip. He felt it all the way down to the toes of his hopelessly scuffed boots. "She does know this is a cattle drive we're going on?"

Cash grinned wryly. "She knows."

"A real, honest-to-goodness, eighteen-hundreds' style, dusty, hot, four-state cattle drive?"

"She knows," Cash repeated.

Shaking his head in disbelief, Jesse returned his gaze to the pair of legs that were finding their balance on the rocky ground. Once they were firmly planted, the woman poked her head out of the car. Her long blond hair fanning out in the April breeze, she levered herself from the cab and then towered over the taxi driver as she paid him.

Jesse was too far away to see her face, but he pushed back his Stetson with one finger and squinted against the unusually hot spring sun. What the hell was she wearing? It looked like a skirt, except it was shorter and tighter than any skirt he'd ever seen. He squinted harder at the white strip of fabric that barely covered her thighs. If they were in New York, he supposed she'd look fashionable. But here in Maybe, they had another word for that getup.

This was going to be worse than a bad trip. This was going to be a damn nightmare. If he didn't need the money from this gig as trail boss, he'd blow off the deal right now, Jesse thought.

"Come meet my sister-in-law," Cash said.

Jesse looked back at the woman and her adoring taxi driver. The man was actually reshuffling her bags as she stood smiling and pointing. Some men were total idiots when it came to tall, leggy blondes. Jesse shook his head. He should know. In his younger days, he was one of them.

But those days were long gone. Just like his rodeo career. Ms. Sunny Daye was in for one helluva surprise if she thought this was some Disney trip. Or that he was going to baby-sit her throughout this drive. Reluctantly, he pulled off his work gloves and made his way over to where Cash was already hugging Sunny.

"Sunny, you look terrific." Cash angled back from her, then added, laughing, "But of course I'm biased."

Jesse watched her laugh at his friend's remark and marveled at how much she really did look and sound like Cash's wife. Then he glanced at the short skirt and ridiculous boots, and shook his head. The twins' similarity obviously ended at their features. It looked like he had a bone to pick with his friend for roping him into letting Sunny stand in for Rainy.

"Sunny, meet your co-pilot," Cash said.

Sunny looked at him and blinked. "Do they use that term on cattle drives?"

"No." Cash laughed. When he caught Jesse cringing, he quickly said, "I was joking. This is Jesse Logan. Alias Jesse James Logan, alias The Outlaw.

* * * * *

Be sure you too get to meet The Outlaw!
Don't miss the hilarious sequel to
THE COWBOY AND THE CENTERFOLD:
American Romance #622
THE OUTLAW AND THE CITY SLICKER
by Debbi Rawlins—available March 1996.

BRIDE'S
BAY RESORT

UNLOCK THE DOOR TO GREAT ROMANCE
AT BRIDE'S BAY RESORT

Join Harlequin's new across-the-lines series, set
in an exclusive hotel on an island off the coast of
South Carolina.

Seven of your favorite authors will bring you exciting stories
about fascinating heroes and heroines discovering love at
Bride's Bay Resort.

Look for these fabulous stories coming to a store near you
beginning in January 1996.

Harlequin American Romance #613 in January
Matchmaking Baby by Cathy Gillen Thacker

Harlequin Presents #1794 in February
Indiscretions by Robyn Donald

Harlequin Intrigue #362 in March
Love and Lies by Dawn Stewardson

Harlequin Romance #3404 in April
Make Believe Engagement by Day Leclaire

Harlequin Temptation #588 in May
Stranger in the Night by Roseanne Williams

Harlequin Superromance #695 in June
Married to a Stranger by Connie Bennett

Harlequin Historicals #324 in July
Dulcie's Gift by Ruth Langan

Visit Bride's Bay Resort each month wherever
Harlequin books are sold.

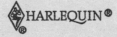

HARLEQUIN ®

BBAYG

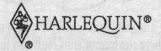

HARLEQUIN®

AMERICAN ◆ ROMANCE®

The Outlaw and the City Slicker
by Debbi Rawlins

This month, American Romance introduced you to the feisty Rainy Daye in The cowboy and the Centerfold (#618). In this woderful tale Rainy's twin sister Sunny made her smashing debut. Being such a strong-willed character, she simply wouldn't go away until she got a story of her own! The Outlaw and the City Slicker (#622) is Sunny's story, and in case you haven't figured it out, she's the city slicker, and the outlaw—Jesse "James" Logan—is a hunk of cowboy, almost too sexy to be real.

So come along and join Sunny and Jesse on a memorable cattle drive, where the humor runs high and the romance is hot!

DR

HARLEQUIN®

AMERICAN ◆ ROMANCE®
®

In Name Only

...because there are many reasons for saying "I do."

American Romance cordially invites you to a
wedding of convenience. This is one reluctant bride
and groom with their own unique reasons for
marrying...IN NAME ONLY.

By popular demand American Romance continues this
story of favorite marriage-of-convenience books. Don't
miss

#624 THE NEWLYWED GAME
by Bonnie K. Winn
March 1996

Find out why some couples marry first...and learn to
love later. Watch for IN NAME ONLY!

HARLEQUIN®
AMERICAN ✦ ROMANCE®

The Magic Wedding Dress

Imagine a wedding dress that costs a million dollars. Imagine a wedding dress that allows the wearer to find her one true love—not always the man she thinks it is. And then imagine a wedding dress that brings out all the best attributes in its bride, so that every man who glimpses her is sure to fall in love. Karen Toller Whittenburg imagined just such a dress and allowed it to take on a life of its own in her new American Romance trilogy, *The Magic Wedding Dress*. Be sure to catch all three:

March
#621—THE MILLION-DOLLAR BRIDE

May
#630—THE FIFTY-CENT GROOM

August
#643—THE TWO-PENNY WEDDING

Come along and dream with Karen Toller Whittenburg!

WDRESS1